MW01599546

A Godsent Governess for his Tormented Family

STAND-ALONE BOOK

A Christian Historical Romance Book

by

Olivia Haywood

Copyright© 2022 by Olivia Haywood

All Rights Reserved.

This book may not be reproduced or transmitted in any form without the written permission of the publisher.

In no way is it legal to reproduce, duplicate, or transmit any part of this document in either electronic means or in printed format. Recording of this publication is strictly prohibited and any storage of this document is not allowed unless with written permission from the publisher

Table of Contents

Prologue

August 1873

Pueblo, Colorado

The soft light from the oil lamps danced on the walls of Frank Clement's small bedroom. The room was sparsely decorated and modest, just like him, with only a bed, a dresser, a small bedside table, and a chair for his attentive daughter. The walls were bare but for but one verse from Corinthians embroidered by Emma's mother and embellished with pink and blue flowers; "Love is patient. Love is kind."

Emma sat in her plush blue wingback chair beside her father's small wooden bed, reading his favorite stories from the Bible. He liked the stories that told of God's great power and strength. Her voice trembled as a lump, hard and unforgiving, formed in her throat, but she attempted to maintain a serene face.

As she read about Moses parting the Red Sea, her father stopped her with a frail hand on her arm.

"My Emma," he whispered, his voice weak, "I hope you always remember that you are unique. God speaks to you. Promise me you will always trust in your visions, in the message God is sending to you. He knows what is best, even if it is not apparent to us."

"Of course, father. I will always trust in God's plan." She placed her hand on top of her father's, struggling to hide her tears, then continued with Moses' story. As she read, her father's breathing became more and more labored.

She set the Bible aside and took his hand, placing her other hand on his forehead, rubbing her fingers along the edge of his salt and pepper hair. His blue eyes, normally clear and alert, were closed, and his skin paled. His breath slowed and became shallower.

Then, in just one moment, it stopped.

He was gone. Now, she was completely alone in the world. Her emotions whirled in her heart like a maelstrom, from panic about what would become of her now that her father had died to an incredible peace, knowing that he was no longer suffering.

It had happened so quickly. Two weeks ago, he had been standing in his usual place in the front of the church, leading the congregation in prayer. Then one day he just could not get out of bed. His breathing had become so labored the past few days, she had known his time was near.

She had sent for the doctor early on, but he could only tell her what she already knew.

"Keep him comfortable. His fate is in God's hands now."

Emma's chest tightened as tears began to well in her blue eyes, the same crystalline hue as her father's, at the memory of the doctor's words. She pushed the loose strands of her golden blonde hair out of her face to prevent them from getting caught in the cascade of sadness streaming down her cheeks.

God's plan was to reunite her parents in heaven today. They were together, where they wanted to be. She may be here on earth alone, but she felt peace knowing that they were smiling down on her from above.

There was nothing for her to do but wait for Reverend Thompson to arrive for a final blessing, though at this point he would arrive too late.

She lightly brushed her father's thinning brown hair, noticing the gray around the edges, and examining the familiar face one last time. He had small lines around his eyes and mouth from smiling and laughing. She had been told that she got her wide, honest smile from him, and she could only hope to be a fraction of the person he was.

She touched her father's lifeless hand and remembered what he had said to her the first time she had had one of her visions, many years ago.

Mother was sitting beside the stream that ran behind the house, with an angel by her side. They were looking out over a group of children splashing in the shallow water.

Emma approached hesitantly, sure her mother would disappear at any moment. She had seen her only in a small portrait her father kept by his bed, but something told Emma that this was the mother who had died to give her life. She could feel it in her soul. She felt an incredible peace inside her and knew she had no reason to fear.

As Emma's skirt swished through the tall reedy grass, her mother looked up and smiled. The older woman's face was flawless and glowing. Calmness and serenity emanated from her kind eyes.

The angel said nothing. But an immense light suddenly seemed to shine from his whole being, illuminating the children.

Emma looked to her mother for some explanation of what was happening but got none. Instead, she was suddenly filled with God's word. She didn't hear it exactly. Rather, she felt it.

Take heed that ye despise not one of these little ones; for I say unto you, That in heaven their angels do always behold the face of my Father which is in heaven.

It was a line from the Book of Matthew.

She was still thinking over what it could mean, what it all could mean, when she found herself lying awake in her own bed.

She leaped up and ran to her father's room. "Father! Father!" She yanked on his arm as his eyes jolted open.

"Yes, my Emma, whatever is the matter?" As always, he was calm and reassuring. Nothing ever seemed to ruffle him, he was so sure of God's plan and presence in his life.

Emma told him what had just happened. "But it wasn't a dream! It was truly happening! I was there, and so was Mother, and the angel and the children. I felt the warmth of the light and felt God in my heart."

"Well then, my Emma, I am sure it was not a dream at all. It was God. You are a very fortunate little girl. God sent a message just for you."

"But what does it mean?"

"That part is a little more difficult. As we know from the Bible, it can be hard to know what God wants. It can be even harder to follow his instructions. That's how Jonah ended up in that whale. But I would say that God is trying to tell you that you have an angel in heaven looking out for you. And so do all the other children. So you would do best to remember that God loves us all, and so we should all love one another."

Emma pondered this a moment, remembering Eliza Marshall's new pink hair bows in church last week. Emma had spent more of the service staring at those hair bows than listening to her father, feeling her heart grow hard with jealousy. She had later ignored Eliza when the blonde girl had waved hello in front of the church. She felt remorse now for the way Eliza's face had fallen at the slight.

Emma nodded to her father. "That makes sense. I could be more charitable toward others sometimes."

"That is what God asks of all of us." Father ran his hand along the top of Emma's head. "Now, my Emma, there are still hours yet until the sun will rise. Do you think you can go to sleep?"

Emma smiled softly now at the memory of his warm voice calling her "my Emma," as he always had, but still a tear unfurled down her cheek. He had also told her many times how fortunate she was that God chose to speak directly to her. Yet, she did not always feel fortunate. Sometimes the visions felt downright inconvenient, and often they were confusing. But she had promised her father that she would trust in her visions and in God's plan.

As she sat now in the wavering lamp light, she wondered what God's plan was for her, now that she was alone.

Chapter One

One week later

Pueblo, Colorado, August 1873

"The Lord is my shepherd; I shall not want."

Emma repeated these words—the words spoken over her father's grave just a week ago—in her head like a meditation. After each line, she stopped to think about its meaning to her own life, trying to see all of the good things the Lord had brought her even amidst her sadness.

"He maketh me to lie down in green pastures: he leadeth me beside the still waters."

She had a home in a town surrounded by the beauty of God's creation. She found immense peace in nature and in this place. Colorado was a striking place to live, with its wide-open blue sky, lush green meadows, and the majestic mountains in the distance jutting up toward heaven. At times, she wondered sometimes what it must feel like to stand atop one of those craggy peaks, to be that close to God and to look down upon His whole creation. It must be a breathtaking experience.

"He restoreth my soul: he leadeth me in the paths of righteousness for his name's sake."

She lived her life by His word, trusting in His plan for her. She knew she was a good and righteous person, thanks to

His presence in her life. She knew He would restore her soul from the sadness she was feeling.

She also knew grief was something that would never fully fade, like a small scar upon delicate skin. She would always yearn for her father. There would always be a part of her missing. But, with God by her side, she knew that the hole in her heart would grow smaller day by day and the sharp pain she felt now would weaken to a dull ache.

"Yea, though I walk through the valley of the shadow of death, I will fear no evil: for thou art with me; thy rod and thy staff they comfort me."

The shadow of death, indeed, she mused. Her entire life had been lived in the shadow of death. Her mother had died giving birth to her. Now, her father was gone as well. However, knowing they were now together in heaven brought peace and stillness to her troubled heart. She had no reason to fear with God and her guardians looking down upon her, and this brought her a sense of calm.

She repeated these verses and her meditations on them, mostly trying to remind and convince herself that all would be well, she should have hope at all times. But she was grieving, and hope was difficult right now.

And so, she kept praying as she hung the laundry to dry in the August sunshine as a gentle breeze ruffled her skirts, a practical dress made of simple green homespun with a white apron over top, around her long legs.

She prayed to avoid thinking about all the things she had lost.

She had just washed her father's linens and the last of his dirty clothes, hesitant to wash away her father's scent— tobacco and leather. She would never again hear her father's gentle voice praying with a young couple in the parlor over their coming wedding. She would never smell the pipe tobacco wafting in from the porch as she finished cleaning up supper. She would never hear him call her "my Emma" again or know the feeling of his strong arms around her in an embrace.

There were a lot of nevers.

A whole week had passed since Reverend Thompson had arrived to oversee the services and her father's burial. The service had been lovely. As a pastor himself, Frank Clements had selected the hymns to be sung and the verses to be read in his last few days. Emma had diligently written down all of his wishes and made sure they were all carried out. But all of that was done now. Reverend Thompson had returned to his home church the next town over, and she was left with a house filled with only furniture and memories.

There was nothing more to do but pick up the pieces and carry on.

The days were not so bad. Emma kept busy with her chores, and the women in town had organized someone to come and visit her each day, just to check in and give her some company. She loved when they would stop by with their children. The energy of children never failed to buoy her spirits.

On Monday, Maggie O'Shannon stopped by with all seven of her children. The yard was in delightful chaos as the siblings played chase, screeching and calling to one another from across the grass.

Emma stood beneath the apple tree between the house and her father's church. She loved the fruit trees around the house—pear, apple, peach, and cherry. They provided cool, refreshing shade to both the house and the church on stifling days like today. She was grateful to God for the abundance of food they always had between the trees and the vegetable garden nearby, its neat rows overflowing now with cucumbers and squash.

Emma glanced at one tree in particular, its limbs heavy with fruit waiting to be canned or made into pies. The two littlest O'Shannons sat by her feet eating the apples the other red-headed children had already managed to gather into baskets. The eldest children were in the tree itself, gathering fruit from the twisting branches.

"Little squirrels, that's what my children are." Maggie O'Shannon shook her head, auburn curls bouncing, and looked up into the limbs of the tree.

"Adorable little squirrels," Emma added, "and very helpful. I could never get all this fruit myself. And I surely won't be able to use them all. You make sure you take what you can carry home."

"Emma, you're such a dear. Always thinking of others, even in this time of grief."

"I'd be much more aggrieved if I let a bushel of apples spoil, knowing there were others who could use them."

Maggie laughed. "You've talked me into it. Of course we'll take some. My children likely will not have any room for their supper tonight anyway. Their stomachs are already full of apples." Maggie paused and looked around at the blue sky surrounding them and the sun shining on them through the shade of the leaves. "What a lovely day."

Emma agreed, but in the evenings when she was alone, the small house seemed cavernous. Every sound seemed to echo loudly against the walls. The house only had two bedrooms upstairs and a kitchen, parlor, and dining room downstairs. It wasn't large. But it was more than she could bear now.

Her father had said many times, "There's no need for a pastor to be ostentatious. I simply need a place to eat, a place to rest my head, and a place to meet with those who come to me for guidance and prayers." He was a simple, humble man, and she missed him so much.

She was so lonely.

Each night, she sat alone at the dinner table and ate the food that someone had kindly brought her that day, missing the conversations she would have with her father over the business of the church or who needed prayers that day. She read the Bible alone before bed, but it lacked some of its meaning when it was not read aloud and discussed with someone else. Her father had always had some insight into God's word or a connection to make to their lives.

"God often sends us suffering to help us see the beauty in what we have and to remind us to be grateful," he would say.

Or, *"This story reminds me of Mr. Hopewell. Do you remember when he got very sick last winter, and even the doc wasn't sure he would make it through. But then, we had the whole church praying for him, and the Lord saw fit to heal Mr. Hopewell. He stopped by just today with some wood for the stove at the church. He's a good man. The Lord sees that."*

Father had helped the words come alive. But reading them silently in an empty house seemed to take some of the life right out of even her favorite passages.

There were few times Emma had ever contemplated a husband, but she wished she had a strong shoulder to lean on at a time like this. It wasn't that she was uninterested in marriage, she simply had yet to find a man who made her heart flutter or someone whom she thought of in those idle moments when her mind wandered. If she ever did daydream about a husband, he was always an unknown man, tall and strong with dark hair and kind eyes.

She knew as well that God would lead her to her husband whenever He saw fit. She was sure His plan held great things for her, and a husband was not on the agenda just yet.

***

After she hung the last sheet on the line to dry, Emma sat in her father's rocking chair on the front porch, intending to peel and cut some apples for a pie, but she was overcome by lethargy.

"Come on, Emma, you can do this," she whispered to herself. "It's a simple task you've done hundreds of times."

But she could not seem to make her arms move. Instead, she gently rocked herself back and forth, admiring the view. The small house stood beside the church, with a lush green lawn between them. Beside the apple tree stood pear and cherry trees, both alive with birds snacking and insects pollinating. The dirt road out front led into town just a little ways to the east. She could hear the horses whinnying and men calling to each other from where she sat. And even farther in the distance were the mountains.

To climb one of those mountains, Emma thought, closing her eyes, *to be that close to God.*

She sat at the table in the back of the church, where she held her Sunday school lessons. Instead of the passel of children who normally surrounded her, there was only one little boy. He was wearing a simple dark shirt and pants with worn spots on the knees. His light brown hair was a little mussed, and she could see a little dirt on his right ear as if he had been playing outside recently.

The small room had four rows of little tables with four chairs each, all facing a chalkboard at the front of the room. Emma did not often stand at the chalkboard. She preferred to sit, to be closer to the children. They seemed to like it when she was closer to their level. It was not unusual for her to sit side by side with a child and work together, as she was now.

"H," she said, pointing to the letter in the book on her lap.

"H," the little boy repeated in his high, clear voice.

She was showing him the letters of the alphabet, his head down, finger tracing the letters. She smiled down at him, feeling strong affection and pride for this little boy. As she named all the letters, he repeated after her but never looked up. She never saw his face.

Emma awoke, still in the chair on the porch, chilled as the sun began to sink behind the mountains. She must have nodded off for an hour or more.

She took her basket of apples inside and pondered the dream.

Why had God sent her the image of this unknown little boy?

She had always turned to her father for guidance with her visions, but he was not here.

His Bible, she thought, placing the apples on the kitchen counter. *He relied on the Good Book for guidance whenever he needed it. Perhaps it can help me now.*

She hurried upstairs to her father's room, where Frank Clement's Bible sat upon his bedside table.

Sitting in her chair beside the bed, she set the book on her lap, much as she had with the book in her vision. It fell open to her favorite passage — God speaking to Aaron and Miriam in the Book of Numbers.

"When the two of them stepped forward, he said, "Listen to my words: "When there is a prophet among you, I, the Lord, reveal myself to them in visions, I speak to them in dreams."

Since she was very young, she had loved that passage because it told of God speaking through visions and dreams like hers. She was reluctant to call herself a prophet but knowing that she was not the only one God spoke to in this way brought some comfort.

But how is this passage related to my vision? Why has God led me to these words? And how are they connected to the faceless little boy?

***

She reread the entire chapter of Numbers before bed that night, sitting in her usual chair by her father's bedside. As she began to ready herself for bed, she contemplated the words.

In the chapter, Aaron and Miriam had criticized Moses, asking why Moses alone spoke to God, Emma thought as she carefully combed her hair, tugging at an especially stubborn knot in her sun-colored waves.

But then God himself came down and spoke to them to explain. She tugged her high-necked nightgown over her head. *Afterward, Miriam was punished for her criticism.*

Emma paused, looking at her narrow nose and bow-shaped mouth in the mirror, to think back on the last few days as she braided her hair.

Have I been overly critical of anyone? Her fingers moved deftly down the length of her hair, expertly plaiting the waist length tresses.

She was certain she had not. She had hardly thought of anything in the last week but making it from one moment to the next.

Surely God wants me to focus just on the verse about visions and dreams. Is He simply telling me to trust the visions, as Father did? She reached the end of her braid and tied it off.

She knew God was trying to tell her something, but as always, it was indistinct, like a reflection glinting in river water. For the first time, she was left to interpret this vision by herself. With all of her previous visions, she had talked it through with her father, and he would help her come to a conclusion about God's meaning.

She decided to turn to God for clarity and guidance.

"Dear Lord, I trust that you have a plan for me, and I trust that you will use me as you see fit. I know that all my suffering will be worth it because it will bring me closer to you. Please, Lord, show me how I can be of use to you. Show me what I am to do with this little boy. Call me to your service, oh Lord, however you see fit. I will trust in you and go where you send me."

She still did not know what the vision and the verse had truly meant, but she felt more peace in her heart than she had in a week. God had a plan for her, and she would place her trust in Him.

Chapter Two

August 1873

Colorado Springs, Colorado

Paul Gilbert stood in the kitchen of his father-in-law's house, where he now lived with his five-year-old son, Aaron.

How in the world had it become my responsibility to make breakfast every day? he wondered to himself, stretching his lanky arms up over his head. *Two years ago I would not have known how to break an egg.*

In reality, he knew how cooking meals had become his responsibility. In a house full of men, someone had to keep their bellies full. Aaron couldn't be expected to help much at his age, and Earle could not do much more than heat some salt pork in a skillet. Paul wasn't much better, but he was at least willing to try.

He watched Aaron playing on the floor, quiet and content for the moment with his tiny wooden horses and cows.

"Clip clop, clip clop." Aaron trotted a horse across the floor by the kitchen table, rounding up the cattle. His light brown hair hung down around his chubby cheeks as he moved the animals across the rough wooden planks.

It brought Paul some peace to watch his son looking so happy, but the feeling quickly passed. His wide shoulders tightened, and he reached a long arm up to massage the tense muscles.

Every time he looked at Aaron, he was transported back to the previous year, hearing the screams of his wife and child all over again. Feeling the searing heat from the flames licking at his back. The acrid scent of smoke filling his nostrils and the taste in his mouth, down his throat. The adrenaline rushing through his veins.

Paul was a man in turmoil most of the time, and he could not quite seem to move beyond a feeling of constant underlying anger since the death of his wife.

As he hacked at a loaf of hard bread he had baked the day before with minimal success—it tasted close enough to bread and did not seem to give anyone a stomach ache—Paul became aware of the smell of smoke wafting from behind him.

The odor sent his body into a state of high alert. His breaths became shallow as his heart rate accelerated. He could feel sweat beading up all over his body. Preparing for a roaring flame, he whirled around to find the source of the smoke.

The eggs!

Smoke billowed from the cast iron pan on the stove. Paul snatched it off the heat, but in his haste, he forgot to pick up the flour sack towel from the hook. His hand burning, he threw the pan on the floor and let out a loud expletive.

"Aaahhhh!" The boy wailed, startled by the clamor from across the room. He clenched his favorite wooden pony in his hand as his father scooped him up onto a chair and tried to console him.

"Shhh. It's fine, little one. It's fine." Paul rocked from side to side in the chair, trying to soothe his son. "I'm sorry I made so much noise."

Aaron had outbursts frequently. He had suddenly be crying and screaming, sometimes he would throw or break whatever was in reach. More than one plate had been the victim of Aaron's tantrums.

Usually, Paul had no idea what might have set the boy off. This time, however, he was fairly certain that the loud noises and the smell of smoke had done it. Paul was still working on slowing his own heartbeat. After experiencing a house fire with tragic results, it was only natural to be wary of smoke and flames for a while.

"Mama!" Aaron always cried for his mama, even though she had been gone a year. "I want my mama!"

Even a year later his son never seemed to want him, only the mother he would never get back. The mother who had sacrificed herself for her son.

Paul continued his rocking and shushing, kissing the top of his son's head, and wishing he could make everything better for both of them. He knew it was futile. Nothing would ever be good again. Not with Laura gone forever.

Lord knew taciturn old Earle was not helping much. Even though this was Earle's house, he had left the daily work over to his son-in-law when his daughter had married. And now the daughter was gone, leaving Earle in a dark mood much of the time. Most days, he sat on the porch and watched the sun move across the sky until it was time for supper.

Paul smoothed his son's light brown hair and wiped at the tears on his cheeks, ignoring his own burned hand for the moment. He could tend to himself later, right now he needed to calm Aaron and start breakfast over again.

As the sobs faded to soft, chirping hiccups, Paul tipped Aaron's chin up toward his own face. "I'm sorry for yelling, son. I should not have said such a word. I didn't mean to frighten you."

The little boy nodded his acceptance, still sniffling. "I'm hungry."

"I know you are, son. I am too." Paul helped Aaron climb down from his lap. "You go play outside a bit. I'll go get more eggs to start breakfast again. I made a right mess of the last one."

Aaron nodded again, then went and sat on the wide plank porch near where Earle was already perched for the day, rocking back and forth in his old chair.

Paul looked back at the mess he had made of the kitchen and shook his head. The eggs were blackened and scattered across the floor. The fat he had used to grease the cast iron pan was sprayed across the front of the stove and the wall. He got down on his hands and knees and cleaned it all up.

His life sure was not going the way he had planned, but whose did? Rather than continue to brood, he got to work scraping the eggs off the wooden floor boards and scrubbing the pan before heading back outside to gather more eggs from the chicken coop, a task he had completed once already today. His hand throbbed throughout his chores, but he ignored it.

As he stomped his way out the back of the big white house toward the chickens, he encountered Holt Daniels making his way across the wide green lawn between the bunkhouse and the stables.

"Mornin', Paul. Beautiful day, isn't it?" Holt looked up at the receding dark of night to the west and the orange spreading across the eastern horizon and took a deep breath.

The gray-haired man had worked on the ranch for Paul's entire life and had become the man Paul had turned to for guidance and advice since the death of his own father years ago. Holt had a pleasant disposition, typically seeing the bright side of a situation and always finding a possible solution to any problem. He could often be found with a smile on his face and had the deep creases around his eyes as proof.

Paul grunted and kept his clear blue eyes focused on the chicken coop. He didn't even glance at the sky. "I already burned breakfast and made my son cry, so I'm not sure I feel the same way as you. I'm headed out to the henhouse to get more eggs." Paul wrinkled his nose at the prospect. "Woman's work," he huffed.

"Well, now, why don't you just pause for a moment and look at that beautiful day dawning? It's barely even started yet. It hasn't been determined. There's still time to turn it around."

Paul shrugged sullenly, like a teenage boy.

"Is that all that's bothering you? Some burned eggs?" Holt gave him a fatherly look. The empathy and sincerity in his eyes made Paul want to confide in him. There was no reason to be short with Holt. He had not done anything wrong.

He took a deep breath. "I just do not know how much longer I can do this. I cannot be both father and mother to the boy. I cannot run the house and the ranch both. I can't. I can't do it all." Paul shook his head in defeat.

"Sounds like you need a woman."

"I ain't interested in marrying again, Holt." Paul's voice hardened.

"No, not a wife. Just a woman." The men moved toward the chicken coop together. "You need a woman to run the house and help with Aaron. The boy runs wild—yells, hits. You're right that you can't handle that by yourself, and you do not have to."

Paul's brows drew together, and he shifted on his feet. "What do you mean 'I need a woman?'"

There was a low whistle from behind them, and they turned to see Shaw McCormick, one of the farmhands, standing behind them. "You need a woman, huh? Don't we all? I could use a pretty little thing to dote on me."

Shaw was a good-natured man of twenty-three, usually found with a broad smile on his tanned face. He was known to joke around quite a bit, but he was a good worker who truly cared about the land and the animals.

Holt chuckled at the younger man. "I was just telling Paul that he needs a woman to help take care of things around here." Holt then turned back to Paul. "Hire a governess for the boy," Holt clarified, his tone firm.

"Make sure you hire a pretty one. Us farmhands could use something nice to look at every now and then," Shaw added, smiling jovially to indicate that he wasn't being serious.

"Not sure how much control I have over that," Paul responded through gritted teeth.

"You just need someone who can keep Aaron out of the stables and cowshed while we're working. Someone who can do the housework for you." Holt leaned against the side of the coop while Paul leaned in to gather the eggs. "Keep you from having to collect eggs from these ornery old hens every day."

"Invite a stranger into the house?" Paul's voice echoed from inside the chicken coop, sounding offended.

"Well, yes. You have plenty of space in that big house. There's room for a governess."

"A pretty governess!" Shaw reminded them again, then scooted quickly out of the way of Holt's teasing smack, aimed at his upper arm.

"Get to the barn, you rascal," Holt playfully ordered Shaw, who took the instruction to heart and walked away to tend to the horses.

"I don't know. I'm not sure how Earle would feel about it," Paul replied cautiously. "It is his house, after all. It does not seem right for me to just invite someone to come live with us without consulting him."

"This may have been Earle's house and land, but you're the man in charge now as far as I see it. Seems to me if you decide you're going to do it, there's not much he can say. And I'm sure he would appreciate the improved quality of the food."

Paul still hesitated.

"Just think about it, Paul. And then think about all the work you have to do around the ranch and in the house. Consider the benefits of having a woman around. Not just for yourself, but for your son. Someone to teach him right from wrong, how to be kind and strong."

"How would I even find such a woman? All the women in Colorado Springs are married with their own children and houses to take care of."

"Put an ad in the newspaper. I see those sorts of things all the time."

Paul nodded, clearly considering this possibility. He could hire a woman to take care of all the household chores that he dreaded, and that he frankly was not very good at. The house could be clean again. She could teach Aaron to read and write, and somehow maybe the boy would become a little calmer. Maybe a woman's gentle touch was what he needed to help him become the sweet little boy he had been before. If that was even possible. Could any of them ever be how they were before? Could they ever recover from the aftermath of the fire? Of losing Laura?

Holt squeezed Paul's shoulder in a farewell gesture and continued on his way, and left Paul to ruminate as he repeated the task of gathering and cooking eggs.

Having a woman around would mean he could tend to the livestock in the morning, rather than collecting eggs. It would mean that he would not be the one tasked with cooking the eggs, or cleaning up after the meal either.

By the time the table was set for breakfast, he was convinced. He broached the subject with Earle as the man served himself the newly cooked eggs.

"I think I'm going to put out an ad for a governess."

"Whatever for?" Earle asked, frowning at the hard bread he had just attempted to bite into. Earle was a grumpy man on the best of days, but he was never deliberately unkind. He never criticized the work that Paul did, but neither did he offer help or solutions.

"To take care of Aaron. And the house. Things are not going as well as I'd like, and I think a woman could help."

"Things are just fine. We're all fed. Aaron's fine. We do not need another woman in this house." Earle's gray eyebrows drew together seriously. His tone said that he was final in his opinion on the matter.

Aaron sat silently beside Earle, dipping his bread in his eggs with his wooden animals on the table beside his plate. Paul sipped his coffee as he considered his next words.

Holt had said that Paul was the man in charge now, but he still felt that he should respect that this was Earle's house first. It was Earle's family land. However, it was his son, and he would not risk his son being an uneducated hell-raiser.

"I need more help. Aaron's been having more and more bad dreams. He doesn't know his letters yet. He runs around this ranch and gets in the way of the work that needs to be done. A woman can take care of him, teach him, and help him to become a real man who can help us on the ranch instead." He looked his father-in-law in the eye. "I think a governess is the best choice. For Aaron."

A slight, accompanied by a rough grunt, was Earle's only response, but Paul knew that was the only approval he was going to get from the man. Aaron was the man's only soft spot, though he hid it behind a hard veneer most of the time.

Paul nodded as well, silently acknowledging that the plan was made.

That evening, after the usual argument with Aaron over bedtime and finally getting the boy to sleep, Paul sat down at the small desk in the front room. It was a cozy room, decorated by Earle's late wife Amelia, with family portraits on the walls and white lace curtains at the windows. Over the large fireplace hung a wreath she had made from dried wheat and wildflowers from this very ranch.

Paul opened the desk drawers and took out a pen and paper. But that was as far as he could get. He did not know what to write.

What does an advertisement for a governess look like? What words should he use? He didn't want to sound desperate, and he didn't want to let on that his son was difficult. He didn't want to scare the women away.

He considered what he needed a woman to help him with, and decided it was best to just write a list based on that. After a few attempts, revisions, and crossing the whole thing out twice and starting over, he had an advertisement that looked serviceable. He read it over a few times, wondering what Laura would think of him now. Would she be ashamed that he couldn't care for himself and their son without another woman's help?

"Wanted – Governess for my 5-year-old son Aaron and housekeeper for our ranch house in Colorado Springs, Colorado. Must be able to cook, clean, sew, read, and write as well as perform other household chores. Apply by letter to Mr. P. Gilbert, Colorado Springs, Colorado."

He decided that he would ride into town the next day to place the ad.

Chapter Three

September 1873

Pueblo, Colorado

"Hello, Emma!"

Emma waved at Mrs. Miller, who was walking toward her on the boardwalk in the bright noon sunshine. "Good morning, Mrs. Miller. How are the children?"

"You sweet thing, always asking about the children. You truly do love working with the little ones, don't you?" the dark-haired woman asked.

Mrs. Miller had three young children who had all been in Emma's Sunday school classes. Felix, the rambunctious seven-year-old, loved the Bible stories that involved battles or fights, and Emma always had to remind him that suffering was not a game. His younger sisters, twins Mary and Anna, had bouncy golden curls and always wore matching bows, but the similarities ended there. Mary took after Felix and would rather be climbing the trees with the boys. Anna was content to sit quietly and read her Bible or make headdresses from the clover flowers blooming in the churchyard. The Miller children were dear to Emma, just as much as all the children in her class, and she hadn't seen them in too long.

The women crossed the muddy street together, adeptly avoiding the puddles and horse droppings littering the middle.

"I do love working with the children." Emma's brow furrowed. "And since the church is closed while we wait for a new minister, I surely miss them. I love teaching Sunday school."

"I'm sure the new pastor will be happy to have a willing teacher when he gets here. Have you heard anything about getting a new preacher in?"

Emma shook her head. "No, Reverend Thompson said he'd send word once he had a man on the way. It was so kind of him to help."

The two women walked together into the general store. The earthy smell of leather mixed with the strong musk of lamp oil and the tang of vinegar from the pickle crock. It was a strange mix of scents, but one that was as familiar and comforting to Emma as her own home.

She had always loved coming to Carson's General Store. She liked all of the colors of fabric and ribbons in the sewing department and in the array of candy and spices on the counter. As a child, she would stand and watch the men in the front playing checkers while her father made his purchases, watching the black and red pieces jump across the board and cheering for the winner.

"Howdy, Mrs. Miller, Miss Clement! What can I get for you ladies today?" Matthew Carson asked from behind the counter, surrounded by his store's array of groceries and dry goods. As always, he was impeccably groomed in his striped shirt, wool vest, and Carter's General Store apron. His wife had embroidered the store's name right across the front of it in shimmering emerald green, and they were both mighty proud of their shop.

Emma indicated that Mrs. Miller could be served first, as she wanted the time to peruse the shelves.

Mr. Carson mostly carried the typical things his customers needed or asked for—salt pork and dried beef, canned fruits and vegetables, sewing supplies and fabrics, fragrant soaps and paraffin candles, lamp oil, nails and assorted hardware goods. All the little things that were necessary to just live life in a small frontier town.

But Mr. Carson would often add in a few unusual items or new products that no one had seen yet. Once, when Emma was twelve, Mr. Carson had gotten a little music box into the shop. It served no practical purpose and cost quite a bit of money, so she knew better than to ask her father to buy it for her, but she had to stop and listen to it each time she came into the shop. It had been shaped like a tiny piano with delicate pink roses painted across the lid. It played a song she had never heard before or since, as it wasn't a hymn, but it was beautiful.

A man had eventually bought it for his wife as a wedding gift, and Emma could only imagine how wonderful it must be to have a gentleman buy you such a lovely gift simply as a token of his affection. She had never had a man court her, none had ever caught her eye, and now she was worried she was getting a little too old to find a husband.

Today, Emma had come to the store for a few food items and nothing more, since the supply of food from neighbors was running dry. But truthfully, she also wanted to do something to get out of that house, so she strolled slowly and with no purpose around the store.

She perused the beautiful fabrics and ribbons in the sewing department, wishing she had any reason or enough money for a new dress. The fashion magazines placed among the fabric and notions showed the current trends in ladies' dresses—lots of ruffles with bustles and trains. She reminded herself that not only was her simple clothing far more practical for life out West but also that she should be grateful to God for what she had, which was plenty.

She peered curiously at some small tools hanging on one wall. As a city girl, she did not know for sure what any of the farming implements might be used for, but it seemed that many of them were just large knives of some sort.

The floorboards creaked under her feet as she turned toward the household goods. She might need more laundry soap soon, but that was not a necessity just yet. There was a lovely smelling new bath soap that Emma imagined smelled the same way a very beautiful and fancy woman in a real city must smell. The kind of woman who would go to the opera and have gentleman callers.

She was certain these were all things she had read in a book somewhere. Probably here in this very general store in the book display. This thought made Emma turn toward the small stand of newspapers, magazines, and books.

She was leafing through a new kind of publication, a Montgomery Ward mail order catalog, when Mr. Carson called to her. In her haste and distraction, she knocked a stack of newspapers to the ground.

"Oh, my, how clumsy I've become," she muttered to herself. Attempting to straighten up the papers, she could not quite seem to get the pages back in order. As she attempted to properly refold the crumpled paper, an advertisement for a governess caught her eye.

She gasped. It mentioned a little boy named Aaron.

Her mind flew to her favorite Bible verse, the one she had read only days before after her vision of teaching a little boy: *When the two of them stepped forward, he said, "Listen to my words: When there is a prophet among you, I, the Lord, reveal myself to them in visions, I speak to them in dreams."*

For a moment, she was frozen, staring at the advertisement. Aaron and Miriam were the two people God had called forward. The name appearing again in this advertisement did not seem like merely a coincidence.

She heard God's voice calling out to her, saying, "Emma, this is your path."

Emma clutched the small cross that hung around her neck.

"Miss Clement?" Mr. Carter called again.

"Emma, dear." Mrs. Miller touched Emma's shoulder. "Have a lovely day."

Jolted out of her reverie, Emma said good-bye to Mrs. Miller and took the newspaper with her to the counter to make her purchases, thinking over the job. It must be what God was telling her.

"I'd like this Colorado Springs newspaper, please." She placed it on the counter so Mr. Carter could ring it up.

Never fazed by what his customers bought, and not one to ask any questions, he simply added up her purchases on his notepad and then gathered her remaining items as she directed.

Emma could hardly stand still as her groceries were totaled and packaged. She just wanted to get home and compose her letter. She knew—just *knew*—that this was her path. This was God's plan. She was supposed to go take care of this little boy. She could do everything the advertisement required. She had been taking care of herself and her father on her own for years.

On a whim, she had bought herself a few pieces of hard candy. She popped a lemon candy in her mouth as she walked down the boardwalk, back toward home. As the candy, tart and sweet, melted on her tongue, she began to feel lighter than she had in weeks. She had something to look forward to, something to hope for.

As she walked, she formulated her response to the advertisement. She would need to introduce herself and explain her qualifications. She would need to sound capable but also like someone who would be kind and patient with a little boy who she supposed must not have a mother. Just like her.

Dear Lord, she prayed, *If this is what I'm meant to do, I will follow Your lead and Your message. Help me to be strong and courageous and to make the right choice.*

After putting her groceries away, Emma sat at her father's desk in the sitting room. She found paper, ink, and a pen and thought over the choice. After a few minutes of prayer, she put pen to paper. She knew just what she wanted to say.

Chapter Four

September 1873

Colorado Springs, Colorado

Dear Mr. Gilbert,

My name is Emma Clement. I am writing in response to your advertisement for a governess. I would very much like to help you take care of your son and your house. I assure you I am qualified.

I am twenty-two years old. I have lived in Pueblo my whole life with my father, who was the pastor at our town church. I have been running our household since I was fifteen. I am a skilled cook and a satisfactory seamstress. I am fully capable of completing other necessary household chores as well.

I have also been teaching the children in my father's church for the last six years. Children bring me such joy, and I truly feel that teaching them and looking after them is my calling in life.

As of yet, I am unmarried and have no children of my own. Since the recent passing of my father and the subsequent closing of the church, I have no one and nothing to keep me in Pueblo.

I would very much like to take on the advertised position.

Yours truly,

Emma Clement

The letter had arrived in town only two weeks after Paul had placed the advertisement. The Colorado Springs paper was only published once a week, so he was quite surprised to get a response so quickly.

The woman sounded enthusiastic and capable. The only thing that bothered him was that she was a pastor's daughter. Surely she was used to talk of God in the house and prayers over meals. There was none of that in his house. Nor would there be.

He considered the letter during the entire ride back to the ranch from town. The long dirt road gave him plenty of time to think as he absently patted the neck of his horse, Fritz. He ruminated over the idea of a Sunday school teacher in his house.

The more he thought about it the more uncertain he became about the whole idea. Not just about having a preacher's daughter in his house, but having a woman in his house. Laura had only been gone a year. It seemed impossible that it had been an entire year, and yet the past year seemed endless. The hole in his heart grew wider each day. He did not know if he could handle having another woman around, reminding him of her all the time.

By the time he arrived at the stable, he had almost talked himself out of the whole thing until Holt saw him. The ranch hand rode across the corral on the horse he was training.

"I know that look," the older man said, tying his horse to the post by the door. "What's troubling you?"

"I got a response to my advertisement for a governess." Paul had dismounted and was beginning the process of removing the saddle and blankets from the horse. He took the bit from Fritz's mouth and gave him a carrot to snack on from the nearby bin. He glanced at Holt but cared too much about his animals to stop what he was doing.

"Then why do you look so upset? That's good news!" Holt took a brush from the bin nearby and helped Paul brush down the horse. "Unless she's not any good? She doesn't like children?"

"No, she sounds just about perfect," Paul grumbled, a storm brewing in his expression despite the fact that this should be good news.

"But?" Holt put on a fatherly tone, as if trying to draw the whole truth out of a small child who was withholding the details of his wrongdoing.

"She's a pastor's daughter."

"And?" Holt looked at Paul around Fritz's hind quarters, his brow furrowed.

"I do not want some woman talking about God in my house."

"Sounds to me like she'll be a fine, upstanding woman. She'll know right from wrong. And she'll be able to teach Aaron right from wrong, too."

Paul nodded, but still did not look convinced.

"That's not everything, is it?" Holt gave Paul the look of a father eliciting a confession out of a child.

"I'm just not sure I want a woman in my house so soon. And how will this affect Aaron? He barely even had time to know his mama, and now I'm going to just throw some other woman at him?" He continued to brush Fritz, vigorously working the sweat out of the animal's hide.

"I'm not sure Aaron's going to see it that way. I think you're worried that somehow this will be seen as replacing Laura." Holt placed a hand on Paul's shoulder. "Nothing is further from the truth. No one could replace Laura. She was a fine woman. A governess is hired to help, no different from those boys out there in the fields."

Paul didn't have any time to respond. There was a high-pitched screeching coming from the house. The only thing that could make that sound was Aaron—he must be hurt. Paul's heart leapt out of his chest in alarm, his body leaping into high alert. He took off running, making it across the yard, up the back porch steps, and up the interior staircase to Aaron's room in record time.

The little boy was screaming like a demon, red-faced with tears running down his cheeks, as he threw anything and everything he could reach. His bed was disheveled, the blankets tangled on the floor. His toys were strewn about the room, laying wherever they had landed when he'd thrown them. Articles of clothing lay in wrinkled heaps all around the room.

The boy looked as if he were about to tear the curtains off the wall when Paul snatched him and held him tightly, as he had done before, while Aaron thrashed and wailed.

As always, Aaron cried out for his mama. And as always, Paul gritted his teeth against his own pain and whispered what he hoped were soothing words.

But this was no ordinary crying child. This was one of the episodes Aaron had started having after the fire. He would kick and punch and scream louder than Paul thought was possible for such a small person. Paul had come away from these episodes with quite a few bruises and even a couple of bite marks, but he could never tell what had started them. Afterward, Paul typically needed to take a few deep breaths, followed by a few moments to collect himself. Sometimes, he would go to the front room to talk to Laura's painting about it, but nothing much made him feel better.

"Mama!" Aaron's voice was getting weaker, tired, and his limbs were going still. Paul stroked the boy's hair and watched as the blue eyes, much like his father's, drifted closed and he fell asleep.

Paul lifted his son easily and placed him on the small bed. It would have to be remade later. For now, the child needed some rest and the father needed to respond to the letter he had received today.

This latest outburst made it clear. He needed help. He could not keep doing this by himself, and Aaron deserved more than what Paul alone could give him.

Dear Miss Clement,

I was glad to receive your letter inquiring about the governess position. You sound like you are highly qualified and exactly what I am looking for in a candidate.

I would like to offer you the position of governess, provided you can start right away.

As payment, you would have your own room in my house and food provided for you, in addition to a small monthly salary.

In your response, please let me know when I should expect you.

Yours,

Paul Gilbert

Paul reread his letter. It seemed sufficient, but he had never been very flowery with his writing. Laura used to joke that if he wrote poetry, it would probably just be rhymes about horses and cows.

"Roses are red, that cow is brown, I'd like to take you on a drive into town," she teased. Her face, bright and full with

laughter, disappeared behind a tree as she said it, enticing him to chase her. He lunged, catching her around the waist, and they fell together into the grass, laughing breathlessly in each other's arms.

Paul could not imagine what would make him laugh like that now. He missed her. Each and every day he missed her.

He went to the front room to look at the portrait of Laura hanging on the wall. She had given it to him as an engagement gift, and it had somehow survived the fire. In it, she was smiling brightly, wearing a yellow dress with lace ruffles that she had proudly made for herself. She had wildflowers woven into her dark braided hair around the crown of her head. It was how he liked to think of her, smiling and laughing, and so he was glad to have the painting to look at now that she was gone.

He sat in the wingback chair nearby, settling into its dark blue velvet, and gazed up at the portrait. He often talked to her when something was troubling him, and he thought now he might owe her an explanation.

"Laura. Dear Laura. Soon there's going to be another woman in this house, a governess for Aaron. Someone who can cook without starting fires or turning bread into bricks."

He looked down at his rough, callused hands and nervously picked at the dirt beneath his fingernails.

"I think we need her. It's hard to care for three men and a house and a ranch. It's difficult for me to be the only parent to our son."

Paul looked back up into Laura's eyes, smiling impishly down at him. His heart clenched at the sight, unknown emotions tightening their grip.

"But don't think I'm trying to replace you. You'll always be his mama. Your picture will stay right here no matter what, so that Aaron will always know your pretty face. This new woman will not be his mama, just his caretaker. Someone to keep him out of trouble and teach him the things he ought to know. You said many times that education is important, and Aaron doesn't have any yet. This woman is a teacher. I'm sure he'll be reading and writing in no time."

He smiled sadly up at his wife, trying unsuccessfully to make light of the situation.

"She'll be here, but so will you. I'll make sure of that. I'll never stop missing you or loving you. Never. You're a part of me. So much so that I don't even remember meeting you. We just always knew each other.

"I do remember the first time you kissed me. *You* kissed *me.* You were nine years old and I was eleven, and we were back behind the cowshed, both of us covered in dirt." Paul chuckled softly to himself at the memory.

Laura's brown strands tumbled out of their loose braids, hay and grass sticking out of them in every direction. She was wearing a blue and white checkered dress with holes in it that her mother had given up patching. As a child, Laura had gone where the boys went and did what the boys did, having no care for being gentle with her clothing. If her skirt got caught on a tree branch, she just yanked until it came loose and kept climbing.

She had suddenly leaned over and kissed him as they watched a frog jumping through the mud.

After he ripped his face away, he wiped his mouth with the back of his hand and exclaimed, "What did you do that for?"

"'Cause I've never done it before and you were here," she said defensively, crossing her arms. "I saw Winnie Edmonds and Andy Pierce kissing at the picnic last weekend. I just wanted to know what it was like."

"So? What did you find out?" he asked, curious about kissing as well, but unable to admit it to a girl.

"Didn't seem like anything special to me." With that, she kicked at a clod of dirt with the toe of her boot and ran off to find the other boys.

Paul sighed at that boy he had once been. "But the next time, *I* kissed *you*. You were sixteen and so pretty and I could not help myself. That's when I knew that we were meant for each other." Paul had had this conversation many times with this painting. It was one of his favorite memories of his wife.

It was at the annual town picnic. She wore a brand new dress with no holes or patches anywhere. Her chestnut hair curled with pretty blue ribbons holding it away from her face, showcasing her high cheekbones and pointed chin. With the smattering of freckles across her nose and cheeks, he thought she looked like a mischievous fairy and told her so right before he kissed her behind a stand of willow trees by the river.

When they had pulled away from one another, Paul felt stunned and a little embarrassed. He thought he was probably about to be smacked for his impertinence.

Instead, Laura touched her lips reverently and looked him right in the eye. "What took you so long?"

"What?" He took a step back, surprised and confused by her response. He had expected anger that he had had the gall to kiss her, not that he had taken too long to finally do so.

"I've been trying to get you to kiss me all summer, you nincompoop. What took so long?" She shoved his shoulder, displaying a shadow of her formerly tomboyish ways.

"I...I didn't notice."

"You didn't notice? You didn't notice all my new dresses?" She held out the skirt of her pristine white and blue striped dress, not a speck of dust or a wrinkle to be found, unlike her childhood dresses that were full of holes and stains from outdoor exploits. "How I always found you alone in the barn?"

"Well, how was I supposed to know?" He threw his hands in the air in frustration. How could she be upset with him when he had not had the slightest idea that she was interested in him?

"Oh, never mind. Just kiss me again." She wrapped her hands around his neck and pulled their faces together. That's the kiss that had sealed the deal.

From then on, they were more inseparable than they had been before. She liked to say that God had meant for them to be together and there was no keeping them apart.

"God has more plans for you, my love." The high, lilting tone of Laura's voice shook Paul out of his reverie. He blinked hard, convinced he was losing his mind. He just needed sleep. That wasn't Laura's voice. It was only his imagination.

He missed her every day, and he could not see how her God would make her die if he wanted them to be together. He had no interest in a God who would rob him of a wife and his son of a mother.

Chapter Five

September 1873

Pueblo, Colorado

"Push! Push the lid down!" Hallie Jacobs commanded. She had one arm leaning hard on the top of Emma's trunk and one attempting to close the clasp. "It's almost there! Can't you push any more?"

"I am sitting on the trunk, Hallie, how could I possibly push it more than using my entire body?" Georgina McPherson retorted, her normally prim and neat black curls askew atop her head from the efforts of attempting to enclose all of Emma's worldly possessions, as well as many of her parents' into a single container.

Georgie and Hallie were Emma's two best friends. The girls had all grown up together, and their mothers had often substituted for Emma's, teaching her to sew, cook, and behave like a lady. They girls were inseparable, and now Emma was parting from them. The prospect made Hallie and Georgie, who fought like sisters on a normal day, even testier than usual.

"And don't you dare comment on my physique!" Georgie continued, before Hallie could tease her about her wide hips. "I am fearfully and wonderfully made, just the way God wants me, and Thomas Covey agrees."

"Thomas Covey!" Hallie stood abruptly, shocked at this new information. When she stood, however, she also let go of the trunk, sending Georgie tumbling feet over face onto the floor.

"Hallie! I thought you almost had it!" Georgie's voice was muffled by the fabric of her own skirt, which now covered her face.

Emma, who had been packing away the possessions that wouldn't go with her to Colorado Springs, came rushing into the room at the cacophony of Georgie hitting the floor followed by the clunks and clangs of items springing out of the trunk.

"Goodness, girls, whatever is happening in here?" Emma reached down to help Georgie right herself. The other woman ran her hands down her skirts and patted her hair to assure herself that everything was in place.

"Thomas Covey is courting Georgie!" Hallie exclaimed, her face alight with glee for her friend. They were all of marrying age, but their parents expected a certain quality of man that was hard to come by in a frontier town.

"Thomas Covey! The banker's assistant?" Emma turned to Georgie, her face showing the same excitement as Hallie's. "He's so handsome!"

"He's charming and sweet, too." Georgie began to blush, a flush of pink spreading across her cheeks behind her freckles. "He said my hair was the color of a lake at midnight. And he brought me some sassafras candy from the general store because he noticed I like them."

"Tell us everything!" Hallie took Georgie's hand and pulled her over to the edge of Emma's bed. All three girls sat to share and gossip for one last night before Emma had to leave.

***

Emma watched her brown leather trunk, filled to the brim with her possessions and mementos of her parents, being loaded onto the train. Georgina and Hallie stood with her on the train platform to see her off. She had said goodbye to their parents, who felt as much like hers as theirs, already so that she could spend her last few minutes in Pueblo with her closest companions.

"Oh, Emma, I'm going to miss you so much!" Georgie threw her arms around her friend's neck and squeezed her one last time. Her dark hair whipped around her head, curls bouncing wildly.

Emma laughed lightly at Georgina's typical melodramatics. They had already had this conversation a number of times in the last few weeks. "I'm going to miss you, too, Georgie. I'll write to you as soon as I'm settled, and perhaps you'll even be able to come visit."

They stood at the small train station in Pueblo. It was just a small wooden platform with a few benches, but it was one of many sights Emma would miss.

She was going to live in the countryside, where there would not be nearly so many buildings or people around all the time. She would miss walking down Main Street and seeing the elegant men's suits in the front window at the tailor's shop and the frilly, intricate ladies' hats at the milliners. She would miss the familiar, smiling faces in the general store. Most of all, she would miss the sight of the white steeple of her father's church always shining like a beacon above the town, guiding her home.

"Wouldn't that be exciting? I would love that." Georgie's face lit up. She was all emotion, that girl. If something was exciting, it was always the most exciting thing she could imagine. If it was sad, it was the most depressing thing on earth.

"Do not get too excited yet. It may not be possible," Emma warned her. "I don't yet know what my living situation will look like or how large the house is. I've been assured I'll have my own room, but there's no telling yet if there's room for more than just me."

"She might even discover this man is just terrible and be back within the week," their friend Hallie added, concern lurking in her voice. She was the worrier in the trio.

"Now, Hallie, don't fret." Emma took Hallie's hands in hers. "I'll write to you, too." Emma dropped one of Hallie's hands and took one of Georgie's so that she held each of them by the hand. "I'll never forget either of you. You're both my dearest friends."

The conductor called for the passengers to board, so Emma picked up her satchel and smiled one last time at the girls she had known all of her life, hoping she looked braver and more certain than she felt. What if Hallie was right? What if there was something terribly wrong with this man? What if she had misunderstood God's message?

She boarded and settled in the ladies' car at a window facing the station so that she could wave to the girls as the train pulled away from the small depot. She watched the familiar buildings pass by slowly at first, then disappearing from view completely, not knowing if she would ever return. She took a deep breath and told herself it would all work out exactly as God intended. She had to have faith that it would.

A small lump clawed its way up Emma's throat every time she thought about saying goodbye to the only home she had ever known, but she knew that God's plan was more significant than her sadness. There was a little boy at the end of this journey who needed her. She took solace in the idea that she could be of use to someone, rather than a lonely unmarried woman taking care of only herself.

Once the train had pulled away from the station in Pueblo and the friends who had accompanied her to the station had faded into the distance, Emma took her father's dog-eared leather Bible out of her satchel. She intended to read but quickly became distracted by the beauty that surrounded her, inside and outside of the train.

An older woman traveling with two young girls caught her eyes. The girls were dressed in matching red plaid dresses, the frothy lace of their collars kissing their plump cheeks as their impeccably curled hair lay neatly tied back with bows. One girl had a red bow and one had white in their shining brown hair. The younger girl, whose feet did not reach the floor, kicked her legs back and forth, swinging them energetically underneath the seat. But the woman with them reached out and swatted the young girl's knee, whispering sharply, "Be still!"

The gray-haired woman glanced at Emma with a dour expression. *The type of governess I hope* not *to become*, Emma reflected. This woman seemed like the type of adult who believed that children should be seen and not heard, who would have the children eat dinner in the kitchen away from the adults rather than all together as a family. It seemed impractical to Emma that children would be expected to eat by themselves with perfect table manners if they never ate with adults who could model those manners to them.

Emma did not believe in being harsh with children, but rather in being compassionate. In order to understand how to behave and why such behavior was important, adults needed to explain and model proper decorum to them.

The little girl squirmed in her seat for a moment but stopped when the sour old woman glared at her with eyes that could curdle fresh milk. To Emma, it was clear that the child just needed a few minutes to wiggle. Children were full of energy and could not be expected to sit perfectly still for long periods of time.

Rather than sit and watch disapprovingly while the two children tried their best not to wiggle and squirm under the imperious gaze of their guardian, Emma continued her perusal of the interior of the train car.

The inside of the train was ornate, with intricately carved woodwork on the ceiling and plush velvet seats. Emma had not expected such luxury. She spent a few minutes examining the floral details carved into the window frame beside her head when she then became entranced by the scene rushing past her outside the window.

She had never left Pueblo before. She entranced by the dazzling colors of the wildflowers in the meadows surrounding the train. It truly was amazing what God could do. The snow was visible on the tops of the mountains, yet down in the valleys the flowers bloomed and the tall green grasses swayed in the wind. Colorado was beautiful all year, but the wildflowers of summer took her breath away.

Emma rested her head on the seat back and gazed out the window at the Lord's abundance of beauty. She didn't take notice of her eyes drifting closed as the warmth of the sun lulled her to sleep.

Abram, an old man, stood alone in his home. He stared into the fire and the voice of God spoke to him as the flames wavered.

"Abram, get thee out of thy country, and from thy kindred, and from thy father's house, unto a land that I will show thee. And I will make of thee a great nation, and I will bless thee, and make thy name great; and thou shalt be a blessing"

"Me, Father?" Abram asked. "I am an old man. I have no children. My life and line are close to the end."

"Yes, Abram. I will bless them that bless thee, and curse him that curseth thee: and in thee shall all families of the earth be blessed."

Abram nodded his understanding and agreement with the Lord's wishes, and soon departed with his family through Sichem and the great plain of Moreh. He camped atop a mountain east of Bethel before continuing into Egypt. Abram and his family faced many challenges before they found a place to settle and multiply.

Emma awoke with the face of a newborn baby in her mind, the child that God has promised Abram. He was sweet, with pink skin and dark hair, and a toothless smile.

Her stomach grumbled, and she took an apple from her bag. She snacked and watched the mountains and wildflowers pass by outside the window as she contemplated this latest vision.

Like Abram, she too had been called away from the land of her people and to an unknown future. She too was sent out across an unfamiliar land. She had also faced her own challenges already in her life, growing up without a mother and then losing her father. She had to admit that she was also getting a little old to still be unmarried and without children and that sometimes bothered her. But, like Abram, she trusted in God's plan for her.

***

As the train pulled into the station at her destination, she hoped that God would bless her the way he promised Abram. She did not need her name to be great, but she did want to be a blessing to others.

Emma stepped down onto the platform into the waning sunlight and said a quick prayer.

Lord, give me the strength to be brave and to be what the Gilbert family needs. Let me be a blessing to Aaron and his father. Let me continue to grow and learn to be the best woman I can be so that I may continue to serve you. Amen.

A tall, handsome man strode toward her from across the station platform, a fearsome scowl pinching his features. Emma startled, both at how drawn she felt to this man despite his glower and at the fact that this distaste seemed to be aimed at her. She stood frozen to the spot, unsure of what to do. She had never been judged so quickly by a stranger before.

"Miss Clement?" he asked, stopping a few feet away from her and removing his hat. He had nicely groomed brown hair that glinted with bits of gold in the sunlight. Emma noted his strong jaw, shadowed by a thin layer of whiskers, and his sun-darkened skin. He looked to her like the very stereotype of a rancher, except for his long, lean frame.

"Yes, sir. I'm Emma Clement." Her voice came out more softly than she had intended. She wanted to sound confident and self-assured, not meek and shy. Unfortunately, meek and shy was what she felt in that moment.

"I'm Paul Gilbert."

"Pleased to meet you, Mr. Gilbert." Emma smiled broadly, relieved that he looked like a reputable man, with nicely trimmed hair and a clean face. He had a nice face, more attractive than she had expected. His waistcoat and jacket were well taken care of and his boots were polished.

He looked as if he had put in his best effort to impress her, and that pleased her. She had done the same, wearing her best blue gingham dress, the one her father had always said made her crystalline eyes shine even brighter. She had tied her blonde waves back with a new blue ribbon that Hallie had given her as a going away gift.

In response to her greeting, he gravely inclined his head and replaced his wide-brimmed hat, tipping it toward her. Then he turned toward the luggage that the porters were unloading.

"Point me toward your trunks and we can be on our way." He began to walk across the platform, then paused and turned back to Emma. "Unless there's anything you need in town before we head back to the ranch. We only get into town once every one or two weeks."

"No, I thank you, Mr. Gilbert. I'm sure I have everything I'll need for a little while."

He nodded again, then walked toward the trunks, simply expecting her to follow him.

So she did. His steps were much longer than hers, she struggled to keep up. He was quite tall and thinner than she expected a rancher to be. The farmers and ranchers she knew were all burly men with large muscles from all of the hard work they performed every day.

"I'm sorry, it's quite heavy," she said as she pointed out her trunk among the luggage being unloaded. The trunk contained all of her clothes and the most important mementos of her parents. Emma, Georgie, and Hallie had eventually all sat on it to get it closed. It was packed to the brim.

Mr. Gilbert, however, thought very little of simply lifting the trunk onto his hard shoulder and carrying it toward a waiting wagon. Emma was amazed that his thin frame contained such strength. Stunned, she simply followed him again.

He had yet to smile, but he had not been rude, exactly. He seemed like a man who did not talk much, didn't have much to say. It made her hesitant to speak, as she didn't quite know what to say to him.

An inexplicable pull, like the tide tugging shells and pebbles out into the surf, drew her toward this man. She could feel in her heart that he needed her, and she could do his family some good. Although she knew very little about him, she sensed upon seeing him that this was precisely where God was leading her.

Mr. Gilbert loaded her trunk into the back of the wagon and then helped her alight onto the wooden bench. His warm hand touched hers lightly, but her fingers tingled at the contact.

He then launched himself up beside her, signaled to the horses, and they were off.

Although Emma had left home this morning and had been traveling all day, watching an unknown world fly by the window, only now did she feel her journey was truly beginning.

Chapter Six

September 1873

Colorado City, Colorado

Paul stood on the platform at the small station in Colorado Springs in his itchy suit, his burning skin acutely aware of the unseasonable heat of the September day. He fanned himself with his hat, but it did very little to stop the sweat gathering on his brow. He shifted from one foot to the other, restless and uncertain, and continued to overheat.

Thankfully, the heat was broken by the wind of the train approaching from the south. This had to be the train Miss Clement was arriving on.

"All aboard for Castle Rock, Littleton, and Denver," the station manager called as the train slowed to a stop.

A few men trickled off the train, but only one woman. At the sight of her, his pulse slowed for a moment.

She's pretty, he thought. *Beautiful, in fact.*

His heartbeat resumed at a galloping pace as heat hurried up his neck. Her golden hair caught in a breeze and blew back from her face in a way that showcased her high cheekbones and pale pink lips. Paul set his jaw in a rigid line.

He stepped toward her, knowing he was scowling but unable to stop the expression. She had no business being pretty. He would have been very happy with dowdy and scrawny.

"Miss Clement?"

She turned toward him. Her blue eyes were striking, intensified by the dress she wore, blue like a robin's egg. Then she smiled wide and bright, displaying a row of straight white teeth. A faint spray of freckles played across her cheeks, giving a playful air to her overall delicate, ladylike features. She was not a tanned, roughened farm girl, but she emitted an inner strength that told him that she could handle ranch life.

He had not been prepared for her to be pretty. He had assumed an unmarried, twenty-two-year-old preacher's daughter must be frumpy and unattractive. He had expected to see her in a dress that fit poorly with unkempt mousy brown hair. He had built a very specific image in his mind of what such a woman would look like.

She said hello and they gathered her trunk, which was heavier than he had expected. What did she have in that thing? All of her worldly possessions? A cast iron pot? Accustomed to lifting bales of hay and sacks of grain, however, he easily hefted the trunk over his shoulder and led Miss Clement to the wagon.

He set the trunk in the back, and then hesitantly took her hand to help her into the wooden bench at the front of the wagon. Her hand was delicate but warm. He didn't like the pleasure he felt at the touch of her soft skin.

They headed out of town, and as the old wooden buggy bumped along on the hard-packed dirt, Paul held his body in a rigid posture, trying to avoid any unintentional contact with Emma beside him. He had to consciously relax his jaw and keep from gritting his teeth.

Why does she have to be pretty, he puzzled, *she has no business being pretty.* and capable woman to help cook, clean, and look after Aaron. He did not want someone that would be a further distraction in his life. He did not need more distractions, he needed less. That's why he had hired her in the first place.

He could sense her keen, gentle eyes on him. Appraising him. She then glanced away, around at the passing farmhouses and fields of cattle and crops. But she looked back to him every now and then, drawing her eyebrows together in consternation. She was clearly curious, as she had every right to be, but he was not willing to open his mouth and convey his irrational anger. When he had to speak, he tried to simply be straightforward without being curt. He didn't want to scare her away.

Eventually, Paul turned the horses down the narrow path worn through the grass between the road and the ranch. He took in his surroundings and tried to see it all through the eyes of a newcomer. On either side of the path was pasture, the grass trampled and eaten by the cattle. Up ahead, the two story farmhouse was coming into view.

Earle and his wife had built a nice house on the eastern side of the ranch land. Two stories with a big porch that wrapped around from front to back, enough room for a large family that they had never had. The whitewashed wood siding was holding up nicely, and there were even flowers around the front steps that Laura's mother had planted years ago, giving the house a cheerful look. In fact, they were a bit overgrown and probably needed to be pruned some. But it looked cheerful nonetheless.

Behind the house were all the farm buildings—the bunkhouse to the right and stables to the left, with pigs and chickens in between. Beyond all of that lay more fields of crops and cows.

Paul thought it all looked quite nice and felt proud. He assumed that Emma was appropriately impressed.

He stopped the buggy just in front of the house and spared Emma a glance. She used a hand to shield her eyes as she surveyed her surroundings. She did not look displeased, which Paul took as a good sign.

"Well, here we are."

"It's lovely." Emma a wide smile brightening her face. "The flowers are beautiful." He nodded again, trying not to notice how the smile lit her up, as if the sun itself were bursting forth from within her.

Paul hopped down from the wagon, then walked around and helped Emma down. She watched as he hefted her trunk up on his shoulder again and then mounted the front porch, where Earle sat in his usual spot.

"Miss Clement, this is my father-in-law, Earle Smith." Paul paused at the top of the front steps, his hand on the door to the house.

Emma inclined her head politely. "It's very nice to meet you, Mr. Smith. I'm Emma Clement. I look forward to living on your lovely ranch."

She looked at Earle expectantly, but he barely even glanced her way. He grunted and went back to staring down the road.

Paul sighed and held the front door open for Emma. She took the signal and stepped into the front room. It was a cozy room with a big fireplace, a few chairs gathered around the hearth, and a small desk. The colorful braided rug on the floor showed that a woman had been here, but the slight covering of dust on the furniture indicated that it had been a while since a thorough cleaning had been done. Along the walls hung family portraits, and Emma could tell someone had gone to a lot of trouble to make this house truly make the inhabitants feel welcome and at home.

"Earle doesn't say much," Paul commented by way of apology once the door was closed. "All the bedrooms are upstairs. Follow me."

He led her to a staircase opposite the fireplace and took a right turn at the top of the stairs, then stepped into a bedroom.

"This will be your room." He set her trunk down on the floor at the foot of the bed, then pointed to another door. "That leads to Aaron's room. I'm across the hall and Earle's room is next to mine."

Emma glanced around the sparsely decorated room. The small bed was made with crisp white linens. Around the room were a bedside table, one dresser, and one wooden chair.

Above the dresser, a small mirror was hung on the wall, and there were thin blue curtains framing the window. It would take a lot to make this room feel like home.

As she examined the curtains, Paul strode to the open window and leaned his head out of it.

"Aaron!" he called down to his son, who was stomping through the vegetable garden behind the house, hopefully not destroying any of their food. "Son, come up here. There's someone I would like you to meet."

A boy of about five, covered in mud, ran down one row of the garden and then through the yard and up the backstairs into the house. Paul and Emma could hear him coming from the clomping of his tiny booted feet through the kitchen and up the inside staircase. Paul sighed, knowing that Aaron was leaving a trail of muddy footprints through the house.

He appeared in the doorway with dirt smudged on his cheeks and his hair sticking out on one side.

What has this boy been up to today? Paul wondered, knowing how Aaron tended to run wild on the ranch and get in everyone's way.

"Aaron, this is Miss Emma Clement. She's going to live here and help take care of you."

"Hello, Aaron," Emma said, getting down onto the floor to be eye level with the messy child.

"Hi." There was no emotion in his voice, and he did not move from his place in the doorway.

"Have you been playing outside today? It looks like you've been having all sorts of fun." Emma attempted to engage him in a conversation. "Maybe later you can show me what you like to do."

"No! I don't want to play with you! I want you to go away!"

Aaron turned and ran back down the stairs and out of the house, and Emma was left sitting on the floor.

Paul watched as her face fell. She clearly had not expected such a response from Aaron, but he wasn't surprised. The boy had been emotional and unpredictable since his mother had died. The most unexpected things would set him off, and he would either run away or scream and break things.

"I'd better go after him." Paul sighed. "I'll let you get settled in."

He tipped his hat and left the dejected young woman.

Maybe tomorrow will be better, he thought.

Chapter Seven

"Dear Lord, I need your help and guidance. Is this truly your plan for me? Is this where you intended to lead me? I'm afraid I misunderstood your message to me and brought myself to a place where I am not wanted." Emma paused in her prayer, watching herself tie her blonde hair back into a braid for the night. After the rough start yesterday, she had made it through one full day at the ranch, and it had not gone as smoothly as she had hoped. It was evident that Aaron needed a lot of help and attention to improve his behavior.

She made breakfast, taking extra care to prepare something that might impress the men of the house, but Paul and Earle ate silently and left and Aaron threw it on the floor and refused to eat. So she cleaned the food up off the floor and allowed him to run outside instead, throwing sticks and hanging from low tree limbs.

But not too much later in the morning, Aaron became cranky and screamed at her that he was hungry.

She tried to engage him with music, singing "Oh, Susanna!" and "Camptown Races," but he ran to his room and slammed the door closed. Later, when he was finally calm and playing by himself, she tried to join, but he threw his toy animals at her and told her to go away. He had no interest in engaging with her at all.

Emma thought of all the children she had worked with and cared for in the past, and she could not remember a single child who had been so difficult to reach. Some had been shy and reluctant but never had a child been so resistant to her presence. She prayed that with a little more time, he would adjust to her. She just needed to remain calm and be nearby, and eventually, he would trust her.

Wouldn't he?

She blew out the paraffin oil lamp on her bedside table and tucked herself into bed, watching the moon rising languidly through the window.

In reflecting on Aaron's reactions to even simple things like breakfast, Emma thought that he seemed to be harboring a lot of anger about something. *What happened to his mother, I wonder*, Emma pondered, *is she at the root of this anger?*

No one else in the house seemed very happy either. Earle sat on the porch and only came in for meals, which he ate in disgruntled silence. Paul seemed strung tight and tense. He also spoke very little, though he seemed more serious than rude.

Somehow, Emma thought, *I left an empty house for a full one and now I feel more alone than I did before.*

***

"Do you know what number comes after ten, Aaron?" Emma and Aaron were seated on the floor in front of the fireplace in the front room of the ranch house on her third day there. She had brought her teaching materials downstairs that morning and decided to start with numbers.

"Nine!" the boy shouted.

"No, that's the number *before* ten. Eleven is the number *after* ten. It goes eight, nine, ten, eleven." Emma pointed to each number in the small arithmetic primer she had brought with her.

When she had brought the book out, Aaron had gently turned the pages and looked at the pictures and words with curiosity, which Emma took as a good sign. Perhaps he just needed something productive and educational to focus on. She had also given him a small notebook of blank pages to practice some writing and drawing in. Children always seemed to like being given their own materials.

"Can you count with me, Aaron?"

"No! No more counting!" Aaron suddenly stood and stomped his feet. His face began to turn red and his eyes squeezed shut.

Surprised, Emma sat up straighter. "Do you know the letters of the alphabet?" She took a deep breath and maintained a calm tone of voice as she reached for the early reader she had brought with her.

"No! No letters!" He took the notebook she had given him and tore a handful of pages right down the middle.

"Aaron, please don't do that." Emma tried to take the notebook out of his hands, but he simply grabbed the next pages and yanked them out as well, throwing the mangled scraps of paper to the floor at his feet. Emma looked down at the scraps and chewed on her lip, disappointed that her gift to the boy was so quickly destroyed. "May I have the notebook, please?"

"No!" He stomped on the paper. "No! No! No! No numbers! No letters! No Emma! Go away!"

Tears streamed down the little boy's face as he balled up his fists and began to strike them against Emma's chest.

She gathered the agitated boy into her arms, holding him close so that he couldn't move his arms any longer, and then spoke calmly to the boy. "Aaron, I will not let you hit me like that. It's not nice to hit others. The Book of Luke says you must 'Do unto others as you would have them do to you.' Please be kind to me."

The boy continued to wiggle a bit, but stilled as Emma stroked his hair and wiped the tears from his cheeks.

"What does that mean?" he asked quietly after a few moments. He looked down as if talking to his feet.

"Which part?" Emma asked, gently nudging his chin up so she could see his face and so that he could see she was smiling and kind.

"Who's Luke?" Aaron rubbed at his eyes and Emma loosened her hold on him.

"He wrote his own book in the New Testament in the Bible, and it says, 'Do unto others as you would have them do to you.'"

"What does that mean?" Aaron sat down on the floor facing Emma, crossing his legs in front of him.

"It means that if we would like others to be kind to us, we must also be kind to them." Emma smiled when she said the word "kind," and then narrowed her eyes and scrunched her nose to help explain the next part. "But if we are mean and hateful toward others, they will be mean and hateful toward us." She gently took Aaron's hands in hers. "Would you like to be hit?"

"No," Aaron said quietly, almost whispering.

"So if you don't want someone to hit you, do you think you should hit them?"

"No."

"See, you understand just fine." Emma smoothed a hand over the boy's hair reassuringly. "People will treat you the same way you treat them. God wants us to be kind and take care of one another, not hit one another. 'Do unto others as you would have them do to you.'"

Aaron nodded and repeated her words, "'Do unto others as you would have them do to you.'"

"Very good!" Emma smiled brightly. "Now, do you know how you can make it right when you've hurt someone else?"

"Say sorry?"

"That's right! And you hit me and hurt me a little, which was not kind. Should you apologize to me?"

Aaron nodded. "Sorry I hit you, Emma."

Emma's heart filled with pride at Aaron's quick change of behavior and incredible understanding of the situation. She was about to accept his apology and move on with her lesson when she felt someone standing in the doorway behind her.

When she turned, Paul was scowling at her. His jaw was clenched and his face was red, with one throbbing vein visible on the left side of his forehead. She had never seen anyone look so angry in her entire life.

Chapter Eight

Around the east side of the paddock, Paul and Holt mended a fence post that had rotted and was about to fall apart. Holt had a good eye for anything that might need maintenance or repairs around the ranch. Without Holt's help, Paul knew this ranch would have fallen apart in the last year. Life had become overwhelming with Laura's death, but with Emma here, he finally had some small glimmer of hope. It was very small at the moment, but it was there.

"No! Go away!" Aaron's small voice carried out to the pasture from inside the house. He sure could be loud. Paul sighed, wondering if his son would ever settle or if he was just always going to be this angry and difficult.

Holt gave Paul a wry look over the fence they were mending. "Sounds like Aaron isn't taking to that woman you hired just yet."

"I'm a little worried that he won't," Paul replied, taking a bandana from his pocket and wiping sweat off of his forehead. "I'll go see what's happening." He turned and started walking toward the house, and Holt followed, trying to support his friend.

"Oh, of course he will. It just takes a little time to adjust. Did you like her right away?" Holt had yet to meet the woman, but he had seen her from afar. She had jumped right in to completing the daily household chores and seemed capable and efficient from what he had seen.

Paul's face hardened in response. His eyes narrowed and his mouth clenched.

Holt was surprised. "From the looks of it you do not like her at all. What's wrong with her?"

"She's too pretty." As soon as he said it, Paul realized how ridiculous that sounded.

"Too pretty for what, exactly?" Holt smiled, but drew his eyebrows together in confusion.

Paul was not sure how to answer that question and was saved from having to respond by mounting the back steps of the house. Aaron's yelling and crying had calmed, but Paul thought he should probably just go in and check on them anyway.

Paul knocked the dirt off his boots outside the backdoor and entered the house through the kitchen. He immediately noticed how neat and clean the room was. Before Emma came, the kitchen had been in a constant state of disarray. Nothing seemed to have a place where it belonged. The counters and table had always been slightly dusty or sticky when they weren't covered in dirty pots and dishes or leftover food. Now, everything was put away and the table was even set with clean dishes for supper.

He was feeling impressed and proud of himself for hiring such an efficient woman—until he heard the conversation Emma and Aaron were having in the next room.

"God wants us to be kind and take care of one another, not hit one another," he heard Emma say.

Heat rose up Paul's chest and he felt his teeth knock together forcefully. She had no right to talk to his son about religion, about God.

Now she was quoting the Bible and Aaron was saying it back!

It was not her place to preach to his son. God had no place in this house, and He had seen to that Himself when He took Laura away from them. When He forced Paul to choose between his wife and son.

Emma turned and saw Paul standing in the doorway. Aaron had apologized and seemed calm, but Paul was roiling inside. Emma's eyes widened in surprise at his entrance and the look on his face.

"Aaron. Go play outside for a bit. Holt is out back." Although he spoke to Aaron, Paul glared at Emma.

The little boy loved Holt, and the affection was mutual. Holt would give Aaron rides on his back and shoulders or swing him around by the arms. It was one of the few times the boy ever laughed.

Emma frowned, uncertain. "Everything is fine now, Mr. Gilbert. Aaron just had a moment of frustration." She stood up from her place on the floor, wiping the wrinkles out of her skirt as she did. "As you can see, I'm capable of handling an outburst. It's expected when—"

"Emma." Paul silenced her with the single word, the first time he had called her by her first name. Only it wasn't a familiar or friendly use of her name. His tone was hard and unyielding like stone. "I do not want to hear any of that again in this house."

"Aaron's outburst? I'm sorry, Mr. Gilbert, but I can't prevent that." Her voice quivered as she spoke.

"Not that. No one can prevent that. If I could, you would not be here."

"I don't understand." She wrung her hands and avoided looking into his angry eyes.

"There will be no more talk of God in this house. He does not belong here."

Emma's light eyebrows drew together, forming a deep line down her forehead.

"No Bible quotes or stories. No prayers. None of it." With each sentence, Paul chopped his hand through the air as if cutting something with an ax—cutting God and religion out of his house.

"But why?" Emma asked quietly, taken aback.

"That's none of your concern," Paul replied abruptly. "You need not worry about my reasons. You simply need to do as I say."

"It's only that Bible stories are an excellent way to teach children how to behave and how to treat others." Emma attempted to explain herself, her voice calm yet confused. "As you saw, that's how Aaron finally calmed down."

"This is not a debate or a discussion, Emma. I do not want to hear it again. That's final." He turned toward the kitchen, but only made it halfway across the room before turning back. "This is the only time I want to have this conversation. If I hear it again, I will find someone else to fill your position and your services will no longer be needed here."

Emma looked forlorn, a glimmer of tears hovering at the edges of her eyes. "Yes, sir."

While she had been strong and passionate a moment ago, now her voice was soft and weak. She wrung her hands as she looked down at the confetti of notebook pages around her feet. Paul felt a small amount of guilt for breaking her spirit, but he felt more strongly that there was no God in his house.

He turned on his heel and followed Aaron's path out the back door and down the steps. He nodded to Holt who had Aaron up on his back, trotting around the yard, but continued to walk out toward the creek. He needed to walk off his frustration, and he knew Holt would understand. Paul often walked the length of the creek when he needed some time to clear his mind.

In Paul's view, he was not the one removing God from his own life—God had left all on his own. He had abandoned Paul and the whole family when He took Laura away.

Paul watched as the clear water trickled downstream across the rocks, with small waterfalls here and there that created a bubbling sound that Paul found soothing. The shade of the trees from the canopy overhead and the tweeting of bird songs gave Paul the impression that he was completely alone, protected behind a curtain of leaves.

Out here, he was able to breathe fully. Some of the pressure that lived in his chest released.

He had once found this kind of relief in prayer and church services on Sundays. He had once been a man who read his Bible and recited scripture. But what good had that done for him? After devoting so much time and effort to faith and worship, the God he had placed his trust in had turned His back.

Paul walked along the bank of the stream, noticing the frogs hopping in and out of the shallow water, spooking a pair of chipmunks who skittered off into the brush. When he reached the big cottonwood tree at the bend in the creek, he turned back and headed toward home.

His walk helped him to feel calmer, but no less convicted that there was no God in his home.

Chapter Nine

The heavy, sweet aroma of a pear cobbler in the oven wafted through the air, settling over Emma's roiling thoughts like a warm blanket over a disquiet child. Emma stirred the batter for fried salt pork for supper. She had already sliced some potatoes and onions and baked a batch of fluffy buttermilk biscuits that were beckoning to her as they sat on the sideboard to cool. She kept her hands busy in an attempt to quiet her mind, but not much seemed to help.

How could she live in a house where God was not welcome? She had been surrounded by His presence for her entire life. Her father was a minister! She had spent most of her life in God's house, and now she was being told that He was not welcome in hers?

Is this why You sent me here, God? She prayed silently, desolately. *I'm sure You were welcome here once. Is it my job to bring this family back to You?*

"Hello?" A woman's voice drifted in through the kitchen window. "Hello, Miss Clement!"

Emma looked out the window in front of her and saw a woman waving at her with one arm and a basket slung over her other. Emma waved back politely. The woman looked friendly, and must be close enough with the Gilbert family that she had been given Emma's name.

The woman ascended the porch steps and let herself in the back door. She had hair so dark black it shined almost blue and skin darkened by hours spent outside in the summer sun. Her broad shoulders and sturdy frame indicated that she could carry her load of the hard work of farm life.

"Hello. I'm Bonnie Higgins. I live next door, just about a half mile down the road from here." She wore a simple blue dress with her black hair pinned up on the top of her head. Her wide mouth and large eyes gave her a look of friendly openness, someone who would listen to your worries and help take on the burden.

"It's nice to meet you, Mrs. Higgins." Emma wiped her hands on her apron, removing the film of flour on her palms.

"Oh, do call me Bonnie," she laughed and waved a dismissive hand at Emma, "no reason to stand on formalities. We women need to stick together out here on the frontier."

Emma's smile widened. A weight lifted off of her chest and she felt as if she took a full breath for the first time in days. She was certain she had just met her first friend here. "Bonnie, then. And you must call me Emma. Please, come in. I'll make us some tea."

Bonnie set her basket on the wide kitchen table.

"I brought you a few things. I've been helping feed these men the last year, so I know how bare that pantry and root cellar are." She unpacked two home-canned jars of green beans, a fresh loaf of bread, and a small crock of butter.

"Thank you so much!" Emma gratefully took the offer and began to store the items. "I had wondered where the canned food came from. I'm certain Mr. Gilbert wasn't canning peaches!"

"Oh, certainly not!" Bonnie laughed heartily. "I hope you didn't have to eat any of his bread. I gave him very specific written instructions when he asked, but he never quite got it right. I think he's too impatient with it."

"No, I didn't. And I can tell that yours is nice and soft. I'm sure it'll be delicious." Emma held the loaf up to her nose and inhaled deeply. "Is there anything better than the scent of freshly baked bread?"

The kettle steamed, so Emma took it off the stove top and poured the hot water over two cups she had already prepared with tea leaves, a luxury that she did not take lightly. Tea was often hard to come by in a frontier town.

"Well, I do not want to taint your judgment, but I am a fairly skilled baker." Bonnie sipped the hot tea and settled back into her chair, feeling at home in the familiar house. "So, Emma, tell me about yourself. How did you come to be here?"

"I grew up in Pueblo where my father was the pastor of a church. My mother died in childbirth, so when my father passed away this summer, I was all alone." Emma's voice caught and she paused, watching the sympathy cross Bonnie's face. "I saw an advertisement for a governess in the newspaper at the general store, and I felt deep inside that God was sending me here. But I'm starting to think that perhaps I misunderstood God's message."

"Why would you think that?" Bonnie put her hand on Emma's, her voice full of concern. "I can see you're already working wonders on Aaron. He's out playing with my boys right now, and he was polite and calm when we arrived. The last time I walked over, he kicked dirt at my oldest and ran away."

"Oh my." Emma nodded, her eyes wide at Bonnie's description. "Yes, he does seem to be responding to me."

The two women chatted a little longer, and Emma learned that Bonnie and her husband John had six children between the ages of twelve and two, three boys and three girls, and that they had both known Paul and his wife since they were all children.

After a time, when she was certain that Bonnie was knowledgeable and trustworthy, and possibly a little bit prone to gossiping, Emma broached the subject that was troubling her most.

"Bonnie, do you know why Mr. Gilbert is so adamant about keeping God out of his house?" Emma picked at a spot of food stuck to the table in front of her, not making eye contact as she asked.

"What gives you that impression?" Bonnie asked.

"He told me, almost yelled at me, that there was to be no talk of God or of the Bible in this house."

Bonnie's eyebrows shot up in surprise, almost meeting her dark hairline.

"I was trying to help Aaron understand why it's important to be kind to others and not to hit me, specifically. So I told him to 'Do unto others as you would have them do to you.' And when Paul heard, he became quite angry and threatened to let me go if he heard me speak of God again."

Bonnie sighed. "He is quite angry at God, understandably. The man has been through a lot this past year."

Emma paused, wondering if she should ask what happened. On one hand, it did not seem right to ask about a private family matter. But Bonnie seemed to be a trusted friend, and she clearly knew what had happened. It seemed important that if Emma were going to stay here and help this family heal, she should know what they were healing from.

"Bonnie, what exactly happened? Mr. Gilbert has told me nothing, and all three of these men are clearly hurting."

"You poor thing! Dealing with these men without knowing what's eating at them." Bonnie shook her head. "I should have known. Men do not like to talk about the hard things."

Bonnie took a long drink of her tea and looked out the window, gathering her thoughts. Emma allowed her the time, but the curiosity made it difficult to sit still.

"Paul's wife's name was Laura. She was a lovely woman, and Paul loved her fiercely." Bonnie smiled at the memory of her friends and how happy they had once been together. "They grew up together. This is Earle's land, but Paul's family lived nearby, and Laura was one of the only girls around. She was practically one of the boys, running through the fields and climbing trees with them." Bonnie sighed sorrowfully, remembering her friend.

"But she was also a true lady. She never lost her sense of adventure, but she kept a clean house with nice things and had some of the prettiest dresses. She was a much better seamstress than I am." Bonnie looked down at her own plain dress. "But that's beside the point. You wanted to know what happened to these poor men around here."

"Yes, but I do appreciate any details that could help me understand." Emma's tea sat forgotten on the table, growing cold. She felt as if she were already learning so much vital information, and she was hungry for more. Any small morsel of information was helpful to her understanding of the family she was serving.

"She and Paul were together almost ten years when it happened. They had a house on the Smith land, but down the road a bit. Paul and Holt and a couple of the hands had built it for Laura as a wedding gift." Bonnie smiled at the memory of the pretty little house, with its window boxes full of flowers and matching rocking chairs on the small front porch. Then her voice became melancholy, and she looked down into her empty teacup. "One day a little over a year ago, the house caught fire. No one knows what caused it, but Laura and Aaron were inside the house and the door was blocked by a wall of flames. They couldn't get to one another. Paul came running from across the fields, but by the time he reached the house the structure was severely damaged. He only managed to save Aaron before the roof collapsed and Laura was gone forever."

Emma's hand flew to her mouth and tears came to her eyes. "Oh, Bonnie, that's so horrible."

"Paul blames himself and God for her death. He was running to save her and she begged him to save Aaron first, so he did. But he never had the chance to go back in for her." Bonnie wiped tears from her cheeks. "They had had a couple of rough years. Problems with some animals getting sick or going missing, crops destroyed by drought or flood. Laura always had faith and said that God would provide, but losing Laura was the last straw for Paul. He felt abandoned."

Emma nodded. "I understand why he might feel that way, even if he is wrong. The Lord never turns his back on us."

"I agree, Emma."

"What about Earle? If this is his land, why does he just sit on the porch all day?"

"He declared himself retired when Laura and Paul married—handed all responsibility over to Paul. But his wife passed soon after Aaron was born, and he lost much of his interest in life after that. When Laura passed, he stopped even walking down to help with the horses much."

From her seat, Emma could see through the doorway and into the front room. Her eyes caught on a painting of a dark-haired young woman with an elfin face and a wreath of flowers in her hair. "That painting in the front room, is that Laura or her mother?"

"That's Laura. It was her wedding gift to Paul. She's seventeen in that picture. Her personality just shines right through the paint with that yellow dress and the flowers in her hair. Bright as sunshine with a little bit of wildness."

Emma could see the painting from where she sat, and she examined it as best she could from this distance. She knew loss well and acutely. She was still grieving her father and it was difficult some days to muster the strength to get out of bed. But she could not imagine how much more difficult Paul's pain was. He had been forced to choose between saving his wife and his child, and no matter who he had chosen, it would have felt like the wrong choice.

"Thank you so much for telling me, Bonnie." Emma cleared the cups from the table and set them in the wash sink, then checked on the cobbler in the oven. "I don't believe Mr. Gilbert would have told me that himself. He seems to need me here, but also to slightly resent me here. He does not talk much."

"He'll open up eventually. Just give it time. For all of you." Bonnie stood and glanced out the window, where she could see her children and Aaron playing a game of chase. "I'd best be going. I need to get started on my own supper. That cobbler you've got cooking gave me some inspiration."

"It was lovely talking with you." Emma walked with her new friend out onto the back porch.

"Don't you fret, I'll be back. You're the closest woman to talk to, and as my husband John would say, I can talk a man's ear off with women's talk." Bonnie laughed, taking the poke in stride. "You just keep looking after these men and let me know if you need any help."

Emma watched from the porch as Bonnie rounded up her children and set off across the tall grass. Aaron ran with them as far as Bonnie would let him, then turned back and stood with Holt on the corral fence.

Already, Aaron was calming down a bit. Bonnie had even noticed it, and his behavior today showed it as well. He hadn't had any outbursts, hadn't screamed at any of the children or hit anyone. And now, he was standing with Holt and watching the horses trot around.

This is where I'm supposed to be, Emma thought resolutely. *I'm already making a difference, and there's so much yet to do.*

She said a quick prayer out loud before going back into the kitchen to finish preparing the evening meal.

"Lord, give me the strength to persevere and to bring You back to this house. They need You now more than ever."

Chapter Ten

Paul watched as Aaron sopped up the bright yellow egg yolk with his toast and took a big bite. Two weeks ago, Aaron had simply smashed the food onto his plate and then thrown it on the floor, creating a sticky yellow mess that Paul had had to clean up. One week ago, Emma had arrived, and already Aaron's table manners were improving.

He felt some of the tension in his chest loosen and his shoulders relax, his jaw unclenching just a little. There was hope after all for his family.

The sound of boots hurrying up the back steps raised everyone's heads from their plates. Holt removed his wide-brimmed hat as he leaned his top half through the backdoor, not even bothering to come fully into the room. His mouth was set in a straight line, his face hard—an unusual look for Holt.

"The horses are gone," Holt said breathlessly, as if he had been running.

The words made no sense. Paul furrowed his brow in response and said slowly, "What do you mean 'the horses are gone'?"

"The stables are all empty." Holt took a couple of steps into the room, but still held onto the door with one hand, prepared to leave with haste. "Shaw went down to start morning chores, and came running right back to the bunkhouse with the news. Every last one of the horses is missing. Fritz, Abraham, Buttercup. Even old Harriet who can barely walk."

Understanding dawned, and Paul's spine snapped straight with newfound tension. His heart speeding with alarm and panic, he leapt from his seat, shoved his feet into his boots, and followed Holt to the paddock. He didn't need to check the stables, he trusted that Holt was right that the stalls were all empty. Shaw was carefully making his way around the perimeter of the big wooden building, checking for any holes, breakages, or evidence of what had happened.

"How do you think they got out?" Paul asked as they jogged toward the pasture.

"If Harriet is gone, they did not get out on their own. Someone led them out." They stopped when they reached the fence. Holt put a hand on the rail and shook it, looking for the weak spot. "I'll go left, you go right. I'll bet there's an obvious spot where someone broke in."

Paul ran a hand along the fence as he walked, jiggling every few feet to find where a post had perhaps been removed and replaced. He found the break in the fence about forty feet away from the stables and called out to Holt and Shaw. It wasn't a loose rail or post, however. It was a spot that had been cut clean through, leaving the fence standing wide open.

"This is the spot we just replaced," Paul said, lowering his face toward the rail, scientifically examining the fence.

Shaw stood back and scratched his head. "Looks like someone just cut right through it."

"Looks like they used a handsaw." Holt inspected the break in the fence as well, running his fingers carefully along the cut. "Someone was dedicated to this and took some time to get it done. That was not an easy task."

"This was planned." Paul stated, his voice dull like the thud of a hammer against a hard nail. "Someone stole my horses."

"Who would steal another man's horses?" Shaw shook his head and pursed his lips, looking unusually serious.

The tightness in Paul's chest returned and twisted even tighter than before. "They stole Fritz. He's a good horse, been with me for years. He never once threw me or steered me wrong. He wouldn't just run off if there was a break in the fence. Someone corralled them out of here"

"Looks like it." Holt agreed. "But who? And why? Especially old Harriet. She ain't worth much but a pony ride for a kid." Holt removed his hat and scratched his head.

"If even that," Shaw added. "She's been favoring her right foreleg a bit lately. Getting her out of the fence would have been pretty difficult."

Paul shook his head and remained silent. He didn't have any answers either.

The men all continued on with their regular daily chores, though there was less to do without needing to take care of the horses and some tasks took more time without the convenience and speed of a horse to ride. Stealing a man's horses was not only an emotional blow—ranchers tended to become attached to the animals—it also caused a multitude of financial problems. He would have to pay to replace the missing horses, and it would be more difficult to complete the tasks that kept the ranch running without them.

All day, Paul thought about those horses. He tried to determine what he could have done to prevent the theft. He walked the fence line multiple times, examining the cut out section from all directions, following the trail of hoof prints as far as he could until they disappeared among the tall grasses.

In the afternoon, he walked over to the Higgins' place to see if they had seen or heard anything suspicious. As he neared the house, he found Bonnie outside hanging laundry on the line.

"Hey, Bonnie!" he called, and waved.

"Well, howdy, Paul!" She pinned the last dress on the line and walked toward him, her wide smile welcoming him as always. "To what do we own the pleasure of this unusual visit? You haven't scared off that dear girl you've hired, have you? You're not starving already?"

Paul shook his head and rubbed the back of his neck, in no mood for Bonnie's good natured ribbing. "No, not at all. Is John nearby?"

Bonnie's dark brows drew together, recognizing the look on Paul's face. "No, he took the boys and went out to the farthest pasture today with the cows. What's got you troubled?"

"Someone cut my fence and stole my horses last night. I was coming to see if anyone here had seen or heard anything unusual." His voice was low and deep, reflecting his dark mood.

Bonnie's hand flew to her heart and she inhaled sharply in surprise. "Oh my goodness. There's nothing I can think of at all. I haven't even heard of any other thefts nearby in the recent past." She put a hand on Paul's arm. "How many horses did they get?"

"All of them. Every last one." He shuffled his feet, feeling restless and needing an outlet for his simmering anger. "It's near impossible to do all the work that needs done around a ranch with no horses."

"I'll be sure to ask John when he comes back, but it won't be until suppertime. We'll be sure to let you know if there's anything to tell." She turned toward the house. "Would you like to come in for some tea or maybe a cup of coffee? I think there are a few bites left of a berry cobbler."

Paul shook his head, his face softening. "No, thank you, Bonnie. That sounds delicious, but I need to get back to the ranch. Holt and I are making a few repairs on the stables that we've been putting off. Might as well put all those empty stalls to good use."

Bonnie nodded and turned back to her chores. "I'll send John or one of the children over this evening, then. And we'll be sure to keep a sharp eye out for anything suspicious."

Paul tipped his hat and turned back toward home.

***

Long after everyone else had gone to bed, Paul sat in the candlelit kitchen with a cup of formerly hot tea beside him and the books for the ranch in front of him. He had a record of the purchase or birth of every animal on this farm. He knew how much his horses were worth, and with the exception of Harriet, he knew someone stood to make a lot of money off of his good choices.

How? Who? The questions had plagued him all day long. He did not need to ask why. The answer to that question was always money, selfishness, personal benefit.

He didn't have the resources to replace all of the horses, or even a fraction of them. He had checked and double checked. He could sell a steer or a dairy cow or two, but the missing horses were well-trained and strong. The work to buy new horses and train them was considerable. There was more than money involved, however, there was also time and manpower to consider. There was other work that needed to be done around the ranch, especially as harvest time came on.

Paul shook his head and took a sip of the tepid tea, then made a sound of disgust and set the cup off farther to the side so he wouldn't make the same mistake again.

The sound of small feet coming down the stairs caught his attention and he turned, expecting to see Aaron. Instead, it was Emma.

"Oh! I didn't realize anyone was down here," she said, wrapping her robe tighter around her white nightgown. Her blonde hair was braided and hanging down her back, reminding him of how he used to tug on Laura's braids to get her attention before he had even known why he was doing it. It made her look young and innocent, like someone who had experienced very little suffering in her life, unlike him.

"Can't sleep." He pointed to the papers spread out before him, which looked more and more like a foreign language the longer he looked at them.

"Me neither." She went to the stove to put the kettle back on, stoking the banked fire that still glowed beneath the coals. "Does this happen to you often?"

"Only in the last year. You?" He admired the way the soft flickering candlelight played across her features, highlighting her softness and femininity.

"I've had some trouble sleeping since my father died." Emma's voice was quiet and hesitant. She took a cup from the cabinet and began to prepare her tea, keeping her back to him. "I suppose you're troubled about your horses?"

"That I am." He looked back down at the nonsensical numbers and records before him and began to tidy them up, stacking loose papers

"There's always something to worry about, isn't there?" Emma sighed and pulled out a chair across from Paul, then sat and sipped her tea. "We all have our own trials and tribulations through life. But there are also ways to find peace. We just have to open our hearts and listen to the world around us."

She paused and drank some more, the steam rising from the cup to partially obscure her face. "I find peace in the quiet moments of life—seeing the sun rise in the sky, that particular silence of a snowfall, watching the horses run around the paddock. All of those quiet moments give me a moment to take a deep breath and calm the busy thoughts in my mind. They take my mind off my troubles for just a minute."

Paul nodded, mostly to himself. He knew what she meant. He, too, found peace in those same things, in the beauty of nature and animals. When he worked with the horses, he often found himself forgetting his troubles and focusing on the motion and feel of the great beasts. Maybe there was hope for him yet.

Maybe a peaceful life was still a possibility for him.

"Where do you find peace, Mr. Gilbert?" Emma asked over the top of her tea cup, holding it as if more to warm her hands than to enjoy the taste.

"You know, I called you Emma last week and you never corrected me." He leaned back in his chair, angling his body toward Emma's. "Why don't you call me Paul?"

A small smile brightened Emma's face as she repeated her question. "Where do you find peace, Paul?"

"I suppose in many of the same places you do. But I also find it in," he paused to gather his thoughts, "watching the flames dance in a fire and the first sip of coffee in the morning."

"That *is* lovely," she agreed, smiling conspiratorially at Paul. "Although, I prefer tea to coffee."

They shared a quiet, companionable moment. Then Paul sighed and closed the record book sitting on the table in front of him.

"Do you think you'll find peace after losing your father? Even with the grief?" he asked.

"I'm certain I will," she replied with conviction. "Because I know that there will be more difficulties in life, but I am strong and I have people who care for me and support me. And I know that I will carry my father with me all the days of my life, in my memories of him." Emma smiled wistfully as if remembering her father now.

Memories of Laura flashed through Paul's mind—playing chase in the fields as children, climbing trees, the way she had looked in her pretty pink dress at their wedding, the love in her eyes when she held Aaron the first time.

They had had years together, their entire lives. He had so many memories of laughter, love, and adventure with her, and thinking of her smile did bring him peace. He missed her every day, but he could always carry her memory with him. Maybe he, too, could heal and find some tranquility in his soul.

He stood and gathered his papers into his arms, then turned to Emma and said, "Good night, Emma." He began to turn toward the front room, to return the papers to the desk, but then stopped and looked back to Emma. "I enjoyed talking with you. Hopefully we can both find some rest tonight."

"Thank you, Paul," she replied, nodding her head in acknowledgment. "Good night."

Chapter Eleven

Dearest Emma,

You've scarcely been gone more than a week, and already I miss you so!

I suppose it's not uncommon for us to go a few days without searching out one another's company, but it was this Sunday when I truly felt your absence. There is still no minister, and so services were not held at your father's church. We went instead to the church on the west side of town, and it simply was not the same. I missed the sound of your lovely voice lifted in song during the service.

And afterward, Hallie was unfortunately ill, and so I had no one to talk to about my most exciting development! Mr. Thomas Covey and I have grown quite close. He has paid me quite a few visits in the evenings, and mother and father have given their approval of the match! Thomas even made intimations that he is interested in marriage and children, and I am certain that he only said those things because he is interested in marriage and children with me!

It seems as if all my girlish fantasies about having a handsome husband who dotes on me and a house full of lively children could all come true!

I hope you, too, are finding fulfillment in your new life. You are a born teacher, and so this little boy is so lucky to have you to work with only him every day. And his family is so lucky to have your delicious cooking and your kind and loving spirit in their presence every day.

Do let me know if I can visit! I simply must see you before I am an old married woman!

Love always,

Georgina

The letter had arrived on her tenth day on the Gilbert ranch, and while it made Emma very happy to receive a note from one of her very best friends, it also made her homesick.

Every day, things improved a bit, but every day something also seemed to go terribly. For every two steps she took forward with Aaron and Paul, she also took one step back. But, she assured herself, that was still forward progress, even if she seemed to be progressing at a snail's pace through molasses.

The reminder of church services made Emma's heart ache. She hadn't yet made it into town for services. It seemed the Gilberts did not attend regularly, which was understandable given the distance from the ranch into town and the amount of time and work needed to keep the ranch running. She had also been cautious thus far about asking for too much. She wanted to establish herself as a member of the household before she made any demands such as an entire Sunday morning off and horse to ride into town.

Instead on Sunday morning, Emma had said extra prayers and read a few of her favorite Bible passages. She had made her own personal Sunday service by remembering her father's sermons on the story of Adam and Eve and God creating the world just for them.

This new Sunday ritual would have to do for now.

She read Georgie's letter at least once every day for the entire week after it had arrived. She was very intrigued about Mr. Thomas Covey and Georgie's courtship. None of the three girls had yet had a serious suitor because, while the West was full of unmarried young men, most of them were not considered suitable or "eligible" by their parents' standards.

Emma smiled to herself recalling Hallie's father once declaring, "No daughter of mine is going to attach herself for life to some dust-covered, whiskey-scented cowboy. If you have to live in this house until you're thirty, we'll find you a nice young man who does not waste his time in the saloon or spend all day on the back of a horse."

Glancing out the window, she noticed Shaw McCormick walking toward the barn and the idea of a dust-covered cowboy didn't seem so terrible.

Emma had had the pleasure of making his acquaintance only a couple of days before, as she and Aaron had taken a walk to the stables to find his father. Instead, they had found Shaw sitting on a barrel just inside the doorway repairing a broken bridle.

The man looked like the epitome of a cowboy—clad in denim pants with dirt-covered brown leather boots on his feet, a wide-brimmed hat hanging on a peg nearby. He wore his caramel brown hair long and tied back from his face, though some escaped and hung in his eyes as Aaron and Emma approached.

"Well, hey there, little cow poke!" Shaw greeted Aaron with a wide smile, exhibiting a number of straight, white teeth. When he saw Emma, he stood politely. "Afternoon, ma'am."

"Hello." Emma inclined her head in greeting and introduced herself, hoping to learn this man's name. "I'm Aaron's governess, Emma Clement."

"Shaw McCormick, ma'am, pleased to make your acquaintance." He quickly looked her over and his facial expression indicated that he liked what he saw. He looked back down at Aaron. "I hope you don't mind me saying, Aaron, but your governess sure is pretty."

Emma felt a blush spread across her cheeks at the cleverly given compliment.

"She's nice too!" Aaron replied. "And she makes real good biscuits."

"Really, now? I sure do love me some good fluffy biscuits." He smiled again at Emma. "We cook our own meals up in the bunk house, and we haven't had any good biscuits in quite some time."

Taking the hint, Emma politely offered her services. "Perhaps I can bake a batch for the farmhands some day soon. Aaron, would you like to help make biscuits for the men?"

"Yeah!" He looked proudly up at Shaw. "I'm real good at cutting the circles with the biscuit cutter."

"I'm sure they'll taste even better then." Shaw ruffled the boy's hair. "Want to see what I'm doing here?" He bent down and began to explain the leather work he was doing.

Emma couldn't help but admire the sharp angles of Shaw's jawline, which sported just a little stubble, and the strength evident in his muscled arms and shoulders. He looked like he had been born to ride a horse and work the land. She had never imagined that she would find such a rough and tough man attractive, but his gentle way with Aaron showed her that while his appearance may be rugged, his character was anything but.

Reflecting again on Georgie's letter, she found herself daydreaming about a courtship for herself. As she washed the dishes, she looked out the window at the bright white clouds floating across the blue sky and imagined looking up at that same sky from a picnic blanket, seated beside a tall, handsome, brown-haired man.

In her imagination, they lay back on the blanket and held hands, watching the clouds float by and pointing out the shapes that reminded them of something they knew.

"That one looks like a great Grizzly bear!" her suitor exclaimed.

"That's not a bear! It's a carriage transporting a beautiful bride to her wedding." Emma laughed.

"A bride, you say? Are you trying to put the idea of marriage into my head?" He laughed as well, and then looked over at her. *"Because if that is your aim, I'm afraid you are too late. Marriage is already much upon my mind these days."*

"It is?" She turned her head expectantly toward her suitor, only to find the face of Paul Gilbert smiling at her.

Emma shuddered out of her reverie, a blush rising up her cheeks at the image of Paul as her suitor.

She continued washing the dishes, scrubbing vigorously at a particularly stubborn piece of food on the plate in her hand. The only reason Paul had been the man in her daydream, she assured herself, was because he was a single man nearby. He was the one she interacted with the most, and so he was foremost on her mind. That was all.

***

"And what comes after the letter *G*?"

Emma and Aaron were sitting together at the kitchen table a few days after Georgie's letter had arrived, sharing an afternoon snack of crisp, fresh apple slices. They had picked the apples themselves just a few minutes before from one of the fruit trees beside the house. She had found that an afternoon snack helped to keep Aaron a little calmer later in the afternoon, when he had a tendency to get cranky.

"*H!*" Aaron exclaimed proudly, taking another apple slice and happily kicking his feet under the table. "Then *I* and *J!*"

"Well done!" Emma clapped and leaned forward encouragingly toward him. "Keep going. What's next?"

After two weeks, Emma's life had fallen into a rhythm. As the rosy sunrise filtered in through her window, she got herself ready for the day, using the cold water in the pitcher on her dresser to wake up and wash off. She would say her morning prayers while watching the sunlight begin to spread from the horizon out over the vivid green landscape, the beauty of a new day reminding her of God's abundance and grace. Her favorite prayer recently was once she had come across in her Common Book of Prayer.

Then she would go to the kitchen and get the fire started in the coal stove so that she could heat the kettle for her tea and Paul's morning coffee.

Throughout the ritual of opening the stove, *God be in head and in my understanding;* removing yesterday's ashes, *God be in my eyes and in my looking;* lighting the kindling, *God be in my mouth and in my speaking;* and adding the wood and coal, *God be in my heart and in my thinking;* Emma prayed for a good day, for patience for both herself and Aaron, for healing for Paul's heart and a return to faith. *God be at my end and at my departing.*

She liked the reminder that God was with her always, even in the difficult moments, and that He would always be there. She simply had to invite Him in.

As the sun rose, Emma would open the doors and windows around the downstairs to let in the fresh morning air, and then set to work on breakfast. She went out the back door to collect the morning eggs and to find a few things in the garden, usually some tomatoes and greens to go with their morning eggs. She would collect eggs again in the afternoon with Aaron, because he loved running outside and interacting with the animals—though Emma was working on getting Aaron to be a little less aggressive with the chickens. He liked to spook them and make them squawk, but Emma was concerned one might retaliate one day.

This particular afternoon, Aaron had been a good afternoon helper and an excellent student. He could already say the whole alphabet and count to twenty, though he often got a little mixed up around fifteen.

"*P, Q, R...F?*" Aaron continued his recitation of the alphabet.

"*S. F* comes after *E*," Emma corrected, her tone soft as Aaron's brow furrowed in confusion.

She was particularly thankful for this good day, because the previous day had been more difficult than most.

Yesterday, it seemed as if Aaron had woken up grumpy. He had thrown his toys when he was told it was time to clean up, narrowly missing throwing one of his favorite wooden ponies into a pot of stew. He had screamed and kicked and cried during his morning lesson and threw an egg at a chicken. Emma had been able to calm him a few times, but nothing worked for very long. He would soon be throwing things, screaming, or crying again.

Whenever Emma would become aware of her heart beginning to pound from Aaron's tantrums, she would take a few deep breaths and repeat her morning prayer to herself.

God be in my head and my understanding. This boy is sad and struggling. He misses his mother. His feelings are understandable, and I am here to help him heal.

The question she kept asking herself, however, that she could not seem to answer was how to reach this boy without showing him the wonder of God. Without using stories from the Bible, she wasn't sure how to teach Aaron the life lessons he so badly needed. For her, God and Bible stories made the world make sense and gave her strength and hope each day. How did someone raise a child without these things?

Overall, however, the child had warmed to her and was calming a bit. Some days were just harder than others. A fact, she reminded herself, that was true for everyone, including herself.

She was still grieving her father, and there were still days when she would rather stay in bed under her warm blankets than get up and begin her chores. There were moments when her father's face suddenly came to her mind and her breath caught for a moment. But knowing that God was by her side all the time took some of the weight off her shoulders and lessened her grief.

"*R, S, T, U,*" Aaron chugged along, all the way to the end of the alphabet.

"Good job!" Emma clapped again for Aaron and handed him the last apple slice. "Let's clean up and we can go down to the creek and find some frogs. Would you please put the plate in the wash sink?"

Aaron obediently took the plate they had used for their apples and carried it to the small wash sink that sat beneath the kitchen window. He liked having a task that he could complete successfully, Emma had found.

As they walked across the pasture to the creek, Emma pondered other ways she might be able to help the boy. She had found a few strategies, like an afternoon snack and lots of time in the sunshine, that helped most days. But she was not trying to just help him make it through a day, she wanted to help him get through life. The answer she continually returned to was God, the one thing that was expressly forbidden.

***

Emma found herself surrounded by people, all dressed in long robes, watching a man as he climbed on top of a rock to speak. A spark of recognition registered in Emma's mind. He had shoulder-length dark hair and a full beard covering the lower half of his serene face. She had seen him before. He was Jesus, the son of God.

She heard a voice speaking only to her, reading the lines from the Bible, "And seeing the multitudes, he went up into a mountain: and when he was set, his disciples came unto him, and he opened his mouth, and taught them."

And then he did. Jesus told them of all the ways they were blessed people. "Blessed are they that mourn, for they shall be comforted."

Emma's breath caught. He was speaking to her.

"Let your light so shine before men, that they may see your good works, and glorify your Father which is in heaven."

This last line repeated in her mind as the people around her faded and she felt the warmth of the rising sun on her face.

She woke up the next morning with a new conviction. God wanted her to teach Aaron about Him, and she would do it in just the way Jesus taught the crowds—outside.

Paul had forbidden her to mention God in his house, but he had said nothing about mentioning God outside of the house. Much as Jesus told the crowds not to hide their light under a bushel basket, God's word could not be contained.

And neither could she.

Dearest Georgie,

I so loved receiving your letter! It brings me such joy to know that you are so happy in your match with Mr. Thomas Covey. He sounds like a delightful gentleman who will surely propose marriage very soon!

I appreciate your kind words. I do love teaching and Aaron is learning so quickly! He has received very little instruction on his letters and numbers, but we are moving along briskly through my first primer. He will be reading words and adding simple sums in no time!

However, I have stumbled across an unexpected challenge with his father, Mr. Gilbert. While the family does not attend weekly church services, I assumed due to their distance from the church, I wrongly assumed that I could use stories and lessons from the Bible to help instruct Aaron on proper and polite behavior. His father, however, feels differently. I have been forbidden to mention God at all in my teaching. It seems as though the tragedies of the last year have hardened his heart against the Lord.

It saddens me greatly to think that anyone could live a life without God's presence. I am certain that I cannot do so. And so I have determined that I will not let Mr. Gilbert's anger impede my ability to teach his son to be a good, faith-filled man.

I miss you and Hallie every day! Please share this letter with her. You must both continue to write to me. I love hearing about your happiness. It provides something joyful for me to think about among the frustrations of life here.

All my love,

Emma

Chapter Twelve

"Daddy! Look at the dragonfly!" Aaron trotted after the winged insect, one hand raised in the air as if he could catch it.

"I see it. That's a big one," Paul responded. He and Aaron were walking along the fence line on the back pasture, far from the house. Paul had been checking every inch of fence over the last couple of weeks, making sure it was all in good repair and no other animals had been taken or could get out on their own.

There had been no trace of where his horses had gone, but they had informed the sheriff, Boone Holliday, and all the area ranchers. Everyone was keeping a closer eye than normal on their livestock, and the sheriff was on alert for any word of a horse thief.

That morning at breakfast, Aaron had turned to Paul and said, "Daddy, can I come work with you outside today? I can help! I'm big and strong." The boy had then held up his arms and flexed his muscles to show just how strong he had become. He had never asked to spend time with his father like that before, and Paul's heart softened a bit at the question.

"That sounds like a fine idea!" Emma had said, smiling broadly. "But only if you won't be in the way and your father's doing something that's safe for you to be around."

Paul had acknowledged that it was a good day for Aaron to accompany him, and after breakfast off they went. For the first half of the walk, Paul had expected the energetic boy to run off, but Aaron stayed nearby and only ran a few feet ahead before stopping to let his father catch up.

Aaron also noticed everything. Paul was astounded at the details that caught his son's attention, from a ladybug on a flower to the hawks circling in the distance, he was aware of so much.

Paul was not only astounded at how observant his son was, but also by how much he was enjoying spending this time with his son. Weeks ago, a morning walk like this would have been nearly impossible—Paul would have spent more time attempting to contain and corral his son than completing the task he had come out here to do.

Instead, when they had come to the fence that needed inspection, Paul had explained what he was there to do, and Aaron had declared himself in charge of the lower half of the fence.

"You're too tall, Daddy," Aaron had told him. "You can't see down here. And I can't see up there. We can work together!"

Paul's chest swelled with pride. Aaron was learning to work with others, an important skill on a ranch, and Paul could not help feeling impressed. "Yes, sir. That is an excellent idea. Are you going to be a foreman one day?"

"I'm going to play with the ponies like Holt!" Aaron ran a hand along the fence as they walked, taking his job seriously.

"That sounds like a fine idea." Paul smiled to himself, looking down at the tiny brown head in front of him.

It had been nearly a year since they had spent such a peaceful, enjoyable morning together, and the sensation was so foreign to Paul. His heart swirled between feeling relief and confusion and worry. Relief that they could have such a lovely time together again, confusion at why it was happening now and how it had come about, and worry that it would be a long time before it happened again.

He decided to just allow himself to enjoy his time with his son and let the future come as it may.

***

"Flour, please. Five pounds," Emma told Samuel Billings, the rotund owner of the general store in Colorado Springs.

The gray-haired man eyed her suspiciously, flicking his eyes back and forth between her and Paul as if he expected them to do something he considered improper at any moment. Paul rolled his eyes. The man was a holier-than-thou gossip, but he ran the only store in town so it was impossible to avoid him altogether.

"Mr. Gilbert?" Emma turned toward Paul. They had been careful not to refer to one another by first names in public. That was something Mr. Billings would certainly have considered far too familiar for a man and his hired help. "Should we get a few pieces of candy? I think Aaron would enjoy the surprise when we return."

They had left Aaron in the care of Bonnie, who was more than happy to add to her brood for the afternoon. Aaron was so excited to play with the other children that he had hardly noticed when Paul and Emma left.

Paul nodded to Emma. "Certainly, Miss Clement. And a few pieces for yourself, too, if you'd like."

Emma smiled like a child being offered a treat, and he saw how she must have looked at Aaron's age, a tiny blonde angel with a smile that could melt all the snow on the nearby mountain tops. Her beaming face chipped off a small piece of the ice surrounding his heart.

"Which flavors do you like, Mr. Gilbert?" Her head was bent, examining the bins of candy in front of her. Paul watched the way she ran her fingers along each label. "You should have some, too."

His eyebrows raised, taken aback that she would think to give him a treat as well. He never got treats for himself, but he had to admit to himself that he wasn't sure why. Candy wasn't reserved for children. "I like the horehound and sassafras the best. Aaron favors the cherry, I believe."

She nodded and turned back to continue placing her order, causing Mr. Billings to waddle briskly back and forth behind the counter fetching her things.

To fill the time, Paul wandered to the other side of the store to consider some farming implements. They had come to town so that Emma could restock some necessary items for the kitchen, but he was always interested to see if anything new had arrived that could make ranch life a little easier.

"Oh, hello, Mr. O'Kelley!" Mr. Billings called from behind him.

Paul, shadowed by a saddle that hung from the rafters above him, turned and saw Caleb O'Kelly sauntering through the door, his white-blonde hair curling out around the edges of his hat and the characteristic sour look on his face.

"Afternoon, Mr. Billings." Caleb removed his hat and nodded a greeting at Emma, who smiled politely, but not enthusiastically.

"Seamus, could you complete Miss Clement's order, please?" Mr. Billings handed Emma off to his assistant and came out from behind the counter to talk to Caleb.

Paul returned to Emma's side to complete the purchase.

And to avoid Caleb.

He thought back to the many times throughout their childhood that Caleb singled him out for some sort of challenge, most of which Paul had won and all of which were silly and unnecessary. Generally, Paul only accepted the challenge because he knew the alternative was being constantly pestered by Caleb and being called a coward until he gave in.

"What's the matter, Gilbert, are you yellow?" Caleb taunted Paul endlessly until he gave in. "You afraid I'm going to beat you?"

The two boys and other children their age were all out at the edge of a pasture with their rifles, practicing shooting and loading. They had lined some rotten apples up on top of a fence and were trying their best to hit them. Paul had managed to hit the most, but that was not saying much. None of the children had proven to be a very good shot yet.

"I bet I can hit three of those apples before you even hit one," Caleb challenged. He started loading his rifle again and set it up on his shoulder, squinting down the sight.

Paul sighed and lifted his own rifle to his shoulder, rolling his eyes at Caleb. The boys each took a few shots, and Paul hit three apples in a row, each one exploding with rotten flesh upon contact with the shotgun shells. A roar went up among the boys.

"That was incredible!" John Higgins raised his arms up over his head. "No one has hit three in a row!"

Caleb threw his rifle down on the ground and scowled.

"Come on, Caleb, that was just lucky!" one of the boys said. "You can't be mad about that."

In response, Caleb spit on the ground at Paul's feet, then picked up his rifle and stalked off in the direction of his family's ranch.

"That was pure dumb luck. You're just lucky," he sneered as he passed the group of boys slapping Paul on the back. "Of course. He gets all the luck."

To say that Caleb was an unpleasant man would be an understatement. He had harbored a deep hatred for Paul for their entire lives, and it was never clear to Paul why that was.

He just knew at this point in life that it was generally best to avoid interacting with the man whenever possible.

"Well, Mr. O'Kelley, you're back again? You still have your eye on that self-raking reaper in the catalog? We can get it ordered for you today!" Mr. Billings sidled up to Caleb's side, stretching his suspenders out with his thumbs. He smiled an ingratiating smile, doing everything he could to make a big sale.

Mr. Billings was as unctuous as Caleb was scornful, and a bad taste developed in Paul's mouth as he listened to their conversation. He would normally avoid eavesdropping, but he trusted each man so little that it seemed important to know what they were up to.

"I sure do, Mr. Billings," Caleb replied, running a hand over the soft leather of a bridle hanging beside him. He fingered the price tag dangling from it and seemed to be considering the item, but then turned to Mr. Billings instead. "I thought it over after I bought that new plow yesterday, and I decided I need it."

"You've become my best customer, Mr. O'Kelley. That farm of yours must be having an excellent year!" Mr. Billings, talking loudly enough for anyone in the store to hear, took a catalog from a shelf and opened it to the page he had referenced a moment before.

"Things are looking up, that's for certain. I recently came into some money, so I'm—" Caleb glanced around the store and stopped talking abruptly when he noticed Paul standing at the counter, watching out of the corner of his eye. Caleb cleared his throat and looked back to Mr. Billings and the catalog. "Let's get this thing ordered."

"Yes, sir! I'll get the paperwork started right away." Mr. Billings grinned from ear to ear as he located pen and paper and began writing the order.

"Here's your total, Mr. Gilbert." Seamus, clueless to the interaction across the room, distracted Paul from his eavesdropping. He smiled broadly at Paul, his freckle covered face blushing when he glanced at Emma. "Would you like to pay cash today, or shall I add it to your account?"

Paul pulled some paper money from his pocket and paid the bill, then he and Emma turned toward the door with their purchases. As Paul pulled open the door and stepped aside for Emma to pass through in front of him, Caleb O'Kelley turned and sneered at both of them. His eyes narrowed to slits and his thin lips hardened into a straight line.

Keeping his face impassive, Paul tilted his head slightly at Caleb to acknowledge the man, but left without a word. Emma looked back and forth between the two men, a deep crease forming between her brows.

They made it about five steps down the boardwalk toward the carriage before Emma asked, "What was that about?"

"What do you mean?" Paul kept his eyes straight ahead and pretended innocence.

"You and that Mr. O'Kelley. He smiled nicely at me and Mr. Billings when he came in, but he certainly did not seem to like you very much." Emma placed her parcels in the crate in the back of the wagon. She fixed him with an admonishing look, as if he were a misbehaving child. "And you were not terribly polite either, if I'm being honest."

Paul shook his head and rolled his eyes at the thought of Caleb, removing the waxed paper package of hard candies from his pocket.

"He's been like that since we were kids. Mean, jealous, competitive. He would always try to outrun me or climb higher in a tree than I did." He popped a horehound candy in his mouth and offered the bag of candy to Emma, who took it and rummaged through it for her favorite flavors. "I noticed it when we were young, but I've never been sure why he's that way with me. He wasn't like that with any of the other children nearby."

"I'm sorry. I know how that can hurt when someone seems to dislike you." Emma's voice was soft and consoling as she took a lemon candy from the package and placed the rest of the candies in her pocket for later. "Do you know how he came into such money? A self-raking reaper sounds like quite a contraption."

"I don't, and it is. It's a very expensive and new contraption that he has no business affording, so far as I can tell." Paul helped Emma into the carriage, trying not to notice the softness of her hand on his calloused one, and then walked around the back to get settled in for the drive home, turning Caleb O'Kelley's purchases over in his mind. O'Kelley owned a neighboring ranch, but he was notorious for not taking good care of his animals or crops. He was also known to be a gambler. "I'm not sure this money of his was obtained honestly."

"Perhaps it was an inheritance," Emma said diplomatically, knowing nothing of the situation.

"More likely a successful gamble at the saloon." Paul worried the candy around in his mouth as he directed the horses out of town.

Something about Caleb coming into money rankled him. The way Caleb had stopped talking once he saw that Paul was nearby made him even more suspicious. Something about this situation was not quite right, but he couldn't put his finger on it.

Chapter Thirteen

Dearest Emma,

I'm so sorry to hear of your troubles in Colorado Springs! What a sad way to live, without God in one's heart. I do hope you shall hold strong to your beliefs and not let this setback prevent you from helping Aaron—and his father—see how to live a faith filled life.

Life here is much the same as always, except that Georgie is simply over the moon for Mr. Thomas Covey. You cannot imagine how many times I have heard about the "marvelous luster of his shining copper hair" or how his eyes are "much the same color as the clear sky in the month of May." I believe any day now, Georgie will begin to write and recite her own poetry about Mr. Thomas Covey!

Truly, I am very happy for her, and so I do not mean to disparage her. I suppose I am perhaps a bit jealous of her happiness and success in making such a wonderful match. They really are a fine match. You should see the way he smiles at her and how she bats her eyelashes and blushes at the mere mention of his name. I think indeed we should expect to hear wedding bells for our dear Georgie!

Love always and forever,

Hallie

***

"Holt? Shaw?" Emma called into the stables, finding Shaw raking out the stalls of the three horses Holt had managed to purchase in the last few weeks. Nowhere near the number of horses they'd had before the robbery, but it made ranch life a little easier.

"Mornin', Miss Emma!" Shaw smiled broadly and swept the sweat from his brow with one tanned forearm. His brown hair was damp at the ends from humid summer air. "How can I help you on this fine day?"

"Could you point me toward Bonnie's house?" Her cheeks turned pink and she lowered her eyes. "I seem to have some trouble finding my bearings out here in the countryside."

Shaw laughed pleasantly. He walked toward the open barn door, his gait slightly bow-legged from decades spent on top of a horse. "No need to be ashamed, city girl. You're still new around here. If we ever visit Pueblo together, you'll have to lead me around."

Her heart made a little leap at the thought that she and Shaw might ever travel anywhere together. She quickly reproached herself. That was never going to happen, and she was being a silly girl full of daydreams.

"I suppose that's true," Emma replied, thankful that Shaw did not tease her.

They stood together at the entrance to the building, and he pointed to the east. "See where the tree line comes to a point right there? Once you reach that point, you'll be able to look straight ahead and see Bonnie's house. Same on the way back."

"Thank you, Shaw. I'll remember that. That's very helpful." Emma sighed, relieved that the directions were so simple. In a city, finding your way around was much easier. Roads and buildings were often labeled for reference. Here, there was a lot of wide open space and landmarks that changed from day to day.

She was not sure how she would ever keep her directions straight, and this unsettled feeling did not only apply to finding her way outdoors. The confusing directions she got from Paul within the house prevented her from feeling as if she belonged as well.

"Thank you again for those fresh biscuits. They were mighty delicious. And the jam you made reminded me of my mama. There's not a higher compliment I could pay you than that." Shaw looped his thumbs in the waist of his pants and grinned down at Emma.

Emma smiled back at him, but found that she had trouble meeting his eyes. She always felt a little shy and self-conscious around this attractive young man. "You're very welcome, of course. And thank you. I'm sure your mother must be a wonderful woman."

"I'd best get back to work." Shaw began to walk backward into the stable to finish his work, keeping his eyes on Emma. "Have a nice visit with Bonnie. Tell her I said hello."

"I certainly will. And thank you for your help."

Emma set out across the pasture toward the tree line, which she also knew concealed a small creek. She and Aaron had explored that creek a few days before and found some frogs, which he had loved to catch and hold onto, while Emma preferred to watch rather than touch. They were fat little mud-colored things with spots, and she did not enjoy the slimy feeling in her hands as they attempted to squirm their way out.

Today, Aaron was enjoying another morning with his father. They had set off to check on some cows, with Aaron promising not to get too close to the big animals unless his father deemed it safe. It lightened Emma's heart to know that Paul and Aaron had begun to spend time together. It was good for the boy to get to know his father.

And since Aaron was occupied and taken care of, Emma had the morning free to take a few of her fresh biscuits and some homemade pear jam over to Bonnie's for a visit. She hummed a hymn as she walked, singing the words in her head while she contemplated her latest letter from Hallie, with a small basket swinging in her hand.

She found that she understood Hallie's feelings of jealousy over Georgie's courtship. It was strange that it was possible to feel so happy for her friend while also feeling a little forlorn to be without a beau. She thought it would be so lovely to have a man smile at simply the sight of her or someone who made her blush at only the thought of him. Shaw made her blush with his effusive compliments, but she found that it wasn't his approval she truly wished for.

When Emma reached the end of the tree line at the creek, she looked ahead, and there was the small stone farmhouse, just as Shaw had said.

She knew that the Lord would provide for her in due time. Perhaps she was meant to find a husband here in Colorado Springs. Perhaps there was a man nearby who was handsome and kind and filled with the love of the Lord.

She began to mentally list the attributes that would be most important in a husband. He must be gentle with children and animals. He must have a genuine smile, one that went beyond his mouth and into his eyes, showing true joy. He must have strong arms to wrap her in when she needed his strength and support. He must attend church every Sunday and take to heart the words of the minister and of the Bible. His faith was the most important characteristic of all.

As she approached Bonnie's house, Emma could see the children, all as dark-haired as their mother, gathering eggs from the chickens and picking some vegetables in the garden as she approached and called out.

"Hello!" She raised a hand over her head and waved, setting aside her thoughts of a future husband and Hallie's letter.

"Emma!" Bonnie's six-year-old, William, came running toward her, a few of his siblings following behind. "Is Aaron with you?"

"Not this time, William. I'm sorry." She ruffled the boy's black-brown hair and smiled into his freckled face. "I'll be sure to bring him over soon."

Without responding, the boy turned and ran back toward the house, yelling to the other children. "It's just Emma. Aaron's not with her!"

Emma chuckled, knowing they were not intending to sound as if they were disappointed that she was here. She was glad that the children enjoyed playing with Aaron, even if he was often difficult. Bonnie said he was a novelty for them, as they were used to having only each other to play games with.

Bonnie stepped out on the front porch and waved. "Hello, Emma! I've got the kettle on. Come in and have some tea."

Emma smiled at her friend. "That will go well with the biscuits and jam I brought."

"Did you bring me more of that delicious pear jam of yours?" Bonnie wriggled her fingers in delight, like a child being handed a sweet treat.

"I did. I even brought an extra one to tide you over until the next visit." Emma mounted the porch and hugged Bonnie. The woman enveloped Emma in her warm arms.

"Ooh!" Bonnie squealed with delight. "You know the way to my heart. You discovered it far too quickly, when I have yet to find yours."

The two women entered the kitchen of the small one-story house. Emma began to unpack her basket at the kitchen table while Bonnie prepared two cups of tea.

Bonnie and John Higgins' house was simpler than the ranch house Earle and his wife had built, with fewer rooms and rough-hewn furniture, but it was filled with much more laughter and love.

Emma sighed, wishing she could restore the happiness to the Gilbert ranch. It was so nicely decorated with fine furniture, lovingly handcrafted embroidered pillows and wall hangings, and the portraits of smiling family members. It had clearly been full of love once. But footsteps echoed through the house now rather than laughter. Meals were often eaten in lonely silence, not enlivened by friendly conversation and a recounting of the day. The beauty of the Gilbert house was nothing compared to the warmth she felt in Bonnie's.

"Now, what is that sigh all about?" Bonnie asked, raising one thick eyebrow and blowing on the steam curling out of her teacup.

"This house just seems so full of love and life." Emma stared down into her tea, swirling the liquid so that the tea leaves danced in the bottom. "The ranch house has an atmosphere of sadness. Or anger. There's no warmth or laughter."

Bonnie shook her head and clucked her tongue, sadness etched into her features. "There was once, believe it or not. Even Earle was once a mostly pleasant man. I can remember a town picnic eight, maybe ten years ago? Was Mary born yet?" Bonnie's eyes veered toward the ceiling, lost in her own accounting of time. "Well, never mind, we'll say eight years ago, before Earle's wife died, and not long after Laura and Paul had married. There's always music and dancing at the picnic, and Earle got up on stage with his fiddle while Paul alternated dancing with Laura and her mother all night long. He never left the dance floor, just laughing and twirling until the women called uncle."

"I can't imagine any of that happening now!" Emma's eyes widened and her eyebrows drew together in shock. "Earle plays the fiddle?"

"He's a right good fiddle player, too." Bonnie was smiling at the memory. "And Paul is a fine dancer. He pulled me out onto that dance floor a time or two. That man has some fancy feet that I could barely keep up with." Bonnie leaned in conspiratorially. "I preferred the slower dances with John, anyway."

Emma laughed and shook her head. "I pray someday I can witness Paul dancing happily!"

"It'll happen. The grief becomes less and less as time goes on." Bonnie sipped her tea and sighed wistfully. "I miss that version of Paul. He has such a lovely smile."

"I don't believe I've ever truly seen him smile. I'm not sure he even has teeth in there." Emma thought back over the many expressions of Paul Gilbert, most of them involved a furrowed brow, narrowed eyes, pursed lips, and a clenched jaw. When his face relaxed, however, she was able to notice his cornflower blue eyes with long dark lashes, like his son's, and his wide, full mouth. *He* is *quite handsome*, she thought, *but he appears so sullen most of the time that his attractiveness did not show through often.*

"Oh, Emma, you do have a way with words." Bonnie laughed and leaned back in her chair, settling in. "So, tell me, what was it that happened in town the other day? Paul's whole demeanor changed between when you both left and when you came back. I know that he tried to hide it from Aaron, but I know that man and I could tell."

"It seemed to shift when we ran into a man named—" Emma paused, searching for the man's name in her memory.

"Caleb O'Kelley?" Bonnie suggested, sitting up straighter and raising one eyebrow.

"Yes! So, the distrust between the two men is well known, then?" Emma sipped her tea.

"For those of us who have known them both since we were all children, it is downright obvious that Caleb harbors some unknown hatred for Paul. As far as I can tell, Paul never did anything to Caleb to cause it, but it has always been there."

"The look that man gave Paul was the coldest look I've ever seen. He reminded me of a snake."

Bonnie snorted. "Snake is right. That man is often up to no good."

"So, you don't know what the cause of this animosity is?"

"Well," Bonnie started, seeming to consider her words carefully, "all I know is what one of my brothers supposedly heard from Caleb once years ago. Caleb is simply jealous of all that Paul has. Paul had two loving parents growing up, and Caleb had a good-for-nothing daddy and an overbearing big sister. Their farms neighbor each other, and Caleb has had trouble after trouble with his crops and his livestock while Paul has had none. I think to Caleb it seems that Paul gets everything, and he gets nothing."

"How could he still feel or act that way, knowing that Paul has lost his wife?" Emma rested a hand over her heart, feeling pained that someone could hold such negative emotion for so long.

"At this point, it's so deeply seated that the hatred may never go away," Bonnie said, matter-of-factly.

Emma stared down into her teacup, wondering how this hatred affected Paul. It must hurt him to know that someone felt so much animosity toward him. To believe that nothing could be done to change O'Kelley's feelings must only compound the wound. Paul had so much pain in his life already, it hurt Emma to know that there was even more that he must suffer.

Even if he never smiles, Emma thought, *perhaps I can help lift some of the pain from Paul's heart.*

***

Emma had not even reached the stables on the ranch before she heard Aaron's wailing and screeching from inside the ranch house. He sounded like a wounded animal, but she knew this was more than likely another one of his unpredictable fits.

She hurried her steps, and finally broke into a run when she heard something crash to the ground in the kitchen. She hurried up the back steps and through the back door, to find Paul sitting on the kitchen floor with Aaron beside him kicking at the table. A chair was sideways on the ground, which Emma concluded was the loud clang she had heard from outside.

A vein popped out on the left side of Paul's forehead as he watched his son writhe. The hoarseness of Aaron's voice told Emma this fit had been going on for a while, and Paul had run out of ways to calm the boy.

Paul looked up at Emma and shrugged, confirming that he had given up.

Emma sat down on the floor beside Aaron and calmly took his hands in hers. She spoke to him so softly that she could hardly even hear herself over Aaron's squealing. "Aaron. I'm going to help you calm your hands."

He fought back, but she was strong and held his hands to his chest as she modeled taking deep breaths in and out, blowing into his face and smiling. He flinched at first, surprised by the air being blown into his face, but his hoarse screaming stopped, and his hands stilled.

"Can you breathe with me, Aaron?" Emma wiped his tear-soaked cheeks with the edge of her apron, continuing to take deep breaths. "Breathe in." She took a big breath in. "Then let it out." She let it go.

She repeated the narration of her breathing a few more times, slowing her own racing heart, as Aaron began to mimic her inhales and exhales. After a minute or two of deep breaths, Emma helped Aaron sit up and straighten his clothes.

"Aaron, I think you need a few minutes to play quietly. Would you like to go sit with your grandpa or play with your animals by the fireplace?"

"Play with my animals," he responded quietly, rubbing at his eyes and sniffling. He had worn himself out.

"Alright, you go find your animals and play for a bit. I'll get a snack together for us."

Aaron trotted into the front room and Emma and Paul were left alone on the floor.

Paul had sat silently a few feet away during the entire interaction, watching with his lips pursed and eyes narrowed in consternation. Emma did not quite know what to make of his expression but that he once again looked sullen and brooding.

"Thank you, Emma, for calming him down." Paul shook his head and ran his hands through his hair.

His words sounded kind and heartfelt, but Emma could see that he was upset that he could not seem to do what she had done. She wanted to reassure him that he was doing a good job, that he was a good father to Aaron.

"You're very welcome. I'm glad I can help." They stood and Emma reached down to right the chair Aaron had knocked onto the floor. "You are doing a good job, even if Aaron acts out sometimes. We've all lost someone we love, and that can be very difficult. Grief can take a long time to lessen, but it does over time."

She looked up at Paul with a comforting smile that quickly faded when she saw the way he was looking at her. Rather than an expression of relief or understanding, his face had gone hard, his jaw stiff and eyes guarded.

"That's none of your business," he said, his voice stiff and terse. "Don't talk to me about grief. You know nothing about what this family has been through." He turned quickly, grabbed his hat off a peg by the door, and left without looking back.

Emma huffed and shook her head as she watched his figure retreating toward the stables. She wanted to call after him that she certainly knew about grief, as she was still experiencing it on a daily basis. She wanted to point out that she would not be here in his house if her father had not died suddenly, leaving her utterly alone in the world.

She wanted to say any number of things about her own suffering, but she knew none of it would help Paul. He was one frustrating man. He wanted her to help Aaron, but did not want to share with her exactly what she was helping him to overcome.

As far as Emma was concerned, Aaron's fits were much simpler to deal with than his father's utter refusal to open up.

Chapter Fourteen

Unable to find Holt in the stables, Paul walked off his frustration with himself by making a lap around the garden, then the chicken coop, before heading down to the creek again.

Once he made it to the creek, he found that rather than needing to walk off excess frustrated energy, he felt exhausted by Aaron's outburst. It was an exhaustion that had built up over the last year and that he carried deep into his bones.

He sat on a wide, flat rock along the bank beside a spot where the water fell about a foot down to the next level of the creek bed. Tadpoles swam around in the eddies at the top of the falls, and dappled rays of sunlight shone down through the leaves overhead.

Paul let out a loud, deep breath. Grief had worn him down. He had lost his wife in a manner that was sudden, violent, and unpredictable. He had been given no time to prepare for her death as he would have if she had been ill. He had been socked in the face with it, and it never seemed to get better or go away.

He picked up some pebbles from the ground near his feet and began to drop them one by one into the water, watching as they created concentric circles in the surface of the stream. The small waves started out strong and then grew larger and weaker as they distanced themselves from the site of the impact.

There were days when he thought about Laura more than others, but never one where he felt at peace with her loss. Some mornings she wasn't the first thing on his mind anymore, but he quickly remembered her absence when he rolled over and found himself alone in the bed.

And there were other days when her memory felt like a rock sitting on top of his chest, pressing harder and harder with each step he took and each movement he made. The effort of making in through those days felt akin to Atlas, holding the weight of the world on his shoulders forever.

Paul ran out of rocks to toss into the water and looked up at the sky. It was starting to look like it might rain soon, and so he supposed it was time to head back toward the house. No use getting soaked.

Rather than go in the back door, Paul circled around to the front of the house. Earle was in his typical spot on the porch, staring out across the fields at the road.

"Afternoon, Earle." Paul sat on the front steps and faced the same direction Earle was looking.

"Howdy." Earle kept rocking in his chair. "Sounds as if Aaron had another outburst."

"He sure did. But Emma came back from Bonnie's and got him calmed right down." Paul shook his head and looked down at his boots, which were covered in dust and mud from his walk. "Laura was a rather high-spirited child, wasn't she?"

"Oh, that she was." Earle smiled sadly at some memory, the same expression he often wore when he thought of his daughter. "She could throw quite the hissy fit if she did not get her way. Usually, she wanted to go run in the fields with all you boys. Then there was the period when she was around seven or eight that she declared she was going to wear trousers. Her mother would not hear of it. There was quite a showdown."

Earle was being uncharacteristically chatty, so Paul made the decision to take advantage of the moment and ask the fellow father for some advice.

"What did you do about it? How did you prevent it or keep it from escalating once it started?" Paul removed his hat and hung it on his knee, leaning forward and rubbing a hand over his face. "What did you do?"

"I'm sad to say that I can't help you much. Her mother did most of it. I was too busy making sure this ranch kept running." Earle sighed and shook his head, looking off into the distance. Paul could tell that Earle wasn't really seeing what was in front of him, but rather was lost in his memories. "I wish I had done more, though, spent a little more time with both of them when I had the chance. I'd give just about anything to spend just a few more moments with my girls."

Paul nodded his agreement, wishing the same thing. He would give anything to see Laura's smile, hear her laugh, caress her face one more time. Anything to have one last memory that was something other than her screaming for him to save Aaron while she was surrounded by flames.

"We're lucky, though," Earle continued.

Paul's head shot up, his brows drawing together as he looked at Earle as if the man were crazy. "Lucky?"

"We have Aaron," Earle stated with conviction. "One small piece of Laura who's still here with us, for us to enjoy. I know I don't do much around here, but I do enjoy the times he comes and sits with me on this porch."

"What do you two do when he sits out here with you?"

"Sometimes he brings a book out with him, or I just tell him stories of my own. He asks lots of questions and laughs a lot, just like his mama."

"What kinds of stories?" Paul didn't know that Earle had any stories. In fact, it had been a long time since he had heard Earle speak so much at one time.

"The same stories my Pa and Grandpap used to tell me," Earle said as if it were an obvious answer. "Great men like George Washington and Daniel Boone. When he's older we'll get around to Rip Van Winkle and the tale of the Headless Horseman. Not sure he's ready for those just yet."

Paul hadn't known that Aaron had spent much time with his grandfather, but it was clear the two were fond of each other, and he was grateful for that.

But no matter what Earle thought, he certainly did not feel lucky.

***

After his conversation with Earle, Paul retreated to the front room. There was not a sound in the house, and so he assumed that Emma and Aaron had gone outside to play or upstairs for an afternoon nap.

He sat on one end of the settee with his head in his hands for a moment, then looked up at the portrait of Laura.

Leaning his elbows on his knees, he examined her pretty face again, so bright and full of life. He had seen this portrait for years now, but it seemed each time he looked at it he noticed something new. Today, he noticed one loose curl that looped around her ear lobe, further contributing to her fairy-like qualities. She was always a little uncontainable. Even her hair could not be fully restrained.

He sighed and began speaking aloud to her. "Oh, Laura, you were truly the light of my life. Yet here I am, stuck in this darkness." He raked a hand through his short, brown hair, then stared down at his boots again.

"Why?" He spoke down toward the floor. "Why did you leave? You left not only me, but your father and your son. We are helpless without you. And hopeless too." He smoothed his hands down his face and looked up at Laura's face again, his chin resting in his palms.

He felt a lump begin to form in his throat and swallowed hard to try to make it go away.

"I miss you every day. And I'm so afraid that one day, Aaron's memories of you will all fade, and he won't remember you at all. He's so small and young. He needs a mother. He needs *his* mother—you."

He heard a quiet shuffle behind him and turned to see Emma attempting to sneak away with a sewing project in her hands, the strings dangling behind her as she moved.

"Oh! Emma!" He felt his cheeks heating up and reddening, and hers reflected the same embarrassment at being an accidental intruder on a personal moment. "I didn't realize you were there."

"I'm so sorry. I should have made myself known when you came in from the porch." Her voice trembled a bit. "I'll leave you to your musings."

She began to move toward the stairs, as if to retreat to her bedroom.

"No, no, it's all right." He motioned her toward him with a wave of his hand. "Come sit with me."

She nodded hesitantly and moved to sit on the other end of the settee on which he sat facing his wife's portrait. She placed the sock she had been mending on her lap and fidgeted with the loose strands of yarn.

"Emma, I want to apologize." He didn't look at her but looked down at his shoes instead.

"Oh, no, it's not necessary!" She reached out as if to touch his arm, but quickly moved her hand back onto her lap.

"It is necessary. I was rude earlier when all you had done was help Aaron." He raised his head to look at her, still leaning forward with his forearms resting on his knees. "I am sorry for how I spoke to you."

"Apology accepted," Emma said, her eyebrows drawn together in consternation. She chewed on her lip, looking as if she wanted to say something further.

Rather than give her the chance to continue a conversation he did not particularly want to have, he got up and went into the kitchen to find himself a small snack, leaving Emma sitting alone before the painting of Laura.

He did feel slightly guilty for not explaining himself to Emma, but he could not admit to the woman that he felt completely out of control—that his life had been out of control for a year and he hadn't the slightest clue how to get it back into one piece. He didn't know how to be a parent all by himself, and it seemed no one around him had any sound advice.

He found a small bit of bread and cheese laying out on a plate on the kitchen table and began to nibble on them as he walked toward the stables. Doing some hard labor was always a good way to take his mind off his troubles, and he was sure Holt had something for him to help with.

Chapter Fifteen

Emma lay in bed, unable to sleep after her confusing conversations with Paul. She had recited every prayer she could think of, tried counting sheep, and nothing seemed to relax her enough to lull her to sleep.

Her stomach grumbled.

I might as well get up and find a snack. Perhaps then I'll find some rest.

She got out of bed, located her robe, and snuck quietly down the stairs. She found some fruit and a small cornbread muffin in the larder and decided to take her snack outside under the stars. Perhaps some fresh air was what she needed.

She nibbled on the cornbread as she wandered toward the garden, looking up at a clear sky filled with stars.

"You ever wonder what those are made of?" A deep voice came from the darkness.

Emma squeaked and her heart nearly leaped out of her chest. Clutching a hand to the opening of her robe, she turned to see Shaw standing at the fence of the chicken coop nearby.

"Sorry, Miss Emma. Didn't mean to startle you." He sounded truly apologetic, though Emma couldn't make out his facial expression in the dark.

"Good evening, Mr. McCormick," Emma gasped, recovering her breath and attempting to speak normally. "What are you doing out so late?"

"I was just finishing up some work in the barn and stopped to admire God's creation before I settled in for the night." He swept an arm in a wide arc overhead to indicate the expanse of the sky.

Emma was pleased to hear him mention God. "Are you a religious man, Mr. McCormick?"

"I was raised in the church if that's what you mean. Went to services every Sunday we could, said prayers over every meal."

"My father was a minister," she told him. "My whole life has been about God and His word. I find myself missing it here. I would love to attend a church service in town on Sundays."

"Well, what's keeping you from going?" Shaw asked, his tone indicating that attending church seemed like a simple task to him. And truthfully, attending church should be a simple task. She was an employee in this house, but she was still a free and independent woman. Paul's rules against God did not apply to her personal behavior and faith life.

"Truthfully, I'm not sure where to go or how I would get there." She chuckled at herself. "It seems like an awfully long walk into town from here."

"I can help with that," he offered. "I'd gladly hitch up the wagon and accompany you on Sunday morning."

"Could Holt and Paul spare you for the whole morning?" Happiness built in her chest at the thought of being able to attend a church service again, but she attempted to tamp it down and not count her chickens before they hatched.

"I'm sure they could. Paul and his family used to attend every week themselves." Shaw's voice was confident.

Emma felt a grin spread across her face and hoped that Shaw could tell how happy he had made her. "Thank you so much, Mr. McCormick. I would like that so very much!"

"My pleasure, Miss Emma." He plopped the hat he had been holding on top of his head and tipped it toward her. "Now, I need to get to bed. I have to be up with the sun, and I'm sure you do, too."

"I do, indeed." Emma sighed. "Thank you so much for your offer, Mr. McCormick. I'm very much looking forward to Sunday now!"

Shaw inclined his head again in recognition of her gratitude, then turned toward the bunk house. "Good night. I'll see that you get back in the house safely."

"Good night, Mr. McCormick." Emma smiled again and walked back to the house, her steps and heart both feeling as light as air.

***

"Emma! Look how fast I can run!" Aaron took off at lightning speed toward the tree line that marked the halfway point between the ranch house and Bonnie's place.

"Oh, goodness, Aaron!" Emma exclaimed. "How will I ever keep up?"

She followed along behind the boy, walking at her normal pace rather than running, knowing that he would tire of running by himself and eventually stop to wait for her to catch up.

It had only been a day since she had made this same trip, but she needed a woman to turn to after her interactions with Paul the day before. He had been curt with her after Aaron's outburst, and then had apologized but provided no explanation. He wasn't being very kind, and he was leaving her confused and a little hurt.

"Hurry up, Emma! I found a grasshopper!" Aaron had stopped running and was now crouched in the tall grass, looking down at the ground.

She had promised the Higgins children that next time she visited she would bring Aaron with her, and she was a woman of her word, so here she was trekking across the fields again with an enthusiastic five-year-old as her companion.

She caught up to Aaron and his insect friend just in time to see the large bug hop away, startling Aaron. He leapt backward and fell on his bottom, but then quickly recovered and began to trot along beside Emma.

"How long are we going to stay?" Aaron asked, pulling at a long blade of grass.

"I'm not sure. We'll go back home before lunch." Their visit was unexpected, and she did not want Bonnie to feel obligated to include them in the midday meal, not with all the children of her own that she had to feed.

"And I can play outside the whole time?"

"You most certainly may. But if the Higgins children have some chores to complete, it would be kind of you to help." Emma ruffled Aaron's light brown hair, noticing that it was getting a little long. She wasn't sure who had been cutting his hair until now, but she would need to find out. That was not a skill she had ever practiced. "The faster the chores are finished, the more time you'll all have to play games."

"There's William!" Aaron pointed to the boy who was running toward them across his family's field. Aaron himself went running toward William, and when the two boys met, they ran off together toward the creek where a few of the older Higgins children were gathered, their dark heads huddled together and studying something interesting on the ground.

Emma continued toward the house, where Bonnie stood on the porch churning butter and keeping a close watch on her children. An array of small clay crocks lay around her feet.

"Well, hello again! I didn't think we'd be seeing each other quite so soon," Bonnie called when Emma was within hearing distance.

"I didn't expect it either," Emma admitted, slowly mounting the porch steps. "But I needed someone to talk through my troubles this morning. And Aaron was more than happy to accompany me."

"I need to finish up this butter, but it's almost there. Have a seat and tell me what's troubling you." Bonnie waved a hand toward a small wooden porch chair nearby.

Emma sat and looked down at her hands, picking at her fingernails as she considered her words.

"You know that Aaron's been a bit difficult," she began.

"That's putting it mildly from what I've heard." Bonnie raised an eyebrow at Emma. "No need to sugarcoat the truth, Emma. I know how it's been over there."

"Well, he has these fits sometimes, outbursts where he kicks and screams and breaks things and everything you can imagine." Emma looked up at Bonnie, whose face showed concern and understanding. "He was having one yesterday as I returned after my visit here. I was able to help Aaron calm himself, but Paul was clearly upset with himself that he hadn't been able to prevent the outburst, and he was rude to me afterward."

"Rude how?" Bonnie opened the churn to examine the butter, nodded her head at what she found, and poured the buttermilk out into a crock.

"I told him that I could see he was trying and that he was doing a good job as a father, which he seemed to appreciate. But when I mentioned that I, too, understand grief, he told me to mind my own business."

Bonnie sighed with frustration. "That man is still grieving something fierce but will not acknowledge it. And he does not like it pointed out to him, either."

"That wasn't the end of it, however." Emma watched as Bonnie began to scoop the fresh butter out into another crock. "He apologized later for being rude but offered no explanation and simply got up and left after I accepted."

"That seems like a step in the right direction."

"Perhaps, but I just do not understand this hot and cold treatment. He'll be very pleasant one moment and then harsh and hard the next." Emma threw up her hands.

Her chore completed, Bonnie sat in a chair beside Emma. "Maybe you look at it this way instead: you work *for* Paul, but you're there to work *with* Aaron. And that part of the work seems to be going well. You said yourself that you calmed him when his father couldn't. That's understandably frustrating for him, but he does not owe you any explanation for his feelings."

Emma nodded. "I suppose that's true."

"Just keep working with Aaron. He'll heal with your guidance." Bonnie patted Emma's hand. "Paul may just have to grieve on his own. Let him be. Focus on the boy."

Emma nodded her understanding to Bonnie, but not her agreement. She didn't feel that she could solely focus on Aaron. God had sent her here to help the whole family heal, not just one child. The boy could never fully heal if his father didn't as well.

She was glad when Bonnie changed the subject by suggesting they walk out to the creek to see what the children had gotten themselves into.

**

Dearest Hallie (and Georgie),

Thank you so much for your latest letter. I do so love the reminders of home, and that you have not all forgotten me yet!

My struggles here continue, but I am determined that the Lord is present in this house, and I shall not ignore Him. I say my own prayers every day and read from my father's Bible.

However, I am still finding it difficult to teach Aaron without mentioning God at all. God is such an important part of my life, of my every thought, that I cannot teach without Him present. His father remains adamantly against any mentions of faith and the Bible in the house. But I will not let that deter me. When the moment presents itself, I will not hesitate to instruct Aaron in the best way I know how, using the words of our greatest teacher, God's son Jesus.

I have made some new friends, however, in the Gilberts' neighbor, Bonnie Higgins, and a farm hand named Mr. Shaw McCormick.

Bonnie is a joyful, kind woman who has known Mr. Gilbert for all her life, and so she is quite knowledgeable of his particular struggles. I have found her to be vital in helping me navigate Mr. Gilbert's anger and lack of faith. She helped me to see that the tragic passing of his wife in a house fire caused him to feel abandoned by God. And while I can understand that feeling, I am determined to help him move past it and open his heart again.

Mr. McCormick is the very image of a cowboy. Your father would have a fit to know that I have chosen him as a friend! He has kindly volunteered to take me into town on Sunday mornings and attend church services with me. You cannot imagine the peace this has brought to my heart, to know that I am not losing that important part of my life just because my employer has lost his faith in God.

I include you both in my prayers every night, and I have added a new prayer for myself, as well. I have begun to pray for a husband. I feel that God is calling me toward a family of my own, and I know that He will send me a man filled with faith and love. Please pray for me, as well.

I miss you both!

All my love,

Emma

Chapter Sixteen

"Daddy, that witch is scary." Aaron pointed to the picture on the page of the fairy tale book Emma had purchased at the general store when they went into town.

Paul had watched Emma as she browsed the books, specifically looking for something that Aaron would enjoy. There were only a few on the shelf in the general store, and most of them were Bibles or stories of the lives of the saints. When she had stumbled upon the book of fairy tales, she had yelped in delight and quickly grabbed the red leather volume from the bookcase.

"Oh, look, it has pictures!" Emma held the book open toward Paul, displaying a drawing of a princess holding a frog in her hand.

Paul had nodded and said, "I think Aaron will like that very much." Internally, however, he was questioning if Aaron would even sit still long enough to read a story.

Now sitting on the floor in the front room with Aaron on his lap, Paul was reading a story about a witch who captured two children and attempted to eat them. He had been spending more time with his son in the past few days, and he found that he was enjoying it.

"She is, son. Why do you think the artist wanted the witch to look scary?" Paul did his best to emulate the types of questions that he heard Emma ask when she read with Aaron, but he often felt silly, even embarrassed by the things he would say. How should he know what the artist wanted? But Aaron considered every question very seriously.

Every time he saw Emma, however, he felt his stomach clench. He had been cruel to the young woman, and though he had apologized, it was a somewhat empty apology. He could only assume that she knew something of the basis for his grief—he knew Bonnie must have told her some of the story, as his childhood friend was not known for keeping secrets to herself. But still he knew that she needed to hear the story from him, in order to understand the full impact on Aaron and on himself.

He just could not seem to make himself talk to her about it. He couldn't talk to anyone about it. If he spoke of it aloud, it would only make the pain come back full force. It was safer to lock the pain away inside and not let it out again. Laura was in the past, and she must stay there.

"She's scary to tell kids to stay away!" Aaron poked a finger on the witch's face on the page. "If someone is scary, don't go with them! Find someone safe!"

But rather than explain himself, Paul spent time with Aaron reading stories and playing with his wooden animals. At dinner, he told Aaron about his day and asked his son questions. Emma was keeping him occupied as often as possible, even if their occupation was walking to the creek in search of frogs, and Aaron always had a story to tell. Even Earle smiled a time or two when Aaron told of his exploits.

"Yes, son. We all want you to stay safe." Paul squeezed his arm around his son's middle, noticing the scent of grass on the boy's clothes as he tamped down the memories of smoke and flames that had almost engulfed them both the year before.

He inhaled the fresh scent as he continued reading the story to Aaron, feeling at peace for the moment with his son.

***

"All right, what's eating at you today?" Holt asked from atop his new horse.

"What do you mean?" Paul feigned innocence, his voice raising a full octave.

"You have that pinched look on your face and you keep chewing on your lip." Holt pointed at Paul and swirled a finger around to indicate the expression on Paul's entire face. "Something is clearly troubling you."

"I'm afraid I hurt Emma's feelings." Paul sighed and lowered his voice. The guilt rolled around in his stomach.

"Have you acknowledged it with her? Apologized?" Holt drew his horse up to a stop in front of Paul's, forcing the horse to come to a halt. From this action, Paul anticipated a fatherly lecture on the horizon.

"Yes, but I think I managed to muck that up, too." Paul rubbed at the back of his neck, as if he could massage away the negative emotions. "I do not know how to talk about feelings. She's still practically a stranger. I just don't know what to say to her."

Holt shook his head. "You're still hurting over Laura, Paul. It's plain as day. But you can't take that out on Emma. She's here to help."

"She's doing an exceptional job with Aaron," Paul admitted, scanning the horizon to avoid making eye contact with Holt. "And she is actually quite pleasant to have around. She's an excellent cook, as well."

"See, she's good for you, too."

Paul knew this, but sometimes he needed to hear someone else tell him the truth before he could accept it. He did truly enjoy having Emma around. He just couldn't seem to show it. She had a calm spirit, but she was not weak. She was serenity and strength wrapped up together into a small, blonde package.

"Give it some time. You'll get more accustomed to one another." Holt reached out and placed a hand on Paul's shoulder to emphasize his next words. "Just don't take your hurt out on the poor girl. She didn't cause it, and she does not deserve to be treated badly when she's hurting, too."

Paul nodded, remembering that Emma was only here because her father had recently passed away. "You're right. I often forget that she's also in mourning."

"All right, then." Holt jerked his head decisively and gently kicked his horse to get her moving toward the paddock again. "Let's get back to work."

"Have you noticed Emma talking to Shaw a lot?" Paul asked, ignoring Holt's suggestion to return to their task.

Holt looked at Paul sideways, smirking. "Does that bother you, Paul?"

Paul scratched the back of his neck. "Bother me? Nah. I just don't know what they'd have to talk about, that's all. Whatever it is, they sure do smile at each other a lot."

"They smile a lot, huh? Could be they're sweet on each other," Holt suggested, testing Paul's reaction to this idea.

Paul scowled and looked down at the back of his horse's head rather than at Holt. "He's too young for her. He's barely even a man yet."

"Seems to me they're about the same age. He's, what, twenty-three?" Holt attempted to hide his smile from Paul, finding Paul's frustration over the blossoming friendship between the pretty young woman and the cheerful farm hand quite humorous, and rather telling. "They're both allowed to have friends, aren't they? You don't mind Emma spending time with Bonnie."

"I suppose," Paul said glumly. "I just don't want them getting all moon-eyed over each other and forgetting how to do their jobs."

"Sure, of course." Holt squinted and leaned forward in the saddle, noticing a figure on horseback coming toward them from the direction of town. "Is that the sheriff?"

"Sure looks like it," Paul responded, forgetting the previous conversation at the sight of the lawman. He turned his horse and urged him to pick up the pace, the beat of his heart speeding up with every step toward the sheriff.

When they were close enough, he waved and called out. "Afternoon, Sheriff Holliday!"

Boone Holliday raised a hand in return and stopped his horse a few feet away from Paul and Holt. Boone was just a few years older than Paul and had proven to be a good sheriff, always seeking truth and justice rather than allowing himself to be swayed by money or popular opinion. He was also a vigilant man, his eyes continually scanning the horizon and his hand usually resting on the butt of the pistol tucked into his holster.

"What can we do for you today, Sheriff?" Paul asked, a deep furrow forming between his eyebrows. The sheriff was a busy man, and a personal visit from him meant something serious had happened.

"Mostly good news, thankfully," Boone responded, setting Paul at ease. The sheriff tipped his wide brimmed hat back on his head, revealing a thatch of bright red hair that was graying around his temples. "We found your stolen horses."

Paul sat up straighter in the saddle and his eyes widened. "Well, why didn't you bring them with you?" he asked jokingly.

"That's why it was only mostly good news," the sheriff admitted. "They've been resold, and the buyer understandably will not just give them back."

"Who sold them?" Holt's voice was hard. As the foreman of the stables, Holt had taken the horse theft especially hard. He had put his heart and soul into caring for those animals and they had just vanished overnight. He worried about their health and wellbeing. "What's the name of the lowlife who would sell another man's horse?"

"The buyer wouldn't say. Said he promised the man he wouldn't disclose the name. He even got a small discount on the purchase for promising." Boone scanned his surroundings, on high alert at all times.

"Well, if that don't take the biscuit." Paul pursed his lips and shook his head. "Is there any way to track down whoever stole my horses?"

"The buyer did offer a description of the man. Said he was a little on the short side with hair so blond it looked white."

Holt swore under his breath and Paul clenched his jaw. Paul had suspected, but without any proof he had held his tongue. But now, with the description of the man confirmed, Paul's ire rose.

Of course it was a short man with white-blond hair. Of course it was the one man who held onto a childhood grudge against Paul. Who else would have the desire or gumption to break into his stables in the middle of the night and steal his horses?

Boone raised an eyebrow in Paul's direction, acknowledging that they both knew exactly who this mysterious buyer seemed to be describing.

Caleb O'Kelley.

Chapter Seventeen

Caleb O'Kelley. Paul turned the name over and over in his mind as he and Holt silently brushed down their horses ruminating over the new information from the sheriff. *Of course it was Caleb O'Kelley.*

Since they were children, Caleb had felt the need to outdo Paul, to get the best of him somehow. He rarely succeeded, but when he did, he made sure to flaunt his victory tirelessly until the next opportunity for a competition.

"See, I told you I could spit a watermelon seed farther than you could! Mine went farther than yours by a whole hand."

The town picnic always included a seed spitting contest, with prizes for separate age groups. Neither Caleb nor Paul had ever won, but Caleb had always been the better of the two children at this particular event. Paul did not much care if Caleb beat him at spitting seeds, as he didn't feel it was the most dignified competition, even as a small child.

"Paul shouldn't even try to run in this race. Don't you all remember how much I beat him by the last time? I was in third and he was in seventh!"

When they were around ten, the boys had begun a summer-long tournament of foot races. It seemed that each time a different boy won, but Caleb never noticed who came in first, only where he placed in relation to Paul.

"I got you this time, Paul Gilbert! You thought that horse of yours was so special, but mine could outrun yours any day. And he just did."

Twelve-year-old Caleb had trotted his horse in a triumphant circle, the poor animal panting and sweating from the exertion of the race. Paul had not been willing to injure his horse to simply win a race against the other boy, and he patted his chestnut's neck affectionately. He let Caleb have the victory, but worried that he would not take good care of the animal.

Victory over Paul in anything had been an obsession for Caleb all through their childhoods, and the fascination had not faded even now, as fully grown adults.

Caleb probably thought he had bested Paul this time, but his distinctive blond hair was difficult to hide. Even under a hat. The sale of the horses also explained how Caleb had been able to afford all that fancy new farm equipment. Caleb must have gotten a pretty penny for selling off Paul's property.

"Leave me alone, woman!"

Paul and Holt's heads both popped up at Earle's yelling from inside the house. When it was followed by a feminine yelp and the sound of a dish of some sort breaking, Paul dropped what he was doing and ran to the house, knowing Holt would take care of his horse until he could return.

Paul burst through the back door, Earle still yelling.

"Just stay out of my way! I do not need your help! I didn't hire you. I did not ask you here and I don't want you here!"

Earle, red-faced, stood tall over Emma, who was cowering against the kitchen counter. A mug lay on the floor between them with the dark contents slowly spreading across the hardwood.

Emma clutched the counter behind her, and her eyes darted around, searching for an escape. She visibly relaxed when Paul entered, but still looked a little panicked. Paul had never seen the woman look so frightened and instinctively wanted to protect her from the overbearing older man.

"Earle! Stand down!" Paul yelled at his father-in-law. Earle leapt back, startled, and crossed his arms, still directing his narrowed eyes at Emma. "What on earth is going on in here?"

"This woman thinks she can just come into my house and take over." Earle pointed a long, bony finger at Emma. "She thinks just because she's a woman, she can come into this kitchen and rearrange everything and do whatever she wants. Well, this is not her kitchen!" Earle turned and faced Emma again. "And you do not belong here! You can't just come in here and worm your way into this family. You are not a wife or a mother, and you are not one of us. You'll never be Laura, and you'll never be welcome here as far as I'm concerned."

"Earle! Enough." Paul stepped forward and grabbed Earle's upper arm, pulling his father-in-law back away from Emma.

The poor woman was pale and trembling, her eyes the size of the saucers on the counter behind her. Tears were hovering at the edges of her eyes.

"She isn't trying to be Laura." Paul placed himself between Earle and Emma, so that Earle was forced to look at him rather than the distraught young woman. "She's here to help Aaron. If she needs to move things in the kitchen to make her day easier, that's up to her. Unless you intend to begin cooking our supper, don't bother with the kitchen organization."

Earle glared at Paul, the two men holding intense eye contact for a few moments. Then Earle huffed loudly and turned to retreat to his rocking chair on the front porch.

Once he was satisfied that Earle was outside, Paul turned around to address Emma, who was wiping at her cheeks.

She sniffled and found a rag on the counter before crouching down to pick up the broken pieces of pottery on the floor. Paul bent down to help.

"I made him a cup of coffee," she said quietly, still sniffling. "He came inside for a small snack, as he usually does at this time of day, and I poured him some coffee. But when I handed it to him, he swatted it to the floor and started yelling at me." She stood and placed the broken mug on the counter. "I've never had anyone raise their voice to me like that before."

Paul wiped the coffee off the floor as best he could, then placed the stained rag in the wash sink. He shook his head, picking up a large, ragged shard of pottery from the counter.

"This mug is broken, irreparable," he said, his voice deep and melancholy. "And so is this family."

He put the shard back on the counter and walked slowly out the back door, his boots scraping along the floor as he went.

Chapter Eighteen

The day of the annual Colorado Springs end of summer picnic dawned bright and clear, promising a beautiful day for everyone to enjoy the outdoor festivities.

Emma put on her best dress, the blue one she had worn on her train journey from Pueblo, which had a fitted bodice and a wide, full skirt. The combination made her trim waist look even smaller. She brushed her blonde hair until it shined in the morning light and took extra care pinning it up into a twist on the back of her head.

It was nice to have an excuse to put some effort into her appearance, and, though she tried her best not to be vain, she felt quite lovely as she admired herself in the mirror.

Once she was pleased with her appearance, she went down the hallway to Aaron's room. She had helped him choose a nice outfit to wear for the day, knowing it would more than likely be wrinkled and covered with mud by the end of the picnic. He didn't have a proper jacket that fit him, something she would have to remedy, but she had found a gray waistcoat that would do, and she had taken extra care laundering a white shirt for him.

"I look fancy!" Aaron exclaimed, looking down at his outfit. "So do you, Emma." He looked up at the door as his father appeared there. "So do you, Daddy!"

"We all look very nice," Paul agreed. Emma thought Paul looked very handsome indeed. He was wearing a waistcoat and jacket she had not seen before in a shade of deep blue that drew out the stormy hue of his eyes, which were much the same color as hers. He waved his son through the doorway. "Let's get loaded up in the wagon."

The three of them descended the stairs together and found Earle already sitting on the front bench of the wagon, reins in his hands. Emma was at first surprised to see that Earle was joining in on the festivities, but then she remembered Bonnie's story of Earle playing the fiddle while Paul and Laura danced. She quickly peeked around the floorboards of the wagon for a fiddle case but saw none.

Paul helped Emma and Aaron into the back of the wagon, facing backwards, before launching himself onto the seat beside Earle, and they were off.

"I see something brown," Emma said to Aaron. "Can you guess what I see?"

"Cows!" Aaron exclaimed, pointing to the cattle milling about in the pasture beside the road.

"No, not the cows." Emma exaggeratedly shook her head.

"The road!" Aaron's stubby little finger pointed again.

"That's it! Good job. What do you see?" Emma poked at Aaron's belly, making him laugh.

Aaron swung his head from left to right, searching for something. "I see something yellow."

The only yellow things that Emma could see were the wildflowers growing along the edges of the road, but she didn't want to guess correctly right away. That took away some of the fun. "Is there a yellow bird?"

"No!" Aaron giggled, thinking he had her beat.

"Is it my hair?" She touched her head.

"No!"

"Hmmm. What do I see that's yellow?" Emma tapped on her chin and looked around, pretending not to see the flowers. "It's a bumblebee!"

"No! No bumblebees."

"Oh, I see it! It's the flowers by the road!" Emma placed her palms flat on her cheeks, pretending to be surprised as Aaron giggled more and confirmed her guess.

They continued their game all the way down the road and through Colorado Springs to the other side of town, where the lakeside was already bustling with activity.

Aaron barely waited for the wagon to stop moving before he jumped out. "Can I go play? I see Johnny and William." He pointed in the direction of the Higgins children playing chase near the water's edge.

"Sure, son," Paul responded, grasping Aaron's shoulder to keep him from running off immediately. "If you need to find us, we'll be near Johnny and William's parents, alright?"

"Yes, sir!" Aaron stamped his feet with excitement, waiting for the signal that he could leave.

"Now, go on." Paul released his son and Aaron sprinted off toward his friends. He then turned toward Emma, who stood waiting with a blanket and a picnic basket looped over her arm. "Earle and I will get the horses squared away. You go find Bonnie. She's probably helping arrange the food."

Emma nodded and looked out over the celebration that was unfolding before her. There were many tables already full of food and more being arranged as Emma approached. A small stage had been erected near the lakeside in front of an area clear of trees or tables that would be used throughout the day for the games and competitions and then as a dance floor in the evening.

"Yoo-hoo! Emma!"

Emma turned in the direction of the voice to see Bonnie waving enthusiastically at her. Emma smiled, relieved to have found a familiar face, and walked toward Bonnie, who was standing behind a table full of pies in a ruffled pink dress.

"Oh, my, look at all these beautiful pies!" Emma was amazed at the artistry demonstrated in the elaborate crusts, featuring plants or animals, and one with a complete landscape of a farmhouse among rolling hills of dough. "Is one of them yours?"

"It's supposed to be anonymous, but—" Bonnie pointed to a pie with a leaf motif around the middle and an intricate vine of ivy tracing all around the outside edge. "It's my famous apple spice pie."

"It's lovely!" Emma had to hold her own hands to prevent herself from touching it, for fear of ruining such an incredible pastry.

"The judging takes place just before the potato sack races. Wish me the best!" Bonnie walked around the table and looped her arm through Emma's, leading her away from the food. "Our blanket is spread under a tree over here. We made sure to save some space for you and Paul as well."

Bonnie helped Emma spread her simple log cabin quilt on the grass, and the two women sat in the shade to enjoy each other's company while the children played nearby.

After a while, they noticed Paul and Bonnie's husband John playing a game with the children. The two men were standing among the children and following the instructions given by the child who had been chosen as It.

"Look at the two of them," Bonnie laughed, her cheeks pink from sunlight and joviality. "They're three feet taller than any of the children."

When Paul failed to properly follow the directions given by Bonnie's daughter Melinda, he was declared out by the children and had to sit down, looking like a giant in the grass among all the children.

"Oh, look! Aaron won!" Emma clapped as the last of Bonnie's children was declared out and Aaron was the last man standing.

Paul, too, celebrated his son's victory by gracing Aaron with a big grin as he swept the child off the ground and tossed him in the air.

It was the first time Emma had even seen Paul smile. She inhaled sharply as her heart beat a little harder than a moment before.

He had a beautiful smile. It was not just his straight white teeth and full lips that were breathtaking, but the way the smile changed his entire face. His features seemed to relax, and he radiated happiness from the inside out. His love for his son shined through, and Emma smiled in return, feeling her affection grow for both father and son.

He may have found himself struggling after the events of the last year, but Paul truly was an excellent and caring father. She admired the fact that he had been able to admit when he needed help. She sighed to herself, thinking of how wonderful it would be to find a husband who cared about his children so genuinely and was not afraid to hide his affections in public.

She immediately wanted to see him smile again and picked at her fingernails as she pondered how she could make that happen, but she had already been in Colorado Springs for nearly a month, and this was the first genuine smile she had seen from him. It seemed there wasn't much that could bring that about.

"The judging for the pie contest is beginning!" Bonnie leaped up from the blanket, grabbing Emma's hand and pulling her up. She called over to her husband, who brought Paul along with him to watch the judging.

The foursome stood amidst the townspeople, all dressed in their very best, gathered in front of the rough wooden stage, watching as four judges first admired each pie and then tasted a small slice of each.

"Ugh," Paul muttered from beside Emma.

She looked up into his face to see him rolling his eyes in annoyance. "What is it?"

"Caleb O'Kelley." He inclined his head to the right, indicating which direction Emma should look to find the source of his irritation.

Emma looked to the right to find Caleb glaring at Paul. The blond man would look away toward the pie judging for a second or two, but then his eyes veered back to Paul. He appeared to be saying something to himself, as well, and the way his eyes were narrowed, and his lips were pursed told Emma that he was not saying anything pleasant.

"What a strange man," Emma said quietly, so only Paul could hear. He nodded in agreement.

"Strange indeed. And probably dangerous." Paul didn't get the chance to say anything more, as the pie contest winners were announced.

"And in second place," the master of ceremonies called from the stage, "Mrs. John Higgins for her spiced apple pie with a leaf and ivy design."

Bonnie squealed and threw her arms around her husband with delight. Then she hurried toward the stage, clenching her hands with excitement, as if she would lose control of them if she relaxed. The dark-haired woman beamed as she mounted the stage and accepted her ribbon beside the third-place mixed berry and the first-place cherry pie bakers, both older women with graying hair and proud smiles.

The festivities continued with a potato sack and three-legged races for the children. As Paul helped to tie Aaron's right leg to William Higgins' left, Emma noticed Caleb O'Kelley hovering nearby once more. The man never had a pleasant look on his face, even surrounded by a celebration.

Emma continued to see Caleb O'Kelley throughout the day, always hovering on the periphery of the celebration, often glaring in Paul's direction. With his narrowed eyes and stiff posture, the man looked so unhappy and uncomfortable. Emma would almost feel sorry for him if he did not make her so uncomfortable.

***

The Gilbert clan was weary on their return trip home after a long, pleasant say spent in the sunshine. Rather than pulling the wagon up to the house when they arrived, Earle drove straight to the stables to quickly take care of the horses.

Aaron had fallen asleep in the back of the wagon, his head resting in her lap and one small hand underneath his cheek. When the wagon pulled to a stop, Emma was afraid to move, for fear of waking the sleeping child.

"Paul!" she whispered loudly, watching to be sure that Aaron didn't stir. "I need help!

He turned from the bench in front of her and saw her conundrum. "I'll come get him."

He hopped down from the front bench and walked around to the back of the wagon. Climbing part way into the bed of the wagon, he gently lifted his son from Emma's lap and then lowered himself slowly back onto the ground with the sleeping Aaron cradled against his chest. Emma dismounted from the wagon as well, then reached back to retrieve their now empty picnic basket.

They walked together around the side of the stables and along the paddock fence. Emma looked up at the clear, star-filled sky with only a small sliver of moon shining and took a deep, cleansing breath, letting the peace of the fresh air and cricket song wash over her.

"Beautiful night," Paul said quietly, looking up at the stars as well.

"I've always loved the stars," Emma responded. She looked up at Paul, whose muscles had relaxed as his son's head rested on his shoulder, the boy's arms and legs flopping around like a rag doll with each step.

"You know the ancient Greeks told stories about the shapes they saw in the stars," he told her.

"Really? Like what?" Emma's curiosity was piqued. She did like a good story, but mostly she had heard Bible stories and fairy tales.

"Stories about their gods and their warriors." Paul looked down at Emma, his face relaxed, almost smiling at her. "Do you see that group of stars up there that looks like a letter W?"

Emma looked up and found the constellation he was indicating. "Yes. I see it."

"That one's called Cassiopeia." He looked up slightly as he walked, so familiar with the terrain that he had no need to watch his feet. "She was a queen who was placed there as a punishment after she boasted to Poseidon, the god of the sea, that her daughter was more beautiful than any of his sea nymphs."

"Oh, my." Emma looked back up at the sky, wondering what other stories existed. "Where did you hear this story?"

"I read it once a long time ago. I used to have a whole collection of books, but they're all gone now." He cleared his throat, as if trying to clear the emotion from the moment. "But I read them all so many times, I reckon I could recite a fair number of the myths."

"I would love to hear more. And I'm sure Aaron would love them, too."

"He does seem to enjoy a good story. I'll have to tell you both more some time."

Emma felt her heart give a small flutter inside her chest. She suddenly very much wanted to hear the tales of the ancient Greeks, if only to have more time alone in the twilight with Paul.

Glad the darkness would hide the growing flush on her cheeks, Emma nodded. "That would be nice."

They continued silently toward the house, both enjoying cool air and the starlight. Emma smiled to herself as they walked, thinking that this was the first nice moment they had had together. The first moment that was not about Aaron or Paul's anger and grief. They had simply walked and talked about something enjoyable, even if only for a moment.

She held on to the belief that there was hope for them yet.

Chapter Nineteen

Dear Emma,

The town picnic sounds like such a wonderful and merry day! Perhaps we should instate such an affair here in Pueblo. I can just imagine walking arm in arm along the riverbank with Thomas, wearing a pretty lavender dress and carrying a brand-new parasol to shade my delicate skin from the sun.

But listen to me! I fear I am becoming quite vain, for Thomas is always telling me how beautiful I look in the light of the sunset or comparing my dark hair to the beauty of the midnight sky. He is so complimentary! But I must not let it go to my head. Vanity is not becoming in a young woman, mother says.

Did you notice that I have now referred to my beau by only his first name? We have agreed to call one another Georgie and Thomas, and he was so pleased to have permission to call me by my shortened name.

I am so glad to hear that you had a pleasant time with Mr. Gilbert. It is nice to see a glimpse of the man that is more than anger, at God or at you. I was beginning to worry about you, but I can see from your recent letters that he has not always been such a difficult man. I am so glad you also have Bonnie to guide you through your challenges with him.

I, too, would like to hear more stories of the stars! Perhaps Thomas knows some of these stories, and he and I could go for an evening walk beneath the stars. It sounds so romantic that I cannot even stand it!

I pray every day for you, for you to find happiness and peace in your current situation and for you to find a husband as lovely as my beau.

Love always,

Georgina

Emma carried Georgie's latest letter with her toward the barn, reading as she crossed the stretch of green grass between the house and the farm buildings. She, too, hoped for a man who was as lovely as Georgie's beau. Emma was familiar with Thomas Covey but had not spoken to him often. He had always been courteous and friendly, but now she also knew that he was a romantic who was smitten with her best friend. It made her smile to know that Georgie had found someone who cared about her and thought her to be so lovely.

"Mornin', Miss Emma," Shaw called from the corral fence.

She looked up from the letter and noticed that the man she was looking for was standing nearby, smiling. "Good morning, Mr. McCormick!" She changed her direction slightly to walk toward him. "I was just looking for you."

"Just my luck." The man smiled, showing off his sparkling white teeth and tipping the brim of his hat back. "What can I do for you today?"

"I was just coming to confirm that we're going into town to go to church in the morning. I know that we were not able to go last weekend because of the picnic."

"Of course! I've been looking forward to it since we spoke a couple of weeks ago." Shaw grinned, and Emma found herself a little disconcerted that the man smiled so much. She believed him to be genuine, but was he ever serious? Was he ever sad? Was he hiding deeper feelings behind a smile, much like Paul was hiding his pain behind his anger?

"I'll make sure to have the wagon hitched up and ready to go around nine. Services start at ten, I believe," Shaw continued.

"Excellent! I will be ready to go at nine." She glanced back at the house, where Aaron was playing with his animals on the porch. He was inching himself closer and closer to the steps, telling Emma that he was starting to get bored and would soon run down the stairs and be difficult to contain again. "I need to get back to Aaron. I'll see you tomorrow morning."

"See you then, Miss Emma. I can't wait. Oh, and Miss Emma? Please, call me Shaw." Emma felt her heart twirl with joy.

***

"One more pin, please, Aaron." Later that afternoon, Emma held her dress on the line with one hand and held the other out to Aaron, who was helping her hang the laundry out to dry.

Today had dawned bright and beautiful, so Emma had taken advantage of the weather and declared it a wash day. She'd had to enlist the help of some men to fill the pot and lift it over the fire in the yard. Aaron had been very helpful all day, gathering laundry, helping scrub the clothes in the washtub. It was a hot, wet, arduous task, but he had never complained once.

Emma, on the other hand, had an aching back from hours of bending over a simmering pot of hot water and laundry soap to stir the heavy clothing and bedsheets. She was sure that her hair was a frizzy, wavy mess around her face, and she knew she would need to spend a few extra minutes at bedtime rubbing some salve on her hands to prevent her skin from cracking and hurting.

Beside her at the clothesline, Aaron dutifully bent down to take a clothespin out of the laundry basket and placed it in her hand.

"Emma?" Aaron said quietly, looking down at his bare feet and wiggling his toes back and forth.

"Yes, sir?" She lifted a wet bed sheet out of her laundry basket and began to pin it to the line.

"Why did God take away my mama?" His high-pitched voice trembled a bit as he flicked at a tall piece of grass in front of him.

Emma inhaled sharply at the question, her blonde eyebrows shooting together with concern for the little boy. She felt tears gather in the corners of her eyes and her chest grew tight. She tossed the sheet back into the laundry basket and knelt in the grass in front of Aaron, taking one of his hands gently in hers.

"Oh, Aaron. I'm so sorry you lost your mama." Her voice cracked as she ran her loose hand through his hair, resting it on the back of his neck. "I lost my mama, too, when I was even smaller than you. Sometimes, it's very hard to understand why such things happen."

Aaron nodded, tears beginning to spill over and leaving wet trails down each cheek.

"And we may not ever know the reasons, but it's important to remember that she's always with you, just as God is always with you, in your heart." She placed her hand over his heart to show him where he held these two most important figures in his life. She could feel his little heart fluttering under her hand.

"Is my mama with God?" Aaron asked, twisting his fingers together and avoiding looking into Emma's eyes.

"Of course she is." Emma took both of his hands, stilling his wriggling fingers. She said the first thing that came to her mind, a Bible verse. Even though Paul had forbidden her from mentioning God or the Bible in his house, she knew it was the best way to help this small boy find comfort. And besides, they were not inside the house. She squeezed Aaron's fingers and quoted the Book of Romans. "For whether we live, we live unto the Lord; and whether we die, we die unto the Lord: whether we live therefore, or die, we are the Lord's."

"What's that mean?" Aaron finally looked up at Emma, his nose scrunched up and his eyes narrowed, the whole face contorted in confusion.

"It means that we all always belong to God, whether we're alive or not." She swung their joined hands back and forth, trying to get him to relax a bit. "It means my mama and your mama are both with God, and that He's taking care of them. They are free from pain and suffering and watching us from heaven."

Aaron looked up at the sky, which was bright blue and dotted with fluffy, cotton-like clouds. A hawk circled lazily up high in the sky and a couple of robins chased each other nearby. After considering it for a moment, he looked back at Emma. "Up there?"

"Yes, up there." Emma looked up, too, imagining the faces of her mother and father peeking over the edge of a cloud, smiling down at her and waving. In her imagination, they were so happy and peaceful that they glowed from the inside out. She could feel their love warming her heart and she smiled, basking in the vision.

"Always?" Aaron's face was pointed straight up at the sky, as if he were expecting his mother to suddenly appear, flying across the sky like one of the birds that dotted the blue above.

"Always. All the time and every day." Emma poked his nose playfully. "You are your mama's favorite thing to watch."

Aaron graced her with a big grin, displaying his one missing tooth. Emma smiled broadly back at him, scrunching her nose, and wiggling her head, making a silly face.

"What about your mama? And your daddy?" Aaron asked, looking back up.

"They are up there, too. And I know they look down on me."

"Aren't they sad? Being so far away?"

"No, you can't be sad in heaven." This was something Emma's father had told her many years ago when she had asked similar questions about her own mother. She did her best to repeat the rest of what he had said to her on the topic. "Heaven is a wonderful place where only good things happen, and every day is filled with peace. Everyone there has a light heart and mind with no worries. And when they look down on us, they want us to have that same happiness and lightness, and our parents feel proud of what good little boys and girls we are."

"I'm a good little boy?" Aaron asked, pointing a chubby finger at his own chest.

"You certainly are!" Emma waved an arm at the laundry paraphernalia that surrounded them, taking in the pot hanging over the fire, the wash board and tub, the baskets of wet and dry clothes sitting on the lawn, and the clothesline full of linens and clothing waving in the breeze. "Look at all we accomplished today. I could not have done nearly so much work all alone. I greatly appreciate your help, Aaron. Thank you for helping."

Aaron beamed at Emma, his eyes taking in the array of tools needed to wash clothing. "You're very welcome!"

His proud smile was infectious, and Emma grinned back at him. "Do you have any other questions?"

"No," he replied, after pausing to think for a moment. "My mama is in heaven with God and she's proud of me because I'm a good little boy."

"Yes! Good job!" Emma wrapped her arms around the small boy and gave him a squeeze. Then she leaned back and caught his eye. "But I think we forgot one little thing."

"What?" Aaron's arms were wrapped around Emma's neck, and he began to fiddle with the collar of her dress, getting restless.

"Your mama also loves you very much. And she always will. Don't ever forget that either." Emma's voice grew a little deeper, conveying her seriousness.

Aaron nodded. "My mama is in heaven with God, and she loves me and is proud of me."

"There you go!" Emma squeezed Aaron one more time, then let him go. "Why don't you go play for a bit? I'll finish hanging the laundry." She patted Aaron's back as he turned and ran off toward the house, a smile plastered to her face.

She sat in the grass for a moment, proud of herself for how she had been able to explain a difficult subject to the boy and bring some comfort to him and to herself. It helped to remind herself sometimes that while she missed her parents very much every day, they were together and happy and always with her.

Her moment of peace quickly faded, however, when she noticed a man's silhouette visible through the sheet she had already hung, a ghostly figure standing just on the other side of the fabric. She recognized the tall, thin frame and the shape of the wide brimmed hat that sat atop the shadowed head.

Paul had overheard everything she had just said.

Chapter Twenty

Paul pushed aside a damp sheet that hung on the line in front of him and looked down at Emma, who was still crouching on the ground. He became aware of the heat rising up the back of his neck, then spreading around the front of his face to his cheeks and forehead. Even his ears felt hot.

"Get up," he demanded, clenching his fists, his voice rumbling up from his chest.

Emma shot to her feet, smoothing her skirts around her as she stood and avoiding making eye contact as she fidgeted.

"How dare you lie to me." He pointed an angry finger in her direction, jabbing it at her to emphasize each word. His voice was deep and almost emotionless. "How dare you preach the word of God in my home after telling me that you would not."

Emma cleared her throat and looked into his eyes with much effort. When her eyes met his, she straightened her spine and lifted her shoulders, suddenly confident in herself.

"I did not preach the word of God in your house," she replied with conviction.

"Liar! I just heard you." Paul raised his voice, beginning to lose his composure.

"We are outside." Emma spread her arms wide, indicating the vastness of the outdoors that surrounded them. "We are not inside your house. We are in the Lord's house."

"I do not give a fig if you are inside or outside or upside down hanging from the rafters of the barn." Paul was yelling now, looming over Emma's smaller frame. "You will not preach to my son. There will be no talk of God." He held his hands out and began marking off his fingers as he created a list. "No talk of the Lord. No talk of Jesus. No stories from the Bible. No quotes from the Bible. None of it is welcome on my property. As far as I'm concerned, you can burn that blasted book that sits on your dresser."

Emma's eyebrows shot together, and her mouth fell open in shock. "That is my father's Bible!" Now her voice was raised as well. "How dare you! That book is my dearest possession, and no harm will come to it while I am here."

"You're right no harm will come to it because you will not be here much longer." Their yelling had drawn the attention of Holt, who stood at the edge of the paddock fence, and Aaron, who was standing with a wooden pony in his hand at the top of the back porch steps. "Your services are no longer needed here. You can pack your things and you'll be on the next train back to Pueblo."

With a speed Paul had not known he possessed, Aaron flew down the steps and across the grass to Emma. The boy clung to her skirts, raising his voice just as loud as the adults had.

"No! No, Emma can't go! Emma, stay!"

Paul snatched his son from Emma, pulling the fabric of her skirt out of the boy's tiny hands. "Let go, son! Emma is leaving. She's going upstairs right now to begin packing."

Aaron kicked his legs out, striking whatever part of his father he managed to reach, and flailed his arms. Paul struggled to hold on to the squirming child, but he managed to keep his arms around the boy's middle.

"You are wrong, Paul Gilbert." Emma stuck an indignant finger in Paul's face. "You are wrong to forsake God for yourself and for your son. He deserves to know the love and comfort that comes from a relationship with the Lord, from knowing that he is loved unconditionally by God."

Having said her piece, she turned on her heel and marched into the house and out of sight, her hands fisted, and head held high.

Paul stood frozen to his spot in the yard. She had never spoken to him so directly and with such conviction. If he hadn't been so angry, he might have been impressed by her confidence and passion. But his blood was still boiling, his fury only compounded by her insistence that her way, God's way, was the only way.

Aaron finally succeeded in squirming his way out of his father's arms, but rather than run after Emma, the boy took off in the opposite direction. Paul decided to let him go for now. It was probably best to let him run off some of his frustration before attempting to talk with him again about Emma leaving.

As he watched his son sprint toward the creek, he saw Holt shaking his head, which hung low. He couldn't see the other man's face, but if he could, Paul knew he would see disappointment.

He clenched and unclenched his hands, trying to relax the tension in his body, as he walked around the vegetable patch. He, too, needed to walk off some pent-up energy, but Aaron had run off toward the creek, so he chose to stay closer to the house rather than head in his usual direction.

As he observed the butterflies and honeybees fluttering from bush to vine, making his garden more fruitful, Paul wondered about what Emma had said to him.

Was he wrong? Was he preventing his son from having a full life? Paul certainly did not have a fulfilling life at this point in time, but was that because of the terrible cards he had been dealt, or was it because he had turned his back on God? He had believed once, and he had been happy. Were faith and happiness connected?

He picked a couple of newly ripe tomatoes from a bush as he passed, then meandered toward the house to place his harvest in the kitchen.

As he walked, he began to feel guilty about the way he had yelled at Emma. He had overreacted for certain. She may have deserved a talking to, but she did not deserve to be berated in front of Aaron and the farmhands. Seeing Holt's sad retreating figure had driven that home for him. Paul hated to disappoint Holt, his father-figure.

Paul mounted the back steps to the house and let himself in the kitchen, placing his tomatoes beside a small pile of zucchini and onions on the table.

But had Emma not been lying to him? She had agreed not to talk about God or the Bible to Aaron, and there she was quoting scripture and talking about heaven to the boy. What else had she said that Paul hadn't heard? No, he could not trust her.

She had to go.

Furthermore, he needed her out of his house before he did or said something that would be disloyal to Laura's memory. Emma was far too pretty with her contagious laugh and bright white smile. He did not want to look at her long blonde hair floating in the wind any longer. He did not need her steady, calming presence in his house. He did not care if he was able to wake up in the morning now and know that breakfast would be ready and Aaron would be well cared for. He could do those household chores for himself again if he had to, even if he had resented it every time he'd had to cook a meal. She needed to leave before he became irreversibly attached.

Paul found himself sitting at his desk in the front room, fiddling mindlessly with a fountain pen. He opened the drawer to place the pen in its proper place, and there sat his own Bible.

With a well-worn faded black cover, this Bible had once been a part of his daily life. It was one of only a handful of items that had survived the fire that had killed his wife. But the day after her funeral, after listening to the minister quote scriptures about death and hearing multiple people tell him that it was just her time to go with the Lord, Paul had placed the book in this very drawer and declared to himself that it would stay there forever. He was finished with God.

Today, however, he removed it from the drawer and turned it over in his hands. He noticed the texture of the supple leather, soft from so many days and years of being held and read. He saw the worn edges on the pages, and the places that were discolored from the dirt and oils on his hands. The sides of one section were a little darker than the others, and he opened the book to that well-loved section of the Bible— the Book of Psalms.

He started from the beginning, finding many words and verses that spoke to his heart. When he came to the sixth chapter, he felt the words deeply.

"Have mercy upon me, O Lord; for I am weak: O Lord, heal me; for my bones are vexed." Paul paused and read the words again. He did feel weak and vexed, down to his very bones. "I am weary with my groaning; all the night I make my bed to swim; I water my couch with my tears. Mine eye is consumed because of grief."

It was a perfect description of how he had felt for the last year—drowning in guilt, barely keeping his nose above the tide just enough to breathe.

But as he continued to read, he got to the next chapter, which began, "O Lord my God, in thee do I put my trust." The tension in his shoulders and back began to relax. His breathing came more easily, and he settled into his chair to continue reading.

He felt at peace in his heart and mind, if only for a short time, while reading the words that were once familiar, but now carried a new meaning. His life had changed drastically, but the words in this book would always be the same, and there was comfort to be found in that fact.

Paul allowed himself the few minutes of serenity as he continued to read.

Chapter Twenty-One

After marching herself indignantly into the house and up the stairs to her room, Emma threw herself across her bed and sobbed. She cried until her breath could only escape in soft, miserable hiccups.

She could not remember crying this hard since she was a child and had been slighted by another girl. She could not even recall now the specific event that had caused her distress as a twelve-year-old girl, but she recalled crying until she could hardly breathe.

When she finally sat up to find a handkerchief to wipe her cheeks and blow her nose, her father had been there to hand it to her.

"Chin up, my Emma," he said, "though you feel now as though your heart is breaking, the Lord has sent you this trial to show you how strong you truly are." He tucked some loose strands of hair, fallen out of her now disheveled braid, back behind her ear.

"But why would God want me to feel such pain, father? Why would he want me to be hurt?" Emma blew her nose loudly into the pink monogrammed handkerchief that had belonged to her mother. The softness of the fabric and the feeling that her mother was there with her brought her comfort.

"He does not want you to be in pain, my Emma. He wants to show you that you are capable of picking yourself back up. And He is there beside you all the time, never forget that."

She remembered those words now, as she lay across her bed on the Gilbert ranch, likely looking just as disheveled as she had all those years ago.

God is with me all the time, she thought. *I am strong, and He sees that.*

When the tears began to dry up and she could catch her breath again, she wiped off her face and straightened out her hair and began to pack.

She opened the trunk that sat at the foot of the bed and ran her fingers over the mementos of her parents that still lay inside. She had so many memories of her father to help her keep him alive in her mind and heart, and she was so sad for Aaron that he had so few of his own mother. She knew, too, that as he grew older, many of those childhood memories would fade away and be lost forever.

She slowly emptied the contents of her dresser drawers, transferring her petticoats and chemises into the trunk, where they had been placed with great excitement and hope only a few weeks before.

After the last dress had been packed into the trunk, Emma lay across her bed once more, this time on her back. She was confident that she could help Aaron, if only his father would allow her to do so. She did not want to leave the boy, but there was no way she could stay here with Paul. Not with the way he continued to challenge her faith, something so very fundamental to her life that she could not just hide it away and never share it. Not with the way he ran so hot and cold with her, friendly and open one day and then berating her the next.

"I do not deserve to be disciplined and spoken to in such a manner," she said aloud to herself, trying to convince herself that leaving really was the right choice.

There was some commotion out in front of the house, and when Emma looked out the window, she saw that Shaw had pulled the wagon up to the porch. This was her signal that it was time to leave. She supposed it was best to go now and catch the afternoon train back to Pueblo than to wait until morning. Spending one more day in this house simply was not an option.

She went down the stairs and found Paul, Aaron, and Earle all sitting on the front porch.

"My trunk is packed and ready to be loaded into the wagon," she stated plainly, attempting to keep all emotion out of her voice.

Paul nodded silently and went into the house to fetch it for her.

"Aaron." She turned to the boy, who was sitting on the edge of the porch kicking his legs back and forth listlessly. She felt as though a rock had settled in her chest when she looked upon this sweet little boy whose life was being torn apart once more. Her voice broke as she said, "I have to go now."

"I don't want you to go," the boy said quietly, almost whining. He sat with his shoulders hunched and hands clenched in his lap, looking forlorn. He rubbed at his eyes and sniffled, attempting to hide the tears running down his cheeks. But it was the utter sadness in his voice that was almost her undoing.

She dropped to the porch beside him, dangling her legs over the edge of the porch beside his, sitting up straight as an attempt to instill some strength and confidence in herself and her words. "I know you don't want me to, but I have to." Her voice quavered, but she cleared her throat and began again. "I want you to know that I have loved being here with you and taking care of you. I liked teaching you very much. You're a very smart little boy."

"Who will teach me now?" He rubbed at his eyes, trying to keep the tears from beginning again.

"I'm not sure, but you'll be just fine with whoever it is." She placed her arm around his narrow shoulders. "And remember, no matter what happens, God and your mama are always with you in your heart."

"Looking down on me from heaven?" He looked up at her, his big, sad eyes full of tears.

"Yes, looking down from heaven." Emma squeezed Aaron tight and held her own tears back. She could hear Paul's heavy footsteps coming down the interior stairs, and so she stood up and prepared herself to leave.

Earle was sitting nearby, silently observing.

"Goodbye, Mr. Smith," Emma said politely. "You truly have a lovely house and ranch. I enjoyed staying here, even for such a short time."

To her surprise, Earle stood and tipped his hat to her. His face was solemn, but not unkind. There was a softness around his eyes, despite the straight line of his mouth. "I wish you the best of luck, Miss Clement. I'm sorry to see you go."

"Why, thank you, sir," Emma stammered, taken aback by the fact that he was speaking to her at all, much less with such kind words. "I am, too."

Paul had loaded her trunk into the wagon and stood talking to Shaw, who had apparently been given the task of escorting Emma into town.

After giving Aaron one last squeeze, Emma descended the stairs and allowed Paul to help her onto the front bench of the wagon beside Shaw, who lifted one side of his mouth toward her in a conciliatory half smile.

"Goodbye, Emma," he said impassively as she settled onto the bench.

"Goodbye," she responded. No longer having any reason to care that Paul didn't want her to talk of God, she added, "May God bless you all. I hope you can find your way back to him and let him into your heart once more."

Paul's face hardened and he shook his head. "Have a nice life in Pueblo. Don't come back here."

Emma and Shaw rode off toward Colorado Springs. The ride remained silent but for the sound of the horses' hooves on the dirt road and the occasional bird flying by until they made it out to the main road. Shaw sat stiffly beside Emma, staring straight down the road, while Emma contemplated what she would do when she returned home.

Surely a new minister had been found and the house she grew up in would be given to him and his family. The boarding house was not an appropriate place for a young woman to live. She would have to ingratiate herself upon her friends and hope that Georgie or Hallie would be able to take her in for a while. Then she would need to set her mind on either finding a husband or a new governess position elsewhere.

Shaw cleared his throat as they passed by Bonnie's house. "I sure am sorry to see you go, Miss Emma."

She turned toward him, disappointed as well to be leaving behind her new friends and thinking that she would have to be sure to write to Bonnie and tell her how much their friendship had meant over the last few weeks. "As am I, Shaw. But it seems that it is for the best." Her voice broke and she swallowed past the lump still sitting in her throat. "Mr. Gilbert and I just do not see eye to eye on some very important matters."

"I was thinking I might find me a new job somewhere else, too," he said solemnly, finally revealing to Emma that he did have a more serious side to his personality.

"Oh, Shaw, don't leave on my account!" Emma clutched his upper arm.

"No, Miss Emma, that's not why I'd leave." He cleared his throat again. "You see, I grew up on the other side of town, and I had myself a sweetheart a couple of years ago. Her name's Mary Lou." He smiled timidly at Emma, a pink blush spreading across his cheeks beneath his dark tan. "She was starting to talk about getting married and having a house full of babies, and I just started feeling real anxious and restless at the thought of all that. So I came out here and got myself a job on a ranch and left Mary Lou behind without even a word of goodbye."

"The poor girl must have been heartbroken!" Emma clasped her hands over her heart, feeling sympathy for the devastation she imagined.

"She was." He hung his head for a second, feeling ashamed of his behavior, but then raised it again to keep his eyes on the road ahead. "But, Miss Emma, having you around reminded me of my sweet Mary Lou. See, she's a godly woman, too, and she's so gentle with children. She's got a bunch of younger siblings. She even looks a little like you, though she's taller and her hair's a little darker. But you both have a certain way about you that I can't quite describe." He leaned in toward Emma, as if about to reveal a secret. "It's part of why I liked you so much at first sight. You reminded me of my Mary Lou."

"That's so sweet, Shaw." Emma looked down at her lap and examined her fingernails, wishing that a man would feel that way about her, too. "Is she still unmarried?"

"I got a letter from my mama the other day that mentioned another man coming around and courting Mary Lou. She said my window might be closing if I don't do something about it real soon. So, I think I better pack up and head home and see if I can win my girl back."

"I'm happy for you," Emma said sincerely. "I wish you the best of luck."

"I thank you, Miss Emma. I surely hope she won't turn me away at first sight. I would not be surprised if she still was as mad as a hornet at me, but I'm hoping I can turn that around real quick and remind her why she ever loved me at all."

"Would you tell me more about her? How did you meet?"

Shaw became his animated, happy self once again, and gladly told tales of his courtship of Mary Lou all the way into town. Emma laughed along with him and smiled at his romantic descriptions of his sweetheart, glad to be distracted from the purpose of the wagon ride into town.

So little attention had she been giving her surroundings that Emma looked up with surprise when the horses pulled to a stop and Shaw said, "Here we are, Miss Emma."

"Oh!" Emma looked around, suddenly noticing the bustle of the train station around them. "Thank you, Shaw."

Shaw hopped down from the bench and then walked around to assist Emma to the platform outside the train depot. He unloaded her trunk from the back while she walked to the window to purchase her return ticket home.

"One to Pueblo, please," she said to the young man working at the sales counter. "One way."

"Yes, ma'am." He nodded and handed her a slip of paper in exchange for her money. "Boards in ten minutes."

She turned around and found Shaw standing a few yards behind her, holding his hat in his hands.

"I suppose this is goodbye," he said as she approached, looking sad once more. "I greatly enjoyed getting to know you some."

"Thank you, Shaw. I enjoyed your company as well." She reached out a hand and placed it on his forearm. "Thank you for your friendship. Best of luck in whatever your future may hold."

The train whistle sounded, and the conductor called for passengers to load, and so Emma smiled bravely at Shaw through the tears in her eyes and turned to board the train back home.

***

The last time Emma had passed this stretch of countryside, she had been hopeful and excited for an unknown future. Now, passing it in the other direction, her future was once again unknown, but she did not feel at all excited.

She rested her head against the window, focusing her eyes on nothing specific, and tried to clear her mind of her worries for at least a little while.

Emma stood in a dark room, lit only by one kerosene lamp, which illuminated a small bed a few feet away. She looked around her, but the room was not familiar at all. The walls were completely blank and white. There was no furniture other than this one low bed and the lantern on a small table beside it.

As she looked to the bed again, she noticed a small figure under the covers.

She moved forward and leaned down over the figure. It was a young boy, shivering and pale. His pallor had Emma instantly alarmed. She reached down to touch his forehead and found it burning up, causing her to snatch her hand back as if she had been burned. His skin was clammy, and as Emma stood there, he began shivering from the fever.

This boy needs help! she thought, searching around frantically for another person. Finding no one, she looked for a way to find help, but the room had no door or window. They were both trapped inside a box with no way out.

She moved to one wall and began to run her hands over it, hoping for some trick door that would pop open if she touched the right place, but the longer she spent looking for the door that never appeared, the more worried she became.

The boy needed a doctor, not just Emma. She could place a wet rag on his head, if she could find one, but she did not know any remedies or cures or even what the boy was suffering from.

She clawed at the walls while the boy's breathing grew shallower and more labored, but eventually gave up and sank to the floor, exhausted.

Emma's eyes flew open, and her head jerked up so abruptly that she knocked it on the window beside her. Her heart was racing, and her palms were sweaty.

She had to do something. She had to help that little boy. He was so sick and pale that he hardly resembled anyone she had seen before, but she knew in her heart that it was Aaron. It was a message from God that Aaron was going to fall ill. She could feel it in the pit of her stomach.

As her breathing slowed and she got her bearings, she recalled that she was not in that small, enclosed room. She was on a luxurious passenger train from Colorado Springs back to Pueblo, sitting on a plush velvet bench in the women's car.

She could not quite shake the feeling of panic, however. She knew in her heart that the little boy in her vision was Aaron. Her stomach turned over, a sense of foreboding threatening to send her breakfast back up.

This vision had her worried that something bad was going to happen to Aaron. If she were to take it literally, Aaron was going to get sick or injured somehow, and Emma was the only one who knew.

Perhaps the vision was simply telling her to go back to Colorado Springs.

But Paul had explicitly told her not to return. She had broken his most important rule, and she was not welcome on the Gilbert ranch ever again.

It doesn't matter, she told herself. *If I can prevent some danger from befalling Aaron, I have to do it. I have to go back and save him.*

She remembered the last words her father had said to her, "God speaks to you. Promise me you'll always trust in your visions, in the message God is sending to you. He knows what's best, even if it is not apparent to us."

This was one of those visions. This was one of those important moments to listen to God and to trust herself. She took a deep breath to calm her nerves and decided that she would return to Colorado Springs as soon as possible to warn Paul.

Unfortunately, when Emma arrived in Pueblo and talked to the station master, she learned that the next train to Colorado Springs would not arrive until the next morning, so her plans would have to wait.

Seeing that her trunk was safely unloaded and stored beside the station office, she walked down the boardwalk and into town, her home.

She was comforted by the familiar sights. The men playing checkers out in front of the general store, the sheriff mounting his horse in front of the drab jailhouse, and most of all, the white steeple of the church rising high above everything at the far end of town.

She unconsciously made her way slowly toward her favorite place.

She smiled at the familiar faces she passed, who seemed surprised to see her but were too polite to ask why she was in Pueblo. She reckoned they assumed that she was just home for a visit.

As the church grew closer, Emma's steps grew lighter. She smiled and took in a deep, cleansing breath as she stood before this familiar building with its plain white siding and cross-topped steeple, then walked up the path to the front door and went inside.

The sanctuary was empty and silent, so she walked forward and sat in the very front pew, where she had sat during her father's sermons every Sunday for more than twenty years. She looked at the cross that hung on the wall behind the pulpit and found herself praying aloud.

"Dear Lord, please help me during this trying time," she said, folding her hands in her lap. "Give me the strength I need to return where I am not wanted. Speak through me and convince those who will not believe me. Help me to keep Aaron safe and healthy. Continue to lead me where I am needed most. And most of all, Lord, forgive me for not trusting in your plan when I left Colorado Springs this morning."

She would have said more, but the door to the church burst open behind her and she jumped in her seat. Swinging her head around, Emma found Georgina standing in the back of the church, panting as if she had run there.

"Georgie!" She leapt from her seat and rushed back to her friend.

"Emma!" Georgie threw her arms around her friend, as she always did when she was overcome by big emotions. Then she began speaking a mile a minute. "What are you doing here? Why are you here? Are you staying? If we were not in the house of the Lord right now, I would have some stern words for you for not telling me that you were coming home!"

"Georgie, one thing at a time." Emma laced Georgie's arm through hers and turned to lead them both out of the church. "I'm only here for the night."

"Just one night!" Georgie's face fell, her bottom lip jutting out with disappointment. She dropped Emma's arm and turned to face her friend.

Emma contemplated the best way to explain her situation. "There was a small misunderstanding with my employer, Mr. Gilbert, and he asked me to leave. But I know that his son, the boy I was caring for, is in grave danger, and I must return as soon as I can."

"But the next train doesn't leave until tomorrow morning!" Georgie turned her head sharply toward her friend, looking alarmed. "Where are you going to stay? Your house is all closed up now."

Emma smiled sweetly at her friend, hoping not to cause too much trouble with her request. "Well, Georgie, I was hoping I might stay with you."

Georgina began to blush and wring her hands, which perplexed Emma for a moment, until her friend began to speak. "Thomas was supposed to come by for a visit this evening. He likes to stop by after dinner and we sit together on the porch swing with some tea or a piece of pie."

"That sounds so romantic, Georgie!" Emma sighed, imagining what that must be like. "I would love to meet your beau if you don't mind. I think it would help me to be distracted from my own troubles for the evening."

"Oh! But of course! And you certainly must stay with me." Georgie linked her arm with Emma's once more and they began to walk down the street. "Perhaps we should go find Hallie, as well. An evening among friends sounds like just what you need."

Chapter Twenty-Two

The next day was hot and humid, the kind of September day that made Paul long for the cooling of autumn that he knew was coming soon. He felt rivulets of sweat trailing down his spine and the band of his hat grow damp as he and Holt worked to prepare the barn for winter.

"Heard anything more from the sheriff about the horses?" Holt asked as he patched a hole in the side of the barn, where some wood had rotted away.

Paul sighed his frustration. "Nothing. I'm sure Boone's working on it, and I don't want to pester the man."

"I suppose he can't just go arrest Caleb O'Kelley without some real proof."

"No, I suppose not." Paul shook his head. "But who else could it be? Who else has white-blond hair like that around here?"

"The argument could be made that it wasn't someone from around here," Holt suggested, looping his hammer back into his belt. "Which is likely what Caleb would say."

"According to Boone, the buyer said all he was going to say and has no interest in being dragged into any sort of legal matter, so there's no way to prove it either way." Paul wiped the dripping sweat from his brow with a bandana. "We may never know at all."

"And worse, we'll never get those horses back." Holt's face looked pinched, the only indication that he was disappointed at the loss of what he considered his animals, his responsibility on this ranch.

One of the farm dogs began barking frantically, standing at the back corner of the barn. Holt and Paul both raised their heads and looked in the direction the dog was indicating. If the mutt had seen a rabbit or groundhog, it would have gone running after the varmint and pounced, but the incessant barking let them know that someone was coming.

Paul squinted in the sunlight, questioning what his eyes were seeing. It seemed to be Emma running down the road, her hair hanging loose and thrashing about her shoulders, skirts bunched in her hands to allow her legs to move more freely.

"Is that...Emma?" Holt leaned forward, also squinting as if to clear his vision.

"You see her, too, then?" Paul moved slowly toward the road, patting the dog on the head as he went in an effort to quiet the mongrel. He had told her never to return, and in the moment, he had meant it. "I thought the heat was making me see things."

Now, however, seeing her face brought him a sense of relief. He felt the clenching in his chest loosen at the sight of her, imagining that things could go back to the way they had been mere days ago and the atmosphere of peace and calm that had been beginning to settle into his soul could return.

Holt followed on Paul's heels, bewilderment coloring his words. "I wonder what's got her all fired up. I've never seen that girl move so fast."

"I sense we're about to find out." Paul stepped out in front of Emma's path as her steps began to slow.

The poor woman was panting and red-faced as she stopped and stood for a moment, hands on her hips. Her usually neat blonde hair had fallen out of its pins and was hanging lopsided down one side of her back.

"I...I know...I'm not supposed to...come back." She spoke in short bursts as her breath came in stops and starts.

"Pause a moment, Emma," Holt instructed, placing a hand on her shoulder. "Catch your breath."

Paul stood, arms crossed and one foot tapping impatiently, while she took a few deep breaths and attempted to tuck her hair back up into its pins.

Once the red in her cheeks had begun to face and she appeared able to speak, he looked her in the eyes and asked curiously, "Why are you here, Emma? What's brought you running down the road like a loose mustang?"

"I...I had a vision," she began. "Well, it probably sounds silly to you, but I have visions sent to me from God. And—" She halted, unsure how to explain it to Paul and Holt once she saw their reactions.

Paul looked at her sideways, one eyebrow raised, and his head tilted to one side. He glanced at Holt to see his expression reflecting the same skepticism.

"Visions sent from God?" Paul repeated slowly, as if trying to make sense of the words.

"Y-yes," she stammered. "I've had them since I was very young. In fact, it was one of these visions that sent me here in the first place, when I saw your advertisement in the paper."

"What was this vision that sent you here today?" Paul interrupted her in order to get the point of what had her running down the road today but reminded himself to ask her later about the first vision.

"I saw a very sick little boy, hot and sweating with fever, and so pale he looked near death." The words fell out of her mouth so quickly they almost ran together into one. "I knew immediately in my heart that it was supposed to be Aaron, that he is going to fall very ill. And I knew I had to return quickly in order to prevent it. Or help take care of him. I'm not sure which. But whichever it is, I had to return and tell you."

Holt and Paul once again exchanged a look, wordlessly asking the other man if the woman in front of them had lost her mind.

"Aaron is fine, Emma," Paul told her, his voice matter of fact and calm. "He has no fever; his appetite is fine. He hasn't so much as sneezed today, as far as I know."

"My visions always come true, Paul. He may be fine now, but he will fall ill soon, I just know it." Her voice was strong and steady. She truly believed in what she was saying. "I also promised my father in his dying moments that I would always trust in my visions and in the message God sends me. I would not be able to live with myself if I had a vision like this and didn't warn you."

"Well, I thank you for the warning, then." Paul scratched the side of his head, still not certain if this woman had gone crazy or was to be trusted. Although she had come running from town like a banshee, the confidence in her voice nurtured a sense of truth about her words.

She nodded her acceptance of his thanks. "May I see Aaron? Just to assure myself of his health?"

"Certainly." Paul turned toward the house, holding out an arm toward Emma as if to usher her down the path with him. "I'll accompany you. It's about time to break for the midday meal anyway."

Holt excused himself back to the barn, and Paul and Emma walked together, the air heavy with silence. Paul was turning over in his head this idea that Emma had visions that she believed were sent from God and that she trusted so completely in the messages she saw in them. He wasn't sure he had ever had that much faith in God, even when his belief was at its strongest.

"Emma, how do you know these visions come from God?" he asked gently. It was a tone of honest curiosity rather than accusation.

"Often, they feature stories or figures from the Bible," she said. "Sometimes there are angels in them. Sometimes I wake up and have a Bible verse in my head." She glanced at him, finding him nodding his understanding. "When I saw your advertisement in the paper, I had just had a vision I couldn't decipher about teaching a young boy his letters. And when I awoke from it, I rushed to my father's Bible. It opened straight to the page of the story with Aaron and Miriam. Do you know the one?"

Paul did know, his childhood Bible lessons from his mother coming back to him. "God says he speaks through visions."

"Yes, that one," Emma confirmed. "It's always been a favorite of mine. I connected to it personally since I have visions." She shrugged, then continued. "I deliberated over it for days, unsure of the meaning, until I saw your advertisement with your son's name in it. That's how I knew I was meant to be here."

Paul pointed to the house, which came into view as they rounded the barn. "There's Aaron, sitting on the porch."

The pair both watched as Aaron leapt around on the porch in front of his grandfather, seemingly acting out a scene from the book the Earle had perched on his lap. The boy had a stick in his hand that he swung about as he lunged and parried in an invisible fencing match.

Paul noticed Emma's shoulders visibly relax, her spine no longer ramrod straight. Aaron was clearly feeling just fine the way he was running about on the porch.

"I'm so happy he's well." Emma stopped walking and turned to face Paul. He stopped as well and looked into her eyes. The distress he saw there belied her slight smile. "I suppose if you would like me to leave again, I should turn back before Aaron sees me. I don't want to cause the boy any distress by suddenly turning up again after I've left."

"No, Emma." Paul put a hand on Emma's shoulder, noticing the pleasant softness of her pale-yellow dress. "Please, stay."

A gentle smile bloomed across her face, her blue eyes sparkling. "Thank you, Paul. I would like that very much."

"Howdy, Miss Emma," a voice said from the doorway of the barn behind them.

"Hello, Shaw!" Emma's broad smile was now focused on the young farm hand. "I'm back!"

"I see that. Seems like I just drove you out the train station this morning. How did you get back here so quick?" Shaw scratched the side of his head.

"I just could not stay away," Emma replied. "Aaron needs me."

"He sorely missed you this morning," Shaw told her. "He wandered down here to the barn and talked my ear off with all sorts of questions and stories. I think he needs his friend back."

Paul stood watching this exchange, feeling out of place. They spoke so easily to one another, both smiling at the other with genuine pleasure on their faces. He was inclined to believe Holt's suggestion that maybe they were sweet on each other, and he was not sure how to feel about that. It made his stomach feel like it was tied in knots.

Then Emma asked, "Have you talked to Mary Lou yet? Will she have you for her sweetheart again?"

Mary Lou? Sweetheart? Paul's thoughts began to race. *Did Shaw have a young lady in his life already?*

"I tried yesterday after I saw you off." Shaw blushed and looked down at the ground, kicking at a rock. "But she wasn't at home. I left a note for her saying that I'd be back around real soon."

"I do hope she'll have you back." Emma placed a hand on his arm in support. "It's evident you care for her quite a bit."

"You mark my words, Miss Emma, I'll get her to marry me before this year is out." He smiled down at Emma, who smiled back.

Hmm, Paul thought. *It looks like Holt was wrong. It looks like Shaw and Emma are just friends.*

The thought made Paul smile to himself. Emma was not interested in Shaw McCormick after all.

Chapter Twenty-Three

"Emma!" Aaron's tiny voice carried across the grass from the house. "Emma! You're back!"

Emma watched as Aaron leapt off the porch and sprinted toward her, flinging his arms around her legs.

"Daddy, is Emma back for good?" Aaron peered up at his father, unwilling to let go of Emma. She ran her hand through the boy's hair and looked at his father, awaiting the answer.

"Yes, son, she's here for as long as she'd like to be." Paul made eye contact with Emma as he answered his son.

"Yippee!" Aaron let go of Emma and ran in a circle around the two adults, his arms flung wide.

Emma laughed as she watched, feeling as if she too could run around in the grass with glee.

"I'm afraid I've left my trunk at the train station in Colorado Springs," she told Paul. "I wanted to get here as quickly as possible. There was simply no time to hire a carriage."

Paul nodded his understanding. "I'll send Shaw for it. We need a few supplies from town, anyhow."

Aaron made one last loop around Emma and Paul and then halted suddenly in front of them. "Emma! Can we finish that story we started yesterday? I want to know what happens to the little red girl."

Emma held out her hand to the boy and he took it. She smiled at his father as they turned toward the house, excusing herself and Aaron with the gesture. "Certainly, Aaron. Let's finish reading *Little Red Riding Hood.*"

She settled on the settee with Aaron, the book spread across both of their laps so that they could both see the pictures as she read. They finished reading how the hunter saved the little girl from the inside of the Big Bad Wolf, but Emma hardly paid attention to the words she was saying. She relished the feeling of snuggling with Aaron once again, while also worrying about when this terrible sickness she had envisioned might strike.

She kept a close eye on Aaron all day, waiting for any sign of illness, but none came. As the day wore on and he showed no signs of even fatigue or loss of appetite, she began to wonder if she was truly going to be allowed to stay.

She did not want Aaron to become as ill as the boy in her vision, clearly, but now she worried what might happen if he didn't fall ill. If no fever befell Aaron as her vision had indicated, was Paul going to think she was lying so she could stay? Would he think she was not in her right mind? Would he allow her to stay after what she had told him?

He came back to the house to deliver her trunk upstairs to her bedroom and to eat a few morsels of cheese and bread, but otherwise continued about his usual business and said little to her other than typical pleasantries.

In the afternoon, Emma sent Aaron outside to run around and play a bit while she sat on the porch and supervised. When she had done this before, Earle had generally sat silently watching his grandson gallop through the yard and climb trees. Today, however, he turned to Emma and appraised her for a moment.

"My son-in-law tells me you have visions," he said, his gruff voice breaking the silence on the porch and startling Emma.

She kept her face impassive, uncertain where this conversation was going. "Yes, sir. I've had them since I was quite small."

"Visions sent by God?" He leaned back in his chair, his full attention on her.

"Yes. Often angels or prophets appear in them. Sometimes Jesus himself." Emma folded her hands in her lap, sitting up straight in the old wooden chair that lived on the porch.

"What sorts of things happen in them?"

"My very first vision had my mother and an angel sitting beside a stream where children were playing. Then a line from the Book of Matthew came to me, as if a voice was speaking within my heart, and I woke up." Emma placed her hands over her heart, remembering her mother and the calm, reassuring voice.

"And a vision sent you here? To help with Aaron?" He leaned toward her, resting his elbow on the arm of his chair.

Emma told him about the message that had shown her she was meant to come to Colorado Springs, and the vision that had come to her on the train just the day before.

"Well, if that ain't just a miracle," Earle said when she had finished. "I've heard of it happening, but never knew no one who was sent messages from God."

"It does seem like quite a gift," Emma agreed. "But it can also be quite frustrating. I don't always know what God is trying to tell me with these visions. My father was very helpful in talking them through, but now I'm on my own to interpret them. I can only hope that I'm doing it right!" Emma laughed lightly.

"I think you're doing it just fine," Earle said reassuringly, smiling at Emma. "It brought you here, and that seems right."

***

Emma went to bed that night with peace in her heart. She was back on the Gilbert ranch, where she knew she belonged, and Aaron was healthy. She thought perhaps her vision was not a warning at all, but a message meant to send her back to Colorado Springs. She fell into a heavy and dreamless sleep.

But she was awakened after just a few hours by the sound of a small voice moaning down the hall.

"Emma!" Aaron's high-pitched voice called weakly from his room. "Daddy!"

Instantly, Emma was on high alert. Her heart raced, and her hands shook as she quickly threw on her robe and tied it closed. She raced down the corridor to Aaron's bedside, with Paul close behind her from his room across the hall.

Even in the dim light of the candle Paul had lit, it was clear that Aaron was sick. His face was a sickly shade of green and his skin was damp all over. Emma touched his forehead for a second to find it burning hot.

"You were right," Paul said from beside her, leaning over the small bed. "He's ill."

"Yes, and he's quite warm." Emma held Aaron's hand as he looked bleary-eyed at her. "Could you find a cloth and dampen it with some cool water? It will help with his fever, I think."

Paul disappeared to his own room while Emma stayed with Aaron, running her fingers through his damp hair and murmuring to him.

"It will be alright, Aaron," she said. "We'll do everything we can to get you feeling better very soon."

While she spoke, her mind cursed the fact that her visions came true every time, without fail. This was one that would have been best left alone.

Chapter Twenty-Four

Emma sat at Aaron's bedside for hours, her hands clutching his as he moaned and slept fitfully. Occasionally, she would get up to remoisten the cloth on his head. She eventually brought the white ceramic bowl and pitcher from her own room so that she could stay in Aaron's room and not have to go back and forth for simple supplies.

She prayed the Lord's Prayer aloud and asked for God's help in her heart as she did.

"Our Father, which art in heaven," she said.

Please heal this boy, who has already suffered so much.

"Hallowed be thy Name. Thy Kingdom come. Thy will be done in earth, as it is in heaven."

Please keep him safe from further harm, for his father has already suffered so much.

"Give us this day our daily bread. And forgive us our trespasses."

Please forgive any of his sins, cleanse his soul. He is young and has so much yet to learn.

"As we forgive them that trespass against us. And lead us not into temptation, but deliver us from evil."

Deliver this boy, God, from his suffering. Bring healing power into the hands of those who care for him.

"For thine is the kingdom, the power, and the glory, forever and ever. Amen."

She barely registered a soft masculine "Amen" from behind her as she finished her prayer but recognized the deep voice as Paul's.

As she sat and prayed in the darkness, she was vaguely aware of motion in the room every now and then, the swishing of fabric as pant legs rubbed together or the soft patter of bare feet on the wood plank floor.

Paul and Earle alternately entered and refilled her water pitcher or sat for a time in a stiff-backed wooden chair one of them had placed at the foot of Aaron's small bed. They never spoke, simply sat vigil with Emma as she bathed Aaron with the cool cloth or rearranged his blankets.

When she ran out of prayers, she began to recite all the Bible verses she could remember.

A particular verse from Matthew came to her mind, and she repeated it as she ran her hand along Aaron's head and through his hair.

"But Jesus said, 'Suffer little children and forbid them not to come unto me: for of such is the kingdom of heaven.'"

The kingdom of heaven belongs to the children, she reminded herself, *and Jesus welcomes them into His arms. He seeks to heal them, and we should place our trust in the Lord.*

She repeated the verse over and over until it became like a meditation, clearing her mind of anything else, and lulling her to sleep.

She sat in the middle of a vast field of lush green grass, completely surrounded by children. There were children of all ages, all colors, short and tall, boys and girls. They were running, playing, dancing. Some were sitting in groups and singing or playing games together.

Emma found herself smiling, basking in the warmth of the sun and the happiness of the children.

"Emma?" A little girl with a head full of kinky golden-brown curls approached her and knelt down beside her.

"Hello," Emma responded, smiling down into a face of milky white skin with a sprinkling of dark freckles across the cheeks. "What's your name?"

"I'm Miriam. My father told me to come to you." Miriam began to pick at the clover flowers surrounding her.

"It's very nice to meet you, Miriam." Emma reached out and smoothed a strand of hair out of the girl's face. "Who is your father?"

The little girl looked over Emma's shoulder and pointed a pale little finger. Emma turned and saw a familiar face.

One she had seen in many dreams before.

Wearing his long white robes, Jesus stood a few yards away, with a line of sick children before him. He laid his hands on each child's head in turn, saying a few words over each one. When he was finished, the child would stand tall, his coloring would return to normal, and he would throw his arms around Christ's waist.

Jesus smiled down at the child he had just healed, and then pointed to the field where the other children played, encouraging each child to join in the fun.

"Why did your father tell you to come to me?" Emma turned back to Miriam.

"To show you." The little girl tied the clover flowers together into a long chain of little white flowers and long green stems.

"Show me what?"

"Sometimes there are a lot of children who needs His help, but He heals them." She tied the two ends together and held up a clover crown to Emma, who bent down so that Miriam could place it on her head. "If He can't heal their bodies, then He can heal their souls."

"What will he do for Aaron?" Emma asked, worried that this was some sort of warning that Aaron would not be healed.

"Keep praying," was all that Miriam said in reply before she stood and skipped off to join some other children who were tossing a ball around in a circle.

The scene before Emma faded slowly away, but before it disappeared completely, she turned to look back at the children in line to be healed and took comfort that Jesus was there to heal them all.

Aaron could be healed as well. She just needed to keep praying.

***

When she awoke, the sun was shining brightly through the two small windows, with one ray settling right across her eyes. She had slept later than she normally would, as the angle of the sunlight revealed that it was close to midmorning.

She sat up and blinked a few times, bringing her eyes back into focus, and stretched her arms up high over her head. Her back was stiff from how she had been bent over Aaron's bed while she slept. She twisted from side to side, attempting to clear the tension from her shoulders, and heard her back give a sharp crack in protest.

She sniffed the air, detecting the familiar scent of coffee nearby. Following her nose, she turned her head to Aaron's small bedside table, where a steaming cup of coffee waited for her. She sighed and smiled as she reached for it and inhaled the reinvigorating scent. Taking a sip of the still piping hot liquid, Emma pondered which of the men of the house would have done something so considerate.

She remembered her conversation with Earle the day before, the first time he had shown genuine interest in her, asking her questions about her visions. Then the memory of the recent argument they had had over a cup of coffee came to her mind.

She decided it must have been Earle who brought it to her—an olive branch of sorts. What a lovely gesture from the older man, to humble himself to the role of serving her some sustenance, to show compassion by considering the needs of someone else.

As she sipped her coffee, she contemplated her dream from the night before.

Weeks ago, God had sent her a message through a Bible story about a man and a woman, Aaron, and Miriam, that had sent her here to Colorado Springs, to look after a little boy named Aaron. And once again, the name Miriam had appeared in one of her dreams. She couldn't help thinking that this was significant, that God had specifically used the name to catch her attention.

She brushed her hand over Aaron's hot, damp forehead and smiled, feeling hopeful that things would improve with the dawning of the new day.

Beautiful little Miriam had told her that Jesus healed the children. Emma just needed to keep praying. And keep praying she would.

She bowed her head, folding her hands around her warm coffee mug and resting them on the mattress, and once again began to pray.

"Dear Lord, please stay by our sides in our time of need and lift us all up. We are feeling low and afraid, and we all need Your strength to help us through this difficult time." She closed her eyes. "Aaron is so small and still has so much to share with the world. Place Your healing hands upon him, Lord. He needs you most of all."

She took another sip of her coffee, feeling fortified by its energizing powers and the presence of God's love that she felt in this room.

Aaron would begin to heal. She could feel it in her very bones.

Chapter Twenty-Five

Aaron was not improving.

The day had been long and arduous for Paul, watching his son moan and thrash in bed, the sheets getting tangled in his little legs.

He had helped Emma give Aaron a bath in lukewarm water, attempting to cool his body. They had given him small sips of water and broth, trying to keep his strength up, though the boy had likely taken in less than a cup of each throughout the day.

Needing something useful to do besides worry, Holt had ridden into town to fetch the doctor. When Paul heard a horse approaching, he looked out the window in Aaron's room to find Holt riding back alone.

Paul went down the stairs and out onto the front porch to see what the news was.

"Where's the doc?" He held his hands out and looked around, as if he expected the man to suddenly appear before him.

"Went into Denver and won't be back until the end of the week." Holt, still seated on his horse, shook his head, and stuck his tongue in his cheek. "Evidently, his sister's kid is very ill, and he went up to help her. But I stopped on the way back and told Bonnie. She said she'll come by later with some supper and not to worry about breakfast tomorrow either."

"Thank you for that, Holt. That was a good idea." Paul stood on the porch with his hands on his hips, feeling helpless and useless. "Were you the one who collected the eggs from the hens earlier today?"

"No, that was Earle." A small glimmer of a smile played across Holt's face. "Must have been a while since he collected eggs. The man was hooting and hollering up a storm at the poor feathered ladies. Mildred came after him pecking at his ankles, her wings all puffed up like she was trying to intimidate him."

Paul snorted a small laugh, though he did not feel very jovial knowing his son was suffering upstairs.

Holt tipped his hat. "I suppose we ought to keep the ranch running. I'll go make sure the animals are all tended to. I'm sure Shaw is doing everything he can, but a ranch is not a one-man operation."

"I thank you, Holt." Paul inclined his head at the man and turned to go back into the house as Holt rode toward the stables, but another rider coming from the direction of town caught his eye.

He raised a hand to his forehead, shading his eyes in an attempt to see better. He could see it was a woman with her skirts fluttering in the wind and bonnet still tied around her neck but flapping loose behind her.

Bonnie raised her arm and waved when she turned down the path to the house. Her horse was loaded down with packs full of what Paul assumed was food.

He was right.

"I'm so sorry to hear about Aaron," she said, barely allowing the horse to stop fully before dismounting. She began talking a mile a minute as she untied the packs from the back of her saddle. "I brought food for your supper tonight. There should be enough to last you until tomorrow, too. And then there's some fresh bread and butter for your breakfast. I know you'll have your own eggs, so I didn't see the need to bring you any of ours."

Paul walked down the stairs to assist Bonnie in carrying the heavy parcels into the house, never saying a word as she continued babbling. It was a familiar characteristic of hers, this chattering. She had been talkative as a child, always making up stories and asking questions, wanting to know everything that was going on. Paul knew it was best to just let her talk and wait for her to finish before adding to the currently one-sided conversation.

"I left Rachel in charge of the young'uns until John comes in from the fields, so I can stay and help out with whatever you need." Bonnie unpacked and organized the provisions, then turned to Paul with her hands on her hips, looking up at him expectantly. "So, what do you need?"

Paul scratched the back of his head. "Bonnie, truly, you've done plenty. Holt and his men are out tending to the animals. Earle evidently collected eggs this morning. I'm not sure what all needs to be done."

"Earle collected eggs?" Her voice was flat and her face expressionless, so strong was her disbelief at this piece of information.

"That's what Holt tells me." Paul held his arms out to his side and shrugged, shaking his head with his own incredulity.

"I'll believe that when I see it," she muttered under her breath, shaking her head. She rubbed her hands together, ready to get down to work. "Well, I am here, and I would like to help. Perhaps I'll see what Emma might need."

Without waiting for a response, Bonnie hustled up the stairs and into Aaron's room. He could hear the soft murmur of the women's voices as they fretted over the sick boy.

After a day and half the night worrying over his son, Paul was becoming restless. The small bedroom upstairs had gotten close and cramped with more than a couple of people inside, and he had been cooped up inside of it for much of the day. He needed to get out and stretch his legs, do something useful.

He went out to check on the pigs and found their food and water troughs full. The horse stalls were all clean, with fresh hay and barley inside. The chickens wouldn't have more eggs until the morning. His ranch was running like a well-oiled machine, thanks to Holt and Shaw.

His people had taken care of things in his time of need, and Paul's heart felt full at the thought, as if it had grown almost to the point of bursting. Without prompting, Holt had told Bonnie that Aaron was suffering, and without question, Bonnie had dropped what she was doing to come help. Earle had silently taken care of farm chores that he had not touched in years.

Paul had spent the last year lamenting the loss of his wife and the resulting destruction of his family, but a new sort of family had sprung up while he wasn't looking.

He smiled to himself and checked on the vegetables remaining in the garden.

***

The next day, Aaron was regaining his strength. By no means healed, but stronger.

He could sit up in bed and stay awake for short periods of time, though he showed no interest in stories or toys. He enjoyed having someone talk to him, but he wore out quickly and tended to fall asleep after just a few minutes.

In the middle of the afternoon, Paul walked into the room to see Emma reading her father's Bible in the chair at the foot of Aaron's bed.

"Emma?" Aaron's voice crackled as he whispered to her across the room.

She knelt at his side and pressed a cup of water to his lips. "Yes, love?"

He sipped and wiped his mouth with the back of his hand. "Are you worried? Daddy says he's worried about how sick I am."

She looked over her shoulder at Paul, who leaned against the doorframe with his arms crossed.

"No, Aaron, I'm not worried at all." She smoothed the hair back from his forehead, a gesture it seemed she had made hundreds of times in the past few days. "Because I know that God is here with us. And I trust that He will take care of you and help me and your father to help you get better."

"How can you place so much trust in someone who lets so many bad things happen all the time?" Paul asked from the doorway. His tone was calm, merely curious where weeks ago the same question would have been an accusation.

"I believe that God has a plan for us all." She turned, looking confidently into his eyes. Paul found that he was drawn to her confidence, to the strength emanating from within her.

She continued, still speaking to Paul. "And, yes, sometimes that plan may cause us to suffer or to feel pain, but that pain often leads to a greater good." She paused a moment, a shadow of sadness passing across her eyes. "I asked my father this same thing once, and he said that we can learn about our own inner strength so that the next challenge isn't quite so painful. He also said that without the bad times, how would we know how truly wonderful the good times are?"

Paul had never considered this perspective, but it made sense to him. If there was never any suffering or difficulty in life, a person might lose all perspective for good and bad. The smallest of injuries or social slights could feel catastrophic if a person had never experienced true pain. Conversely, how could someone know that they lived a charmed life if they have experienced any suffering? Such a person might believe that such happiness is a mediocre life rather than a wonderful one.

Emma turned to Aaron again and held his hand. "And I trust that God is not finished with you yet, Aaron. He still has grand plans for you. However, sometimes we have to help his plan along, which is why we are praying and doing everything we can to help you feel better soon."

"Then why did God let my mama die?" Aaron asked softly.

"Well, He had a plan for her, too." Emma rested her elbows on the edge of Aaron's bed. "His plan for everyone is to have them in heaven with Him one day, and that's where she is now. He didn't want to hurt you, but her dying was about His plan for her, not His plan for you. He was just ready to have her back in heaven with Him."

Paul had never quite heard it explained that way, that Laura's death was not a punishment for him personally. It was not proof that God was vengeful. It was, in fact, nearly the opposite. God loved Laura so much that He wanted to keep her near to Him. Paul could understand that.

He watched Emma continue to explain her beliefs to Aaron, noticing the long hair she hadn't bothered to braid or pin up today. It looked so soft, he wanted to reach out and feel the waves run through his fingers, watch the light play on the waterfall of blonde as it danced and fell.

"And while God does have a plan for all of us, it's still important to pray," she said. "Praying helps to strengthen our connection with Him. It allows us to lay down our troubles at His feet and know that he can help us bear the weight. So, I'm praying every moment for you to get better."

This all sounded less than believable to Paul. Prayer alone could not heal his son. The boy needed a doctor, but the darn man had gone to Denver, a full day's ride away.

She shifted her body in such a way that Paul could see her bare feet peeking out from beneath her dress. The intimacy of the moment caught him off guard and caused him to lose his concentration for a moment.

He interrupted Emma's lesson on prayer. "I'm going to go fetch the doc. I might be a couple of days, but Earle and Holt are around if you need them for anything. And I'm sure Bonnie would be happy to come help with whatever she can."

"Oh, alright," Emma said, her eyebrows raising in surprise at this news.

He nodded quickly and then left to prepare the things he would need for a ride to Denver and back. He wouldn't worry about extra clothes, but he would need some food and a horse that could handle the long-distance ride.

As he saddled up the horse they had named Sully, he considered the impulsiveness of his decision to ride to Denver and back just to fetch a doctor, but he needed to do something to feel useful. He could not just sit by his son's bedside to fret and pray.

He could not spend any more time cooped up in that small room with Emma.

Chapter Twenty-Six

Aaron's health seemed to ebb and flow. He acted as if he felt better in the morning, after a night of fitful sleep, but by the afternoon his temperature had risen again to levels that troubled Emma. She had indeed placed her trust in God, but she knew Aaron was uncomfortable and suffering.

Emma felt helpless and listless. She had grown accustomed to seeing Paul sitting beside Aaron at the breakfast table, the way he would stop by throughout the day to check on his son, and the atmosphere of strength he carried with him. Without him nearby, she found herself feeling less self-assured.

From her spot at the side of Aaron's bed, Emma heard a rustling coming up the stairs and down the hallway. She looked at the door to see Earle enter the room.

"Thought I could come spell you a bit," he said tentatively, taking three steps into the bedroom. "I'm sure you could use some rest and a minute to yourself."

"Thank you, Earle." Emma smiled at the old man, becoming more and more dear to her every day. She stood and walked toward the door, shaking the wrinkles out of her skirt. "I greatly appreciate the offer."

"Grandpa." Aaron's weak voice drew Earle to his bedside, where he pulled up the chair and sat. "Tell me a story."

"Well, let's see." Earle scratched his chin, his eyes drifting up toward the ceiling as he considered which story to tell. "Have you ever had the story of the day you were born?"

Emma continued down the hall to her room to wash her face and braid her hair, but with the bedroom doors open, she could still hear Aaron and Earle talking.

"No, I never heard that one," Aaron told his grandfather.

"Well, then, I'll tell you that one. It was a good day." Earle cleared his throat.

"Your mama and daddy lived in their own house just down the way, but still on the ranch. And one fine spring day, the kind when all the flowers were blooming their bright colors and butterflies flitted about in the breeze, your papa came galloping over here to the ranch house. I've never seen a horse run so fast! And your papa looked terrified. Like he'd seen a ghost!"

"Daddy was scared?"

"He sure was."

"What's Daddy scared of?"

"Well, see, your mama had started having pains. The kind of pains that mean the baby is on its way. And he didn't know how to deliver a baby. He didn't even know how to hold a baby, but we'll get to that."

Emma could hear the smile in Earle's voice.

"Anyway, your mama had sent him out of the house and over to the ranch house to fetch your grandmama Amelia, who did know a little about delivering babies."

"My grandmama in heaven?"

"Yes, sir. Your mama's mama was a fine lady, and she was so excited to be your grandmama. So, your papa came rushing right over when Laura, that's your mama, sent him. And your grandma wasted no time finding a horse and rushing right over to the house with him."

"Did you go, too?" Aaron coughed, his chest rattling in a way that Emma found unsettling.

"Not just yet. I went the other direction toward town to fetch Marjorie Winthrop, the midwife. That's someone whose job is delivering babies. We rode our horses as fast as we could to get there in time, but you, my boy, had other plans."

"I did?"

Emma laughed lightly to herself at the excitement she heard in Aaron's voice because the story had suddenly become about him rather than his parents.

"You sure did. You see, when your papa and grandmama made it to the house, your mama was out on the front porch waiting for them, and she looked mad. She said to them, 'Y'all are going to help me into that bed in there and get this baby out. I'm not doing this any longer.' And when your mama had set her mind to something, by golly, everyone else better listen. She would not change her mind for nothing or nobody. So, they helped her into the bed. Your papa fetched her some water to drink and then stayed right by her side, holding her hand through every moment of pain. Your grandmama Amelia made sure the room was ready for your arrival, fussing about for warm water and clean wash cloths. She liked to fuss over things. It made her feel useful."

"Then what happened?" Aaron prompted his grandfather, who must have gotten lost in his own thoughts for a moment.

"Then, when your mama said it was time, out you came. Your papa sat right next to her, holding her hands and letting her squeeze the daylights out her fingers, and your grandmama picked you right up, washed you off, and wrapped you in a little cream-colored blanket. Seemed like you were in a rush to get out and meet the world and had no interest in waiting around for the midwife."

Emma thought this description of Aaron still applied— always in a rush to get to the next thing with no interest in waiting around for anything. On a typical morning, Aaron would be itching to get out the door to play before the breakfast plates had been cleared from the table.

"You weren't there when I was born?"

"No, sir, I was not. If I had been, your papa and I most likely would have been sitting out on the porch and letting the womenfolk handle the birth. But because I took off for the midwife, your father was there to see you born. And that's a memory your mama and papa both cherish. They said it was a miraculous occasion."

"When did you get there?"

"I arrived about five minutes too late. We could hear you crying from a half mile away, but Marjorie came with me to the house anyway just to check that everyone was doing alright. When I walked in, you and your mama and papa were all snuggled up together on the bed making funny faces at each other, already so happy to be a family. I went right to your grandma and gave her a big hug. We were all so very happy to have you here with us."

Emma sighed to her image in the mirror, her hair long since braided. They had all been happy once, a family in love with one another. She made herself get up and go back down the hall to Aaron's room.

"I mentioned earlier that your father did not even know how to hold a baby?"

"Right," Aaron confirmed.

"After your mama had nursed you a bit and you began to drift off to sleep, we passed you around a bit so everyone could snuggle the tiny little baby."

"I was a tiny little baby?"

"Everyone starts out as a tiny little baby. You were just small enough to hold right here." Earle indicated the length of his forearm. "But you grew real fast. Anyway, your grandmama held you for a while, and then I got to hold you for a while, and then I passed you back to your parents. And your mama said, 'I'm so tired, I think I'd like to rest. Let Paul hold him for a bit.' And your papa looked even more terrified than when he'd galloped up on his horse earlier!"

Aaron giggled at the idea that his father was terrified to hold him.

"He said, 'I don't know what to do with him!' And I held you out and said, 'Well, you'll figure it out eventually.'"

Emma stifled a laugh from the doorway, imagining the absolute panic on Paul's face, his eyes wide and frantic.

"And he held you at first like you were made of pure bone china and might just break in his hands. But your grandmama gave him a few suggestions, and he settled you right against his chest and you stayed there until it was time for the next meal."

"That's a lovely story, Earle," Emma said. "Your wife sounds like a good woman."

Earle looked over at her, grinning at his own memories. "She was the best woman. A wonderful mother and grandmother." He turned back to Aaron. "She stayed with your mama and papa for a week straight after you were born. I finally convinced her to come home when I told her that I could not stand to eat anymore cold salt pork and biscuits."

Aaron smiled weakly and his eyelids began to flutter.

Earle stayed by Aaron's bed for a few more moments, then Emma took his place sitting vigil by the pale, sick boy.

Chapter Twenty-Seven

Emma and Aaron both dozed through the afternoon, the warmth of the sunlight acting like a soft, soothing blanket over them. But while Aaron slept deeply, Emma was awakened by the sound of heavy boots on the porch steps and male voices from outside the window.

"Paul's not back?" Emma heard Holt ask Earle, worry evident in the tone of his voice.

"No, sir, I reckon he didn't make it to Denver until after dark last night. That's a long ride." Earle's voice sounded slightly worried, and Emma thought perhaps he had been alerted by something in Holt's mannerisms.

"I suppose I'll tell you, so you can keep an eye out as well." Holt paused, and Emma imagined him taking off his hat, as he often did when he had something serious to say. "I saw Caleb O'Kelley prowling around outside the barn a little while ago. I walked over in his direction to go talk to him, but when he saw me, he jumped on his horse and hightailed it back over to his ranch. Shaw and I looked all around the barn and didn't find anything suspicious, but I can't believe that Caleb was up to anything other than no good at all."

Earle harrumphed, making a sound like a snorting horse. "No good, indeed. I never have trusted that boy. Always has a sneaky look on his face."

Aaron stirred in his bed and Emma moved away from the window to give him a sip of water and feel his forehead again.

It was still warm, but it may have been ever so slightly cooler than before. She also supposed it was possible that she was only imagining the difference and it was only wishful thinking.

The men's voices faded as she moved about, and so she heard no more about Caleb O'Kelley. She could not help but wonder, however, what that man was up to. She knew that Paul was suspicious of him, but other than a few grumpy looks, she did not understand what the man had done to warrant such suspicion.

Aaron sipped his water and looked up at her, his eyes glassy and sad, and she quickly forgot all about Caleb O'Kelley.

***

The next morning when Emma awoke and made her way down the hall, Paul was sitting in the chair in Aaron's room drinking a cup of coffee.

"Oh!" She clutched her chest, surprised to see his tall silhouette illuminated by the dim pink light of dawn. "When did you return? Is the doctor with you?"

Paul shook his head. Even in the darkness, she could see the circles under his eyes and the tightness of his mouth. "Got back a couple of hours ago, and I've been here ever since. Doc couldn't come. He's tending to his sister's daughter, who's been sick with rheumatic fever."

"Oh, my goodness. I'll add her to my prayers." Emma silently said a quick prayer as she knelt by Aaron's side and took his hand.

"Aaron has not gotten any better, has he?" Paul leaned forward, his elbows resting on his knees, and peered at his son's small face. The boy looked so frail.

"Not really. But no worse, either." Emma shrugged, attempting to reassure both herself and the boy's father.

"I wish we knew what we could do," Paul dropped his head into his hands, raking his fingers through his hair. "Doc seemed to think we were doing all we could, given that he couldn't come examine Aaron. Cold cloths, water, and broth."

"And prayer," Emma added, looking at Paul out of the corner of her eye. When he didn't show any side of protest or disagreement, she reached over to the bedside table, where her father's Bible lay, and opened it to the Book of Matthew.

Placing a hand on Aaron's forehead as a sort of blessing, she set the book on the bed and read aloud. "When he was come down from the mountain, great multitudes followed him. And, behold, there came a leper and worshiped him, saying, Lord, if thou wilt, thou canst make me clean. And Jesus put forth his hand, and touched him, saying, I will; be thou clean. And immediately his leprosy was cleansed."

She waved a hand toward Paul, gesturing him over toward the bed, to lay hands on his son and pray for healing with her.

She had not expected him to do so, but only hoped he might join her. As she continued reading, she was stunned to feel his warm hand on hers. With his other hand, he reached out and took Aaron's tiny palm in his. Her heart beamed with gratitude that this man, who had once lost all faith, now knelt beside her praying. She could hardly believe it was truly happening, and so she chose not to make a large show of acknowledging the event. Rather, she continued to read the Bible story.

"'Lord, my servant lieth at home sick of the palsy, grievously tormented. And Jesus saith unto him, I will come and heal him. The centurion answered and said, Lord, I am not worthy that thou shouldest come under my roof: but speak the word only, and my servant shall be healed.'"

As they read and prayed together, Emma discovered that she enjoyed the feeling of his warmth and strength and sensed the healing energy of God flowing through them both. It felt right to hold this man's hand in this way, to offer up prayer and hold one another up in this time of trouble.

Paul's calloused hand in hers just felt right.

When Emma's reading came to a natural stopping point, she allowed her voice to trail off, but she and Paul remained kneeling beside the bed, each with one hand on Aaron and their others entwined.

Chapter Twenty-Eight

After two nights in a row spent mostly on a horse, Paul slept heavily and awoke the next morning feeling refreshed and renewed. His back was still stiff, but he was able to relieve some of the tension by stretching and twisting. The autumn morning air was crisp, the summer finally yielding to the mountain snows of the long Colorado winter. Paul took in a deep breath of the fresh air coming in through his window and threw his robe on over his nightclothes to check on Aaron.

He found Emma already sitting at Aaron's bedside, her steaming mug of coffee on the bedside table.

She looked up when Paul entered and smiled. It was a smile he had not seen from her in nearly a week, the smile that shone from inside of her heart and lit up her blue eyes, so that they sparkled like aquamarines.

"His fever broke!" She touched her fingers to Aaron's head again, as if to reassure herself.

Paul's heart lightened, and a smile spread across his face. Aaron was going to be all right.

The sound of a horse trotting down the path caught their attention and they crowded together at the window. A man on horseback was making his way at a brisk pace toward the house.

"It's the doctor!" Paul felt even more weight remove itself from his chest. He hurried to his room to dress, frantically throwing on a clean shirt and pants, then rushing down the steps to the front door.

He opened the door just as the doctor was raising his hand to knock. Doctor Harold Johns stood on the porch with his hand arrested in midair, looking shocked when the door before him was flung open.

"Howdy, Doc!" Paul smiled ebulliently.

"Hello, again, Mr. Gilbert." The stunned man lowered his arm and raised the case he held in his other hand. "I've come to have a look at your boy."

"I appreciate it." Paul stepped aside to allow Doc Harold inside the house and then ushered him toward Aaron's bedroom. "I admit, I'm surprised to see you so soon."

"Yes, well, my sister called for a town doctor soon after you left, once I could convince her that my patients here also need me. My small niece had turned the corner toward recovery anyway, so it was an easy argument to win." He laughed lightly at the silly arguments siblings have.

"Aaron's fever broke this morning, so we're pretty sure he's on the mend." Paul stepped aside once more and allowed the doctor to precede him into the boy's bedroom. Emma, still in her nightclothes, had snuck back down the hall to her own bedroom, but peeked out the door to hear what the doctor had to say. Paul nodded his head to her in acknowledgement.

Doc Harold examined the boy, listening to his breathing and his heart, pressing on and prodding his limbs, looking into his mouth. All the while, he chatted pleasantly at Aaron.

"And what's your favorite story from your fairy tale book? My favorite is *The Princess and the Frog.* It makes me think there's hope for all of us, even the frogs." Doc chuckled to himself, and Aaron just sat letting the man run his fingers along his throat.

Paul's mind jumped to things that Emma had said in the last few days that sounded very similar to the doctor's analysis of the fairy tale. *There's hope for all of us, even the frogs*, he mused, *even the sinners among us have hope of redemption, of eternal life in heaven. Even the lepers and the sick can be healed with faith and prayer.*

"Alright, young man, I think you'll be right as rain in a few days." The doctor closed his case and stood from the chair by the bed. "His lungs sound like they have a little fluid in them, and he's clearly still fatigued. A little bedrest for a few more days, make sure he continues to drink plenty of water, and see if he can tolerate a little more food. He should have his strength and energy back quickly."

Paul's cheeks grew sore from grinning, the muscles unaccustomed to stretching in that direction. He saw the doctor out, thanking him profusely for stopping by.

As Doc and his horse trotted away, Paul turned and walked around the back of the house to gather the morning eggs, whistling "Camptown Races" as he went. When he reached the chicken coop, he began singing softly to himself, despite his inability to carry a tune.

"Camptown ladies sing this song, doo dah, doo dah." He reached down into a nest and swiftly snatched two eggs. "Camptown race-track five miles long, oh de doo dah day."

The chickens squawked at the noise he made, but he paid them no attention. He just continued gathering the eggs and then made his way into the kitchen, where Emma was frying some meat in an old cast iron skillet on the stove and a fresh cup of coffee waited for him on the table.

"Thank you for the coffee, Emma. It surely is delicious." His voice was vibrant and jovial, booming in the quiet kitchen. Emma smiled in response, reflecting his glee.

As he took a long drink of the dark liquid, Paul felt overwhelmingly that this was a good day.

***

After he had seen to some chores and talked to Holt, Paul impulsively rode into town to the church. He had not seen the inside of the church since the day of Laura's funeral, when he had sworn to never set foot in any church ever again. He had been so angry at God that day. But today, he was thankful to God for sparing his son, for sparing them all further suffering and pain.

As he rode, he noticed the beauty of autumn all around him. The leaves were changing colors, from the lush green of spring and summer to the temporary yellows and reds of the fall. The squirrels were frolic about, gathering and burying nuts for the winter. Birds circled above, diving down now and then to snatch worms and grasshoppers from the ground. He reveled in the glory of nature that surrounded him out here in the countryside.

When the town began to close in around him, Paul marveled in the ingenuity of man. To invent such things as wagons, to find ways to pump water right up out of the ground for anyone to drink, and to build such tall buildings— the bank building was four stories tall—were feats of such genius that Paul could not fathom. Such knowledge was certainly a gift from God, and he was thankful for it.

The white steeple loomed over the shorter buildings at the north side of town, shining like a beacon. Paul nodded and tipped his hat to the people he passed, smiling broadly to everyone, as he made his way to the church.

Stopping his horse in front of the building, he dismounted and stood looking up at the cross perched atop the steeple for a moment. A month ago, a hard rage would have settled like a rock inside his heart at the sight. Today, the building seemed illuminated by more than sunlight. It was the light of God welcoming him back.

He walked up the dirt path to the door and let himself into the cool sanctuary. Sitting in the back of the church, Paul considered his surroundings for a moment. A single candle burned beside the pulpit, and sunlight shone through the stained-glass windows that lined the walls. The windows were simple, showing a cross or a dove, but the minister had proudly overseen their installation a few years back. Stained glass was a luxury that not many frontier churches benefitted from.

Paul bowed his head and began to pray aloud, his voice echoing in the empty chamber.

"Thank you, Lord, for sparing my son," he began. "I don't know that I could have handled any more suffering in my life, and so I thank You for sparing me the pain, though I may not deserve it."

He noticed a hymnal laying on the floor near his feet and reached down to pick it up, flipping through the pages mindlessly as he prayed.

"I have been needlessly angry with You since my Laura died, but I see now that You were not seeking to cause me pain. I should be pleased to know that Laura awaits me in heaven, that she is at peace with You."

His eyes landed on a page in the hymnal, and he read the lyrics before him for a moment.

"What a friend we have in Jesus, all our sins and griefs to bear. And what a privilege to carry everything to God in prayer."

Wasn't that what Emma had been saying recently? That prayer was a way of laying down our suffering at the feet of God and allowing him to help us carry the weight?

The next lines of the song made Paul feel ashamed of himself, so much did they sound like himself.

"Oh, what peace we often forfeit. Oh, what needless pain we bear. All because we do not carry everything to God in prayer."

He began to pray aloud again, "I could have used your help in the last few months, Lord, and instead I turned my head and my heart away from You. I suffered greatly because I was determined to face it all alone, without You." He closed the hymnal and set it on the pew beside his leg. "I thank You as well, Lord, for sending Emma to us. She has opened my eyes and heart to You again, and for that I will be eternally grateful to you both."

He stayed and prayed silently for a time, reciting all the prayers and Bible verses he could remember, asking the Lord to help him continue to heal from the suffering of the last year, and praying for Aaron's improvement.

When he left, the rock that had been lodged in his chest for months was gone.

***

The sheriff was sitting on the front porch with Earle when Paul returned to the ranch, so he led the horse to the house rather than the stables. A visit from Boone Holliday was never frivolous.

"Afternoon, Sheriff." Paul dismounted and tied the horse to the hitching post in front of the house. "Wish I'd known you were coming. I could have saved you the trip, I was just in town myself."

"That's what I heard, but I was coming from the other direction, anyhow." Boone stood and shook Paul's hand. "Some more horses have been stolen, this time from Jeremiah Davis down the road."

Paul swore under his breath and slapped his hat on his thigh.

"Seems likely it's the same thief. He used the same method—came in the middle of the night, cut out a far portion of the fence."

Paul looked out over his land, struck by the sting of the betrayal once again. He would never get those horses back, and it pained him deeply.

"He made one fatal mistake, however." Boone raised an eyebrow and the corner of his mouth quirked up. "It's been so dry lately, the horses left clear tracks from the stable, across the paddock, and straight through the field to the O'Kelley place."

Paul's head shot up and his heart rate tripled. "Caleb?"

"Indeed. Left the stolen horses right out in the open in his corral."

Paul snorted, amused, and shook his head. "Has he been arrested, then?"

"Will be once he gets back to town. His ranch hand told me he was in Castle Rock wasting some money on a game of poker. Should be back in the next couple of days." Boone placed his hat back on top of his head and began to move toward the steps. "Thought I would let you know. I'd say there's enough evidence in this case to charge him with the theft of your horses as well."

"Thank you, Boone. I do appreciate your hard work." Paul saw the man off, elated from one more piece of good news on this day, and then went up to Aaron's room.

"What was that I heard the sheriff say about Caleb O'Kelley?" Emma asked, turning from the window as Paul entered the room.

"We suspected him of stealing my horses but did not have any solid proof except for a vague description." Paul stood by Aaron's bedside and looked down at his sleeping son. "But now he is in possession of horses stolen from Jeremiah Davis just last night. Caleb's over in Castle Rock right now, but he'll be arrested as soon as he shows his face here in Colorado Springs."

"Is that why Holt was so concerned about seeing Mr. O'Kelley near the barn?"

Paul's head snapped up in Emma's direction. "What? When was this?"

"Oh, let me think." Emma wrung her hands and furrowed her brow, sensing Paul's unease. "Maybe two days ago? He came to the house while you were away fetching the doctor. He told Earle and I overheard through the open window."

Paul pursed his lips and crossed his arms, internally questioning what on earth Caleb O'Kelley had been doing near his barn. "I'm going to go talk to Earle. And Holt."

Chapter Twenty-Nine

"Emma?" A tiny voice came from behind her in the kitchen, where she was cracking eggs into a bowl and heating the well-seasoned cast iron skillet on the hot stove. Steam began to pour from the kettle, telling her the water was hot enough to make the morning coffee.

Amid the troubles she had been facing in the last week, there was comfort to be found in these mundane, everyday tasks. She found steadiness in the feel of the eggshells in her hands and the sizzle of the fat in the skillet.

She turned at the sound, surprised to see Aaron up and out of bed after nearly a week of illness. Her spirits soared at the sight.

"Well, good morning, Aaron!" Squatting down in front of him, she gathered him gently into her arms and gave him an affectionate squeeze. "I'm so happy to see you up and out of bed!"

Aaron rubbed at his eyes, which were still rimmed in red and purple, the little half-moons shadowing the skin underneath them. He was well enough to leave his bed, but he still needed some time to recover. He leaned into her shoulder for a moment, as if the effort of walking down the stairs had already worn him out.

Emma ran her hand along his hair, which was tangled and matted from days in bed. Perhaps tonight would be a good night for a bath. A little refreshing soak in the tub always made her feel better, so perhaps it would be reinvigorating for Aaron as well.

"Would you like some eggs and biscuits for breakfast?" Emma knelt happily on the floor, basking in the feeling of Aaron's warm little body in her arms. It was a good warm, a healthy warm, not the worrisome intense heat that it had been.

She could feel him nod against her shoulder, and then his raspy voice said, "Yes, please."

She smiled at his politeness. The lessons she had been teaching him had taken hold, even when he didn't feel well.

"Your toy animals are in a basket on the kitchen table if you'd like to play for a few minutes while I cook us some breakfast.

Aaron spent the morning quietly but happily playing with his animals and listening to Emma read stories from his fairy tale book. Since Aaron still needed some time to fully heal, Emma didn't bring out any of the primers or schoolbooks. His body needed to be well for his mind to be ready to learn.

At midday, Emma and Aaron sat at the table to share a small lunch when Earle joined them, looking tired and drawn from the distress of the last week. He had an uncharacteristic shadow of stubble along his jaw, but still had a smile on his face for Aaron.

"Aaron, my boy," Earle said as he sat and stole a slice of an apple from Aaron's small plate. "Would you like to give Emma a little rest and spend the afternoon with me?"

"Will you tell me more stories about when I was a baby?" Aaron asked around a mouthful of bread.

"Aaron don't speak with your mouth full, please," Emma admonished. She attempted to sound stern but could not help but smile. She was so relieved to finally have Aaron back at the kitchen table, happily eating something other than plain broth or bread.

He swallowed the bread obediently.

"I certainly will," Earle replied. "Have I ever told you about the mess you made when you learned how to open doors and bins?"

Aaron shook his head, his mouth once again full of food.

Earle grinned. "It was quite the mess. The whole kitchen was covered in flour and cornmeal, and so were you." He poked his grandson in the belly, making Aaron giggle.

Emma smiled and breathed a sigh of relief. Not only was Aaron healing, but it seemed this family was, too.

***

A small basket into which was tucked a jar of homemade applesauce, a quarter of a cornbread, and some salt pork swung from Emma's hand as she made her way across the field toward Bonnie's home. The food was in thanks for all the help Bonnie had offered in the last week, and now that Aaron was on the mend, Emma felt it was time to properly show her gratitude to her friend.

Aaron was safely in the care of his grandfather, who was delighting in telling stories about Aaron learning to walk and his first words, while also illuminating Emma on the wonderful person Laura had been and the carefree man that Paul had been once.

She was beginning to see glimpses of that man again, though they were brief. She would look over at him at the supper table to find him looking at his son with not just affection, but pride and admiration, a softness around the corners of his eyes and a slight upward tick at the corners of his mouth. She could see that his face had not always been so tight and tense, but that his eyes could dance with amusement at a joke and that he did, in fact, have a rather nice set of straight white teeth hiding behind his full lips.

She smiled and hummed to herself, enjoying the warmth generated by her movements as the cool autumn air nipped at her nose. She had always enjoyed the change of seasons, though autumn quickly turned to winter here in Colorado. In no time at all, there would be snow on the ground.

Emma looked forward to enjoying the snow with Aaron—building snowmen, having a snowball fight, making snow angels. She envisioned bundling up and spending a lot of time playing in the snow this winter.

As she imagined what the ranch house would look like surrounded by a blanket of snow—solid white and sparkling, with that peculiar silence that comes only with snowfall—a man on horseback galloped past, between her and the road. She was startled at first but noted the shock of white, blond hair on top of his hatless head.

Caleb O'Kelley. It had to be.

A sense of dread filled Emma's chest. Something was not quite right, but she could not seem to put a finger on it.

But he was supposed to be out of town. What was he doing heading *toward* town? If he had just arrived home, wouldn't he be traveling in the other direction?

He was purposely avoiding the road by riding across the fields, and he was hurrying away from the Gilbert ranch. Emma's stomach dropped, dread filling her insides.

Swiftly, she turned on her heels, walking back in the direction she had just come from. Bonnie would have to wait. She had to tell Paul that she had just seen Caleb and his actions seemed suspicious.

When she turned, the wind shifted, and she became aware of the scent of smoke. Her first thought was that Holt must be burning some brush or yard waste out in the pasture. But when she looked toward the house, her heart dropped, and her stomach began to roil.

Oh no. No, no, no. Her mind whirled with incoherent thoughts. *Fire. Smoke. Aaron! Where's Paul? How did this happen? I have to get back!*

Emma dropped the basket she had been carrying and picked up her skirts, not caring a whit about exposing her legs all the way to her knees as she ran as fast as she possibly could.

Black smoke billowed into the air and bright orange flames licked at the sky from the second story windows of the house.

It felt as if every step she took toward the house put her farther away, like she was running through molasses. Near the barn she lost a shoe, but she kept running. There was no time to stop. She had to reach the house and check that everyone had made it out.

She had to get to Aaron.

Chapter Thirty

This cannot be happening. This cannot be happening. Paul's mind repeated the words over and over again.

He was rooted to a spot in the yard, staring up at the smoke and flames gushing out of the ranch house, unable to make his feet move.

This cannot be happening.

The flames shot out the open windows, reaching for air, hungry for anything they could consume. Paul's hands began to tingle.

This cannot be happening again.

"Paul! Paul!" Emma was suddenly beside him, red-faced and panting. "Where's Aaron?"

Paul just pointed toward the second-floor window that belonged to his son's bedroom, where he was still recovering from his illness.

This cannot be happening.

"Well, it is happening. And we need to get him out of there!" Emma pulled on Paul's arm, but he did not budge. His breathing was shallow, moving quickly in and out of his lungs.

"What?" Paul asked. *Had he been saying that aloud?*

She hiked up her skirts and rushed across the strip of grass separating them from the house. Catapulting up the back steps, she reached the back door just as a portion of the porch collapsed nearby.

The sound of the wood hitting the ground snapped Paul to attention.

"Emma! Emma, stop! Don't!" he yelled. But the roar of the flames was too loud and her determination too strong. She threw open the door and disappeared into the house.

Holt came running from the fields and stopped beside Paul, out of breath. "Did I just see Emma go into that house?"

Paul nodded. "This cannot be happening again."

"Fool girl, what on earth was she thinking?" Holt leaned over, hands on his knees, attempting to catch his breath.

"Aaron and Earle are both inside." Paul's voice was emotionless, his eyes never left the sight of the house engulfed in flames.

He heard Holt swear beside him and felt him rush away, but his mind barely registered anything. He was completely numb. The tingling in his fingers had spread up his arms and his heart was racing so fast that it took his breath away. He felt as if he would never get a full breath again.

His mind raced, and suddenly he was standing in the small yard in front of his small log cabin last summer as it, too, went up in flames.

"Paul! Paul! Save Aaron!" Laura screamed.

258

Paul could just make out his son's incoherent wailing through the roar of the flames and the crackling of the burning wood. Between him and his family stood a wall of flames, trapping them inside the burning house.

The smoke was heavy and acrid, so he held a bandana over his nose and mouth as he took a deep breath of the air outside and then bowed his head and leapt quickly through the doorway.

The smoke was so thick inside the house that it looked like the dead of night, even though it was near noon outside.

Aaron. He had to find Aaron. The boy was probably playing in his cot in the small bedroom they all shared. He moved to the left, his skin scalding from the intense heat of the fire.

Paul began coughing, despite the cloth over his face and dropped to the ground to get beneath the smoke. Once there, he saw his son's tiny feet a couple of yards away. He crawled across the floor, threw his son onto his back, and told him to hang on tight, then stood up and ran in the direction of the door, now invisible through the smoke.

He burst through the doorway, coughing and hacking from the burning smoke inside his lungs. He blinked his eyes furiously, attempting to remedy the scratching dryness, and saw Holt and Earle dismounting from their horses a few feet away.

Earle took Aaron from his arms, and Paul turned back toward the house to find Laura. She was no longer calling out to him, but he was confident her voice had come from the direction of the kitchen.

But when he turned around, all he saw was the entire roof of the house cave in, squashing out any life that remained inside.

"Paul! My goodness! Where's Aaron? And Emma?" Bonnie clutched Paul's arm, and he startled back to the present. Where had she come from?

Paul looked blankly at his friend. "They're inside."

"What? Oh! Oh, no!" Bonnie put her palms to her cheeks, panic filling her face, her eyes darting around. "We have to help Holt!"

Bonnie ran off toward the water pump, where Holt was filling buckets with water as fast as Shaw could run and empty them onto the flames. The fire was already too large, however, for the water to do much. They managed to put out the flames licking at the foot of the back stairs, but there was no way their buckets could do anything to tamp down the blaze consuming the second story of the house.

Paul collapsed to the ground, an animalistic keening sound escaping from his mouth, coming from somewhere deep within. Earle was screaming for Laura from beside him, clutching the crying Aaron to his chest.

Holt placed a hand on Paul's shoulder, wiping tears from his eyes that had nothing to do with the smoke in the air.

The fire burned on, consuming all their belongings, all their memories, and any will Paul had ever felt to live.

"Emma!" Bonnie's voice was filled with relief when the back door opened again and Emma emerged, Aaron in her arms.

Paul ran forward toward his son, whose limbs swung limply with each step Emma took.

Please, God. Please, please, please.

This cannot happen again.

Chapter Thirty-One

Emma vaulted up the back steps of the house, not caring about the heat or the smoke, and threw open the back door. The heat was stunning before she even reached the house, but that was nothing compared to the blast that hit Emma's face when the door swung open.

Heavy, acrid smoke filled her nostrils and she coughed, choking at the sharp edges of the charred particles of the house floating through the air. The roar of the fire was thunderous, reminding her of the violent cacophony of a springtime storm, when the winds raged, and the thunder howled from the heavens. She had not expected it to be so loud, the house itself crackling as it burned and the window glass shattering from the intense heat.

"Aaron!" She called, squinting into the darkness. It was astonishing how opaque the smoke was, how impossible it was to see anything in the familiar kitchen.

Flames closed in from the front room, the heat searing her flesh. She was afraid the fire would burn her skin, despite the few yards of distance between it and her. The heat was like nothing she had ever experienced before. It was how she imagined the fires of hell would feel, and she knew she never wanted to experience it again.

She had no time to worry about herself, however. She had to get to Aaron. She had to find the small, scared boy and save him from what would be a terrible fate. She had to save herself and his father from any further suffering or grief.

"Aaron!" She coughed, doubled over from the lack of fresh air to her lungs. The smoke burned her eyes, making it even harder to see.

She put her hands out in front of her, reaching out for the table as a touchstone in the room. Once she found the table, she felt certain she would be able to find her way to the front room, where she had last left Aaron and Earle playing and telling stories.

Earle had been having such fun sharing his memories with his grandson. Aaron had only wanted to hear stories of his own mischievous exploits as a toddler, but Earle had persuaded him to save some stories for later and had begun to tell stories that painted an intricate picture of early life on the frontier, of the difficulty of the wagon train journey to Colorado and all the hard work that went into building a ranch from nothing to thriving.

All of that would be gone in an instant.

She hit her shin hard on a chair and fell to the floor, clutching her leg for a moment. As she began to rise, she caught sight of Aaron's small form lying motionless on the floor near the doorway to the front room.

"Aaron!" She gasped. She leaped again to her feet, ignoring the throbbing in her leg, and ran to the boy. Her head began to swim after less than a minute that felt like an eternity of not getting enough air, but she pushed through. She swept Aaron up into her arms. He was unconscious, which made him feel heavier than normal. The dead weight was hard to manage in the thick darkness, but she was able to turn around and feel her way back to the door.

She burst through the back door, still open from her quick entrance, and almost dropped Aaron as she began once again to cough.

"Emma!" Bonnie exclaimed.

Emma had to blink a few times to clear her eyes, her feet moving of their own volition down the back steps. The moment she felt the soft ground beneath her bare feet—she wondered briefly where her other shoe had gone—Aaron's drooping body was lifted from her arms. She watched as Paul lowered Aaron to the grass and Bonnie checked for any external injuries.

Sitting in the grass, coughing relentlessly, Emma looked around at the burning house. She took note of Holt and Shaw throwing buckets of water at whatever flames they could reach, with little success in diminishing the inferno before them. Bonnie and Paul continued fretting over Aaron, prodding at the boy's limbs, and listening to his chest.

Where is Earle, she wondered wildly as she looked around her, hoping to see the older man somewhere nearby with his own water pail. But he never would have left Aaron alone in a house fire, especially after the way he had lost his own daughter barely a year ago.

He must still be inside the house. She took in the cloud of smoke emanating from the house, knowing that it was only getting more and more difficult to breathe every second.

He won't survive much longer, she realized. *He'll suffocate in there! If he doesn't burn alive first.*

He was probably in the front room, in much the same state that Aaron had been in when she found him.

She had to go back in.

"Earle!" She sprung to her feet, determined to save the man who had become dear to her in the last few days. She could not bear the idea of Earle being left alone inside the burning building.

Her feet flew up the back steps and through the back door once again. This time, she covered her mouth and nose with her apron, hoping to decrease the amount of smoke she inhaled. She was overwhelmed again by the sound of the flames consuming everything around her, the wooden house popping and creaking all around her—the ceiling, the floor, and the walls in every direction crackling like kindling.

"Earle!" She called out, only moving the apron away from her mouth for a second. "Earle! Where are you?"

It was futile. There was no way he would be able to see or hear her among the flames and smoke and creaking wood.

She moved toward the front room again, assuming that Earle and Aaron would have been in the same room inside the house.

But she was only able to take a single step before she was knocked to the floor by the impact of half the roof collapsing.

The world went black.

Chapter Thirty-Two

Paul watched in horror as he once again watched a house collapse among roaring flames.

The haunting sound of Laura's frantic screams—wails like a trapped animal—emanated from inside the house. Paul clenched his eyes closed to try to block out the past. Shaking his head hard to bring himself into the present, he quickly took in the scene before him.

This time, unlike the last, only a portion of the roof collapsed on the front side of the house, mostly demolishing the front porch. The gust of air created by the collapse also extinguished some of the flames for a moment.

Paul thought nothing of the flames and the smoke, despite knowing how horrible it would be inside the house and leaped to his feet. He had barely taken two steps before Holt's hand arrested his arm.

"Paul! What are you doing, man?" Holt's panicked face swam in front of Paul's for only a moment. Paul brushed the older man off and sprinted for the house as the flames began to take hold once more.

He covered his mouth with the bandana he kept in his pocket, then burst through the open back door, now hanging drunkenly from one hinge. The smoke had cleared out of the room momentarily, but he knew any second now it would grow thick and opaque, like a solid wall in front of his eyes.

He had to quickly gain his bearings, locate Emma and Earle, and get them all out in one piece.

Emma suddenly came into view as she lifted herself up off the floor, coughing and shaking her head as if to clear it.

"Emma!" he yelled, hoping to be heard over the crackling and growling of the fire.

Her head swung toward him. "Paul? What are you doing in here?"

"Where's Earle?" Paul grabbed her upper arm, determined not to lose track of her in the burning house.

She pointed to the doorway that connected the kitchen and the front room, where a pair of boots and the hem of a pair of brown pants were visible. Paul shoved Emma toward the back door and rushed to Earle's prone body. He could hear the man alternately coughing and groaning, and Paul threw his semi-conscious father-in-law over his shoulder and ran for the back door behind Emma.

At the bottom of the back stairs, all three collapsed on the ground beside Aaron, who was sitting up and drinking water from a bucket with his cupped hands.

Paul and Emma sat coughing side by side on the grass watching as the remaining roof came crashing to the ground, finalizing the destruction of the ranch house.

It was demolished.

He fisted his hair in his hands, in disbelief that once again his entire life had been destroyed, gone up in flames. This time, so many more family memories and precious belongings were lost. The painting of Laura. Gone. All her mother's beautiful lace and embroidery. Gone. Aaron's little wooden animals. Emma's only possessions from her home and childhood. All of it either burned to cinders or crushed beneath the weight of the collapsed roof.

But this time his entire family had made it out alive.

Thank you, God, he thought. *Thank you for sparing us all. Thank you for working through me to save Emma and Earle. And thank you for Emma, who saved Aaron. Thank you thank you thank you for sparing Aaron once more.*

He turned to Emma beside him, her usually light and luminous hair darkened with soot and face black with ash except for two clean streaks running down from her eyes. And even in such a disheveled and filthy state, she still looked lovely. He could not imagine a woman more beautiful than the one who had just run into a burning building to save his family, the one who was mourning the loss of his home right beside him. She was an incredible person, and he had been so wrapped up in his own guilt and anger to fully see it before. He had been incredibly unfair to her.

Without thinking about what he was doing, he reached out a hand and wiped the tears from her cheek. She startled and met his eyes, reaching up to wipe her own face.

"Emma," he began, then coughed again, the smoke still burning his throat. "I can never thank you enough for saving my family. It was foolish to run into a burning building, and even more foolish to do it twice, but having done it twice now myself, I can't say I don't understand." He chuckled to himself. "Thank you. Words can never fully express my appreciation for saving my son."

She sniffled and opened her mouth to respond, but was interrupted by Earle, who was being tended by Bonnie a few feet away.

"I'd like to echo those sentiments," Earle said. "I'm sure I would have died in that house if not for you, Emma. I owe you my life."

"Oh, Earle." Emma reached over and placed a hand on Earle's shin, the only part of him that she could reach.

"Now, I'm not finished. I need to say my piece." He cleared his throat and looked Emma in the eyes. "I was unkind to you and made you feel unwelcome in my house when all you did was take care of my grandson and this family. You did nothing to deserve my scorn and anger, you were simply a convenient place for me to let go of my pent up emotions. It was wrong of me. It's clear now that you were truly sent to us by God. So I'd like to thank both Him and you for everything you've done for us. And for me."

Emma gave up on drying her face, and now tears of a different emotion were streaming down her face. She threw her arms around Earle's neck and hugged him, sobbing out her appreciation for him, almost making no sense. "I'm so glad we all made it out! When I saw your feet, and then the roof, and then Paul came in, and then, and then!"

Earle patted Emma's back stiffly, looking a little uncomfortable with the young woman hanging around his neck.

Emma regained her composure after a few minutes, when Aaron came over and tugged on her dress.

She sat up and wiped at her face with a pink lace-edged handkerchief that Bonnie offered, looking up into Aaron's eyes where he stood beside her. "Yes, Aaron?"

He threw his arms around her neck, much as she had done to Earle a few minutes earlier, and squeezed. She squeezed him back.

Watching the two of them made Paul smile. He was glad beyond belief that they had all made it out of the burning house with no more than some bumps and scrapes. And he was so glad that Aaron and Emma clearly cared about one another. That he had found someone to not only take care of his son, but to love him. A lump grew in Paul's throat, but the dominant emotion was not one of angry or sadness for once. He was happy. He was so incredibly happy that he had found someone so wonderful, someone that his son loved. He had been so lucky that his simply advertisement for a governess had attracted someone so perfect for his family, and he had not felt lucky in a very long time.

"Who do you suppose that is?" Holt's voice cut through the sniffling and coughing among the group.

Paul turned toward Holt and saw that the man was pointing down the road, back toward town. A glance showed a couple of men on horseback moving fast enough to kick up a cloud of dust behind them.

Paul squinted, trying to identify either one of the riders. As they drew closer and turned toward what had been the house until recently, Paul recognized the glint of the metal star on one rider's chest. The sheriff.

Paul held up a hand in greeting but didn't stand from his position on the ground. He was afraid his legs may not hold him up for very long at this moment. He felt weak from the smoke inhalation and emotional toll of the fire.

"Howdy, Sheriff," Paul called.

Boone Holliday dismounted, and his deputy did the same, but stayed with the horses when Boone moved forward.

"Afternoon, Paul." Boone inclined his head toward the other members of the group, then looked toward the house. "What exactly happened here? What started such a fire?"

"I was out in the pasture when I suddenly smelled smoke." Paul pointed in the direction of the field where he had been testing out a repair he had recently made to a tiller. "I turned around and the house was already up in flames. It was already too late to save by the time I made it over here." He shook his head. "I don't know what happened."

Earle chimed in, "Aaron and I were inside the house when it went up. No fire going inside that could have gotten out of control to cause this. Hasn't been cold enough to need a fire in the fireplace yet."

Paul nodded his appreciation at his father-in-law for contributing that information, even if it was relatively little. As he looked back at Aaron, who was now curled up in Emma's lap, his eyes were drawn to Emma. She was chewing on her lower lip, her eyes darting distractedly about as if she were piecing bits of information together and organizing them in her mind.

"Emma? Do you know something?" Paul prompted.

"Well," she started, her hands nervously tugging at the grass beside her, "I was on my way to Bonnie's for a visit. Oh! Bonnie!" She turned with a jerking motion toward the other woman. "There's a basket of things for you somewhere between here and the creek. As thank you for all the help over the last week."

"Now, that's not necessary. Neighbors help neighbors." Bonnie waved a dismissive hand but smiled at her friend.

"Focus, ladies!" It was all Paul could do not to grab Emma by the shoulders and shake the information out of her. "What did you see, Emma?"

"I saw Caleb O'Kelley riding like the wind away from the house." She pointed in the direction the man had gone, toward town. "He was not riding on the road, which seemed suspicious to me. And since Holt had seen him around the barn not that long ago, I thought it seemed important to come back and let you all know that he was on the ranch. Then I saw the smoke."

At the mention of Caleb O'Kelley, Paul's blood began to boil. Heat rose up the back of his neck. Of course, it was Caleb. He felt his jaw clench and he threw a fist into the ground beside him.

"Caleb O'Kelley," he muttered. "First my horses and now this. I swear, if I ever see that man again, I'll—"

"Now, Paul, don't do anything that'll get you put in that jail cell right beside Caleb," Boone interrupted. "Leave it up to the law. My men and I will handle this. You have enough to do to take care of your family. And I'm sure they'd like to have you around for a long time to come, not locked up or worse."

Paul took a deep breath. He knew the sheriff was right. He was not responsible for doling out justice, and Boone and his men had more than enough evidence to haul in Caleb O'Kelley for multiple crimes. They just had to find him first.

He nodded toward Boone. "You're right, Sheriff."

"We'd best be heading back toward town. We'll need to see if anyone else has laid eyes on Caleb." Boone walked back to his horse and mounted. He and his deputy both tipped their hats before they turned and raced back toward Colorado Springs.

Paul watched them go, trying to convince himself that the law would take care of Caleb, that they would find him and catch him and lock him away for good.

But he was also feeling restless and like he would feel a lot better if he could at least give the man a good, strong punch in the nose. He needed to do something, take some sort of action.

"I think I'll go for a ride," he said, hopping to his feet and walking toward the stables, ignoring the questioning eyes of his family. Earle and Emma exchanged glances, brows furrowed. Emma chewed on her lower lip in confusion, shaking the soot out of her hair, while Earle scratched his head. It was clear from their facial expressions that they all thought he might be going crazy.

He saddled up his new horse, Sully, but before he could get his foot in the stirrup, he felt someone clutching his upper arm. He looked down to find a small, delicate hand on his sleeve. He looked up into Emma's face, finding it soot-streaked and concerned.

Chapter Thirty-Three

"Where are you going?" Emma asked, trying not to sound accusatory, but she felt she needed to remind him of his responsibilities. She could tell that Paul was blinded by anger and not seeing clearly at all. "We need you here, and the sheriff told you to leave the work of the law up to him."

He shook her arm off and went back to the business of mounting his horse. "I'm going to find Caleb. He needs to pay for this, and I can't wait for Boone Holliday and his men to get around to it." Paul adjusted his hat on his head and looked down at Emma from atop his horse, looking menacing with his blackened face and strong-set jaw.

Emma considered for a moment. He was not going to be talked out of his mission, she could tell. But in his current angry state, there was no telling what he would do. He was after revenge, and that could lead to dire consequences. As Sheriff Holliday had said, Paul did not want to end up in a jail cell.

"Then I'm going with you," she said definitively. She thought perhaps her presence could at least prevent Paul from doing any mortal damage to the other man. "Let me saddle up Daisy."

"Why on earth would you want to go with me?" Paul asked, watching her scurry about to ready her little mare.

"To prevent you from killing Caleb O'Kelley when you find him." She lifted her saddle up and over the back of the horse, then tightened the cinch around Daisy's belly.

Paul sighed and rolled his eyes. "I'm not going to kill the man. I hope to resort to no violence at all."

She stopped what she was doing and stood with her hands on her hips, fixing him with her strictest teacher stare. She hardened her eyes and clenched her jaw, a look that made children fall in line. "I'm going with you."

He met her eyes, but he was no match for the withering look being directed at him.

"Fine. Hurry up. We don't want Caleb to get too far ahead of us." He angled himself toward the others, who were still sitting in the grass near the water pump. "I'll go talk to Bonnie. I'm sure she can keep an eye on Aaron and make sure Earle is doing fine while we're gone."

He trotted off to talk to the rest of the group, and Emma quickly finished getting her horse ready so that he did not have time to get impatient and leave without her. She hoped he was smart enough to know that she was stubborn and would simply follow after him if he attempted to leave her behind.

Once Emma was mounted and had said good-bye to Aaron, Earle, and Bonnie, Paul turned and rode quickly in the direction of the O'Kelley ranch, leaving Emma to try her best to keep up.

She had grown up more of a town girl than a country girl, and while she was confident on top of a horse that was walking or trotting, she was not exactly comfortable on a horse that was galloping at a breakneck speed. She grasped the reins until her knuckles were white and clenched her legs so tightly around the sides of her horse that her right thigh started to cramp. Her rear end would certainly be bruised from bouncing in the saddle as they raced away from the Gilbert ranch.

When they reached the O'Kelley farm, Paul led Emma to the barn first, hoping to find Caleb's horse in the stables.

But all was quiet on the ranch, except for one lone farmhand.

"Hello!" Paul called, attempting to sound more friendly than menacing, though his face belied his mood.

"Howdy," the farmhand said, leaning on the pitchfork he had been using to add hay to the stalls. He was a large man, with a doughy face that showed no sparkle of life or sign of intelligence. He wore dark blue overalls that were stained with various farm and animal substances and likely years of wear.

"My name's Paul Gilbert. I'm a neighbor from down the road." Paul removed his hat and smiled disingenuously at the man.

"Davy," the man replied.

"Nice to meet you, Davy." Paul replaced his hat and looked around. "Is Mr. O'Kelley nearby? I thought maybe I'd find him working here, but I notice that his horse isn't in his stall."

Davy shook his head vehemently. "No, sir. He ain't been around in a few hours, maybe."

"Did he tell you where he was going? What he was doing?" Paul tried to keep the urgency out of his voice. Davy looked like a man who might get nervous if put under any pressure.

"No, sir." Davy scratched his head. "He was acting a little funny, but that ain't unusual. He has the mood swings, you know. One day he's real happy and the next he's real mad and you never can tell what way it's going to go."

"He was acting funny?" Paul and Emma exchanged a concerned look. "Did he seem happy or angry, or something else?"

Davy paused and thought. "I guess angry. He rode off real fast straight across the field. He didn't even go up to the road."

Emma noticed Paul's leg beginning to twitch in the stirrup, as if his patience was wearing thin. She, too, was growing tired of the conversation.

"Do you have any idea where he might have gone? I need to speak with him urgently." Paul leaned forward in the saddle.

"He might have gone off to his sister's place." Davy scratched his head again. "He goes there a lot."

"His sister Annie?" Paul clarified.

Davy nodded and started to kick at his pitchfork, getting restless with the constant questioning.

"Can you tell me where Annie lives, Davy? Then we'll leave and let you get back to your job."

Davy pointed straight ahead of him, out the barn door. "She lives over yonder at the base of the mountains. Got herself a little log house with a bright blue front door."

"Blue front door, you say?" Paul squinted, as if picturing the houses in the area and picking out the one that Davy was indicating.

"Yes, sir. It's real pretty. I only been there once, though."

"Well, Davy, thank you very much, and you have a good day." Paul tipped his hat and turned his horse around, nodding at Emma to do the same.

Together, they walked their horses to the road, so as not to alert Davy any more than necessary.

"We've got quite a ride ahead of us to Annie's house," Paul said as they rode. "Are you up to it?"

"I'm staying with you." Emma straightened her spine, calling on her inner strength to stay on this horse as long as it took for Paul to complete his task.

"Well, then, hold on tight." Paul kicked his heel into Sully's flank and the horse took off. Emma's little mare followed, trying her best to keep up with the galloping steed.

As they rode, Emma allowed her mind to wander. Anything to take her mind off her aching muscles.

She watched Paul's back as he rode ahead of her. He rode as if he were made for the saddle, with a relaxed posture that allowed his body to flow with the horse. He seemed to be in his natural state among the land and the animals, an aura of ease about him, despite the tension of their particular situation. He was not meant to live cooped up in a small house in the city.

Prayers and hymns came to mind, and she silently prayed and sang everything she could think of.

> *Lord, make me an instrument of your peace.*
> *Where there is hatred, let me bring love.*
> *Where there is offence, let me bring pardon.*
> *Where there is discord, let me bring union.*

Throughout her prayers, her mind continued to stray to the man in front of her.

> *Where there is error, let me bring truth.*
> *Where there is doubt, let me bring faith.*
> *Where there is despair, let me bring hope.*
> *Where there is darkness, let me bring your light.*
> *Where there is sadness, let me bring joy.*

He had gone back into a burning, collapsing house to save her. He had pushed past the demons of his own past to make sure that she did not die in the house fire.

> *O Master, let me not seek as much*
> *to be consoled as to console,*

to be understood as to understand,
to be loved as to love,

She could only imagine the strength it took for him to march into a burning building after the traumatic way he had lost his wife.

For it is in giving that one receives,
it is in self-forgetting that one finds,
it is in pardoning that one is pardoned,
it is in dying that one is raised to eternal life

Despite his moods and his anger, he was truly a strong and caring man. He loved his son fiercely, which she could acknowledge now was at the root of his anger. He was angry that his son would grow up without a mother. He was angry that his son's life had been irrevocably changed at such a young age and in such a horrific way. He was angry that God had seemingly turned His back on them, even if Emma knew that was not true.

Emma found herself admiring not just Paul's inner strength and courage, but the set of his jaw and the way his hair curled around the edges of his hat. She had found him to be handsome the first time she laid eyes on him at the train station, but as they had come to know one another, she had found more aspects of his appearance to appreciate. He had a lovely smile, expressive eyes, and impressive physical strength despite his tall, thin build.

She began to wonder what it might feel like to have his sure, lithe arms wrapped around her. To have his big, callused hand holding hers. She imagined what it might be like to share an evening of pie and conversation on a front porch swing, as she had seen girls do with their gentleman callers back home in Pueblo. In her daydream, she was wearing a frothy, lacy pink dress and white satin shoes. A dress that would be ridiculous to wear and impossible to keep clean on a ranch.

The sun slid behind the western mountains and the air began to cool. Emma became worried that night was going to fall, and they would encounter an angry Caleb O'Kelley in the darkness.

Just as she was starting to believe that her back and backside would both ache for weeks if they went any farther, twinkling lights and a thin stream of smoke from a chimney became visible not far ahead of them.

"Is that Annie's house?" Emma called ahead to Paul.

"Must be," he replied, slowing his horse. They had slowed to a walk a couple of times on their journey, to rest the horses. Paul's horse was stronger and had more stamina than Emma's, and the same could be said of the riders. She was grateful for the short respite.

"I grew up with both Caleb and Annie, but I've never been out here." The cooling air and emerging stars gave the conversation an air of intimacy. Paul spoke low, as if he were sharing secrets.

They continued to move forward at their slowed pace, dismounting once they were within walking distance of the house. Voices were audible from inside the house as they approached, but they quickly gained volume. They could hear a man and a woman yelling back and forth at each other, followed by the sound of something delicate smashing against a wall.

At this indication of violence, Paul burst forward at a sprint. While Emma froze in place and watched, Paul leapt up the two small steps at the front of the house and kicked down the front door.

Then she, too, ran forward toward the house.

Chapter Thirty-Four

The bright blue wooden door flew open and crashed against the wall, hanging drunkenly from its hinges. Paul stood in the doorway and took in his surroundings.

Caleb loomed in the middle of a shabby, sparsely decorated one-room cabin. A small partition separated the bed from the kitchen and sitting area, which was furnished only by a settle and one chair, both cushioned with worn out pillows.

As Paul continued his survey of the scene, he noticed Caleb's older sister Annie cowering in the corner of the kitchen, a wet spot on the wall near her head and shards of pottery on the floor around her feet. She held her hands close in front of her, as if to defend herself from an attack.

It was then that Paul noticed that Caleb was holding a rifle loosely by his side, almost as if he had forgotten it was there.

"I knew you'd come looking for me," Caleb sneered. He looked down at the rifle in his hand, then looked up at Paul as he raised the gun to his shoulder and looked down the barrel.

A high-pitched squeak came from behind him, and Paul reached back and tucked Emma out of sight behind him. He could feel her grasp the back of his shirt and lean slightly to peek around his shoulder as he raised his hands into the air. He was unarmed and wanted to make that clear to Caleb.

"Now, Caleb, I just want to talk. Why don't you lower that rifle?" He made sure to keep his voice level and calm, despite his pounding heart.

"Just want to talk, huh? Always got to be high and mighty. Always got to show off to the women that you're better than me." Caleb began to inch forward, but Paul stood his ground.

"That's not it at all, Caleb. I just want to keep everyone safe. Including you." Paul lowered his hands, but kept them by his sides, palms open and empty.

"You don't care about me! You've never cared about me!" Caleb began to flail his arms about, taking the rifle with him, the end of the weapon waving with no direction around the room. "You've taken everything from me. You always have the better livestock, the better harvest. You won all the contests when we were kids. You got all the girls to dance with you at the town dances. I've never had anything because you took it all."

Paul glanced at Annie in the corner, finding her still frozen and clutching at her heart. Emma's hands tightened on the back of Paul's shirt, twisting the fabric slightly.

"Caleb, I haven't taken anything from you." Paul took one slow step into the house, thinking maybe if he could get close enough, he could get that rifle out of Caleb's hands. "You have a fine farm, with plenty of land and livestock. You have—"

"I have nothing!" Caleb shouted. "You stole everything that matters when you stole Laura!"

"Laura?" Paul drew back for a moment. What did Laura have to do with any of this? What connection did Laura have to Caleb, other than their shared childhood adventures? Had Laura and Caleb had some sort of relationship that Paul was unaware of? The way Paul remembered it, Laura had been attempting to pursue him when they first began their courtship, which implied that she had not been courting Caleb. He also could not remember a time when she had said much about Caleb other than that he was always out to get Paul or out to prove himself superior to Paul. Laura had never belonged to Caleb in any way, and so Paul could not have stolen her.

"Yes, Laura. I was in love with her, and then you stole her. You have to have everything good, don't you? Your fields produce more, you have better horses, your cattle sell best at market. I lost everything when you stole Laura. It's all because of you. My fields hardly produced a thing this year; did you know that? No fancy tools can do anything about bad soil. But my ranch didn't have bad soil until you moved into Earle's place."

Paul was quickly losing any line of logic that may have existed in Caleb's accusations. He obviously had not done anything to harm Caleb's crops. There was no way a man could cause another man's soil to produce poorly. Paul took a deep breath, attempting to maintain his calm demeanor and tone of voice so that perhaps Caleb would also calm down. He had seen it work with Aaron's temper tantrums, so it stood to reason that the same could work with a grown man.

"You know I tried to kill you once." Caleb grew eerily still, and his voice dropped an octave.

Paul startled at this news, his eyes bugging out of his head. "What?"

He felt Emma's small hand clutch his and squeeze. His pulse was racing, and he could tell his palms were clammy as he felt Emma's soothing touch, but knowing that she was there behind him, lending him strength, helped him to slow his breathing.

"I tried to kill you once," Caleb repeated, his voice dark and menacing as he looked Paul straight in the eye. "I went over to that little house you had on Earle's property. This was last summer. It had been real dry, so I knew a fire would spread real quick."

Paul heard Emma's quick intake of breath from behind him, followed by a quiet, "No!"

"I took some dry glass and a little bit of oil-soaked cloth, got out my flint and steel and sparked a little fire. It was real pretty, watching the flames start to dance and grow, making little trails up the side of the house."

Caleb looked at the air in front of his face, his eyes unfocused as he remembered the event. Then he smiled, his lips turning up at the corners in a sinister way that reminded Paul of the devil himself. He squeezed Emma's hand harder, needing the sensation to tie him here to the present.

"Oh, I'd splashed some kerosene on the wood siding all around the house, just to be sure that the fire caught. It sure did catch." Caleb looked over at Paul then, his eyes glinting with malice. The corners of his mouth twisted up into an unnerving grin as he raised his hands up to waist level and wiggled his fingers, mimicking the shape and motion of flames and smoke floating up into the air. "The whole house just went right up—*whoosh*—flames taller than me, higher than the roof."

"How can you be so cavalier about that?" Paul spat. "You killed Laura." He articulated every word.

Caleb hung his head and shook it from side to side. "I know. And that is my biggest regret in life."

He looked back up at Paul, tears beginning to form in the corners of his eyes.

"I didn't mean to harm Laura. I meant to kill you."

He raised his empty hand and pointed it in Paul's face. "You were supposed to die, so that Laura would be alone and need a shoulder to cry on and a man to help around the house. That way I could step in and be her shining hero."

Caleb sniffled, tears spilling over and streaming down his face. "But instead, I killed the only woman I've ever loved. The only woman I ever will love." He looked down at his shoes and kicked at the floor absently, the toe of his boot scraping across the dirty floor.

Paul swallowed hard, suddenly aware of a lump that had formed in his throat that made it difficult to speak. "Caleb, did you start the fire at the ranch house today?"

Caleb's head shot up and his hands clenched into fists. "Of course I did. I did it once before, I knew I could do it again. And I did. Last time I burned your house down, you had somewhere to run to. But where are you going to go now? There's no house at all on that ranch now. I wish the fire had taken you with it. I may not be able to turn your soil rotten, but I can make your life miserable, like you've done to me since the day your mama brought you into this world. I hate you, Paul Gilbert, and for some reason, you just will not die."

He raised the gun quickly and took aim. Something about his demeanor this time was more serious. Paul could tell from Caleb's stance and the determination on his face that this time, the man was going to fire.

Evidently, Emma felt the same way. As Caleb's finger twitched on the trigger, she suddenly leapt out from behind Paul's back, arms in the air as if to make herself bigger.

"No! Caleb, no!" she cried, lunging toward the crazed, armed man.

"Emma!" Paul shouted. He reached out to grasp her dress and prevent her from moving forward into the room any further, but his fingers only met empty air.

The crack of the rifle shot was deafening in the small space, echoing around the room.

A searing heat went through Paul's body and his arm suddenly felt wet and heavy. He dropped to the ground, seeming to have no control of his legs.

Emma was at his side in an instant, crouching in front of him, holding his face in her hands. "Paul!"

"I—I've been shot," he stammered, looking at the red stain spreading down his sleeve from his bicep.

"Yes, you have," Emma confirmed, examining the bullet wound. Thankfully, it was only a flesh wound. The bullet had merely nicked the outer edge of his arm rather than going into the muscle. "You stay with me. Keep breathing. Take nice, deep breaths."

She reached down and tore the hem off her dress. She then held the fabric against Paul's wound. "Can you hold this here? Put some pressure on it. It will help stop the bleeding."

He did as he was told, too shocked to do anything else. "How do you know how to treat this?"

"People like to tell stories of injury and recovery to ministers. I overheard a lot of what people told my father." She wiped at Paul's sweating brow with a soft pink handkerchief. The fabric felt nice against his skin.

As Paul looked past Emma into the room, he saw that Caleb, too, had collapsed onto the floor. The rifle had been tossed to the side, and the man was curled into a ball, rocking back and forth. He held his blond head in his hands as he moaned in agony, an animalistic, guttural sound coming from his mouth.

This seemed to bring Annie out of her stupor, and she rushed to her brother's side, clutching him to her chest and petting his head the same way a parent would soothe a crying child.

Annie looked up at Paul, her face contorted with sadness and grief. "I'm so sorry he did this, Paul. He ain't right. You know that. He's always been prone to these mood swings and aggressive behaviors." She continued to rock her brother side to side, as if they were sitting together in a rocking chair. "Mama and Daddy gave up on him, never tried to help him. But I just couldn't. He has good in him, but the bad is all that people see. Daddy said he'd for sure end up in the jailhouse and washed his hands of his own son."

"Annie, he shot me. He burned down my house. Twice." Paul's voice was flat and straightforward. "I'm going to have to go to the sheriff with this. He probably will end up in the jailhouse now."

"No!" Annie raised her voice, and Caleb startled at the sudden sound. She smoothed a hand over his head once more, kissing his hair. "Hush, Caleb, hush." She turned back to Paul. "Please don't go to the sheriff, Paul. Caleb just is not himself. He didn't know what he was doing. He will not survive in jail; he'll go crazy cooped up like that."

Paul considered this. Caleb clearly was not mentally stable, and everything that Davy and Annie had both said today confirmed that fact.

"I'll keep him with me now. I'll take care of him and make sure he doesn't hurt you or your family again. That ranch is too much for him." Tears were streaming down Annie's face as she begged for her brother's life.

Just then, the thunder of hooves on the ground indicated that horses were approaching quickly from outside.

"Caleb! Caleb O'Kelley!" Boone Holliday's voice boomed from outside the house, "Are you in there? Come out unarmed, with your hands where I can see them."

Annie looked at Paul frantically, her eyes wide and panicked.

Paul's heart softened a bit for the woman who just wanted to take care of her brother, the only one who had never given up on him and always saw the good inside.

There was no time to think through the possible results of what he was saying, and Paul blurted out, "Annie, you take Caleb and go hide in the mountains. Go as far away as you can before you find a place to take shelter. You keep him safe. I'll talk to the sheriff."

Relief flooded over Annie's face, her features softening with gratitude. "Thank you, Paul!"

She leapt to her feet, dragging her brother up by his arm and pulling him after her as she ran for the back door. They left the door hanging open, swinging in the breeze, as they disappeared into the darkening twilight.

"Caleb O'Kelley!" Boone's voice was closer now, and lower, as if he had dismounted his horse.

"He's not here, Boone!" Paul called back and started to get to his feet. Emma stood and held out her hand to assist when he stumbled a bit, still out of sorts from his gunshot wound. "Thank you, Emma. I'm glad you were here with me."

She smiled sweetly at him, accepting the praise that he so rarely gave. "Me, too."

Chapter Thirty-Five

Emma held on to Paul's arm to help him keep steady as they walked outside to talk to the sheriff and his men.

"Have you been shot? What happened?" Boone Holliday rushed forward, his head frantically swiveling from side to side, searching for the culprit. "Where's Caleb?"

"He ran off. He was a little crazed and the gun went off in his hand. I don't think he meant to shoot me," Paul told the men. Emma bit her lip, troubled by Paul's lies about such a dangerous man. But she trusted that he must know what he was doing, even if she felt that Caleb deserved to be arrested and rot in a jail cell as quickly as possible.

"Did you see which way he went?" one of the deputies asked from atop his horse.

Paul shook his head. "Maybe he ran back home? He was not in his right mind, for certain. He could have gone just about anywhere, I suppose."

Boone Holliday nodded, then raised a hand in the air and moved it in a circle, signaling to his men to turn back around and begin the search for Caleb O'Kelley. The sheriff mounted his horse, tipped his hat to Paul and Emma, and rode off in the direction of the O'Kelley ranch.

"I suppose we should go home now." Paul began to walk toward his horse, which stood in the middle of a small meadow nearby, eating clover beside Emma's mare. He moved the fabric Emma had told him to keep on his arm and peered at the wound. "The bleeding from my arm has gone down, but it hurts like the dickens."

Emma found her limbs and bones aching now that the adrenaline from the confrontation with Caleb had faded, her body was screaming for attention.

"Is it possible for us to walk for just a bit?" she asked meekly, not wanting to reveal her particular discomforts.

"That sounds nice, actually," Paul replied. "I could use a little rest from the saddle."

They walked in the direction of their horses, and Sully trotted over when Paul whistled. Daisy followed close behind, content to go wherever Sully went.

Paul took the horses' reins in his hand and led the way back in the direction of Bonnie's house, where Aaron and Earle would be.

Emma was having trouble processing everything she had witnessed today. One man had nearly destroyed many lives with a house fire and a gunshot. Caleb had been determined to kill Paul today. And yet, Paul had let him go.

She ruminated over this for a few minutes as they walked silently across the grass. But after a time, she couldn't keep silent about it anymore.

"Paul?" She knew she was interrupting his thoughts, and she wanted to make sure she had his attention.

"Yes, Emma?" His deep voice sounded a bit distracted.

"Why on earth did you let Caleb O'Kelley get away?" She tried hard to not sound accusatory but failed. Her voice was harsh and angry. "He shot you. He burned down our house. All in one day."

"For if you forgive men their trespasses, your heavenly Father will also forgive you. But if you forgive not men their trespasses, neither will your Father forgive your trespasses."

Emma looked to Paul in surprise. Her brows drew together, and her eyes opened wider as she asked, "Was that from the Book of Matthew? Did you just quote the Bible?"

Paul chuckled. "I did. I've found some comfort in returning to prayer and the Bible recently. Thanks to you." His hand brushed her shoulder for a moment. "And because of that, I know that the damage has been done. Nothing that I or the law could do to Caleb O'Kelley would bring back the house or put the flesh back in my arm."

Emma nodded her understanding. "As far as the east is from the west, so far hath he removed our transgressions from us."

"Precisely," Paul confirmed. "If I had hurt Caleb in any way, then I would be guilty of sins against an unwell man, and that would not make me feel whole again. It would not bring back my house or my wife. It is best that I leave that anger behind me, so that I might move forward in peace."

"That's lovely."

Smiling to herself that she had, indeed, been able to fulfill her task of bringing Paul back to a relationship with God,

Emma felt peace grow in her soul. She felt as if her chest were becoming warm and glowing with the love of God. If it had not been dark outside, she was sure that Paul would have been able to see the wide smile spreading across her face and the pink blush of happiness upon her cheeks.

In spite of everything, it had been a good day after all.

"Emma?" Paul's voice came more quietly through the darkness than it had been a moment ago, lending an air of intimacy to his words. "Have I ever told you anything about my wife?"

She shook her head, although she knew it was hard to see one another. "Not really, no."

"She was a wonderful woman." She could hear the smile in his voice as he talked about his love. "She was beautiful, bright, and mischievous. She was always up for an adventure, even if it meant getting dirty."

"Bonnie told me some, that you grew up together."

"We sure did. Spent practically our whole lives together. But I didn't really pay her much attention until the town picnic the year I was eighteen and she was sixteen. It was like I looked up from our conversation and suddenly noticed how pretty she was. I kissed her right then and there, hidden away behind the willow trees on the banks of the lake. After that, there was no turning back. We were done for."

His words painted a rosy picture in her mind. She imagined the young girl from the painting that had hung in the front room of the ranch house holding hands with a younger Paul. He would have had fewer wrinkles on his face and more joy in his eyes—the joy of young love and innocence.

In Emma's mind, she became the brown-haired girl, and she envisioned what it would feel like to lean against the rough bark of a willow tree as a handsome young man leaned forward to kiss her.

"That sounds awfully romantic."

Emma realized that she longed for such an idyllic love story, for someone to be overcome with emotion for her. She also noticed the feeling that she would not mind if the man who was enraptured with her was the very man who was telling her the story of his first love but turned her focus back to him rather than unpack that particular emotion just yet.

"We courted for about a year and then got married in town in the church. The whole town came, it seemed. She wore a pretty pink dress. I don't know how to describe any of it to you, but she and her mother were both very skilled seamstresses. They toiled for months over every stitch, every small piece of lace and all the layers of fabric."

He paused for a moment, recalling how she looked and the way she smiled at him all the way down the aisle on Earle's arm. A smile was evident in his voice as he continued, his eyes unfocused as they looked ahead, seeing an image in his memory rather than the world around him for the moment.

"All I know is the pink made her face glow as bright as the springtime sun. She looked like a sunrise, like the dawning of a new day and a new chapter of life. Everyone said she was the happiest bride for three counties."

Emma chuckled and hoped that she, too, would find a husband who made her feel so ebullient on her wedding day. "I'm sure it was a wonderful day for you both."

"It was," he agreed. "And we had almost ten wonderful years together. And then, in one day, it all came crumbling down. My whole life changed in an instant."

His mood had turned somber as he once again recalled the terror of the fire that had killed his wife. Paul's back stiffened and his hands clenched on the reins. His jaw grew tense. Emma could almost hear him thinking it over once more, attempting to determine if there was anything he could have done differently that would have allowed him to save both his son and his wife.

"I was out in the fields working, much like today, when I smelled smoke. I turned and saw the flames shooting from the roof of the house." He reached a hand up and raked it through his hair. "I ran like the wind to try to get there, to see if Aaron and Laura were inside or outside, to get them out if I needed to. I could hear them both yelling and coughing inside, but there were flames everywhere. Blocking every doorway, every window." He paused, recalling what Caleb had said about the kerosene. "I guess now I know why the house went up so quickly. It wasn't just the dry summer. It was Caleb spraying kerosene around the house."

Emma nodded her head but remained silent. She was afraid any reminder that she was present would knock Paul out of his reverie, and he would not share any more of his story. She was so eager to hear from him, finally, what he truly had experienced so that she could continue to help him heal.

"I ran to the front door, calling for Laura and Aaron, but the wall of flames in front of me prevented me from being able to easily get in the house." His voice sped up, as if trying to spit out the words as quickly as possible, as if he were reliving the panic of that moment. "And once I did get in, I did not know which way to go. At that time of day, Aaron was usually playing on his cot and Laura was in the kitchen, but those were on opposite sides of the house." He paused as a sob moved through his chest, his voice breaking around the words. "I had to choose."

Emma felt a lump grow in her throat, making it difficult for her to swallow. Tears collected in her eyes, and she allowed them to fall freely. Here in the darkness, no one would see her crying. The horses whinnied sympathetically, as if lending Paul their emotional support.

"So, I mustered up my courage and ran through the flames into the house. I found Aaron exactly where I expected him to be. He was sitting on his cot, frozen in place but panicked. His eyes were as big as saucers, with tears streaming down his cheeks. I scooped him up and ran back outside with him. By then, Holt and Earle had come running, so I handed Aaron off and turned to go back into the house for Laura." His voice broke again, and he stopped walking, placing a hand to his eyes to stem the gathering tears as he sniffled.

Emma stopped as well, and took his other hand, giving it a squeeze of support. She knew all too well how it felt to lose a loved one before you felt ready, though she could only imagine the terror of losing someone in such a violent manner. Paul's fingers curled willingly around hers, warm and rough from years of farm work. They were strong, masculine hands, and she knew that strength carried through from his physical body to his inner spirit. He had gone through so much, had taken time to grieve, and was now beginning to come out on the other side.

"When I turned back to the house, the roof completely collapsed. The house was just flattened. Gone. Laura was crushed by the rafters and burned by the flames."

Paul's chest heaved with a sob, the air coming in and out of his body in hiccupping shudders. Emma could take it no more and threw her arms around this man who had almost been forced to repeat the worst day of his life today. She clasped her arms around his middle, her head resting against the sound of his beating heart.

She said nothing, did not move, and simply offered him her strength to help hold him up as he returned the embrace. His long, thin arms reached all the way around her and then some, and they held on tight to her shoulders. He rested his cheek on the top of her head, now covered in disordered wisps of blonde that had worked their way out of their pins long ago.

They stood like that for a few minutes, holding each other up and lending each other strength in the darkness as they both let the tears fall.

When their breathing had begun to even out, Paul's grasp on Emma loosened and he stepped back. She was afraid for a moment that she had done something improper, but in the light of the moon, she could see a smile spread across his face.

"Thank you, Emma." His voice was deep and gravelly, full of emotion. "For all your help and support today and all these weeks. You are an impressively strong and determined young woman."

"You're very welcome," she responded, feeling a blush spread across her cheeks. She was not accustomed to compliments, particularly from handsome men in the moonlight, and it made her feel self-conscious.

"And I'd like to say I'm sorry," Paul continued.

"Whatever for?" Emma's brows drew together, and she tilted her head to the side in confusion.

"I was unkind to you. Many times. And without reason." He tucked a loose strand of hair behind her ear, and then, rather than removing his hand, he touched it to her cheek. "You were not deserving of my scorn. I was angry at so many things, but none of them were you. And so, Emma Clement, I am very sorry that I ever hurt you or caused you any discomfort."

She held her hand over his, liking the feeling of his warm hand on her face. "Paul Gilbert, I accept your apology and I forgive you."

He grinned down at her, the first smile he had ever directed at her, and the feeling of it was electrifying. Emma felt as if she were the only woman in the world in that moment, and she began to wonder what it might feel like if he were to suddenly bend down and brush his lips across hers. But she knew that even alone in the darkness, or perhaps because of it, he would never allow himself such a breach of propriety.

He dropped his hand and stepped away from her, gathering the horses' reins once more. "It's growing late. Perhaps we should ride home now."

"Yes, I suppose we should," she reluctantly agreed. She didn't feel ready to share him with others just yet, but she was also feeling eager to return to Aaron and give him a big hug.

They mounted their horses, then rode slowly side by side.

Emma looked up and noticed the abundance of stars twinkling across the dark blue sky. "Look at how beautiful the sky is tonight."

Out of the corner of her eye, she could see Paul's head tip up. As they looked up at the stars together, Emma sighed and remembered a time a few weeks earlier that they had done the same.

"Paul?"

"Yes?"

"Would you tell me another story about the stars?"

Chapter Thirty-Six

They'd scavenged what they could from the ashes of the house, though very little remained that was worth saving.

Paul sighed as he looked at the black, charred remains of his life, and turned to Emma, who stood beside him in the waning sunlight of the autumn afternoon.

"I'm so sorry all your things are gone, Emma." His face was drawn tight, and a deep crease that he feared might become permanent formed between his eyebrows. "I know you had things from your parents that are not replaceable."

She took his hand and squeezed it, a gesture that Paul knew was meant to be reassuring. Instead, he was distracted by the softness of her palm compared to the rough calluses on his. He liked the warm feeling of her skin on his and found his scowl becoming a soft smile.

"The things are not replaceable, that's true," she said, tugging on his hand for emphasis, "but the people are more important. We are all healthy and alive, and we will make it through this trying time." She let go of his hand, and he found that he missed her touch immediately. "We have each other, and we have our friends. It was very kind of Bonnie to take me in, and Aaron, too."

Paul chuckled. "I'm not sure that one more child is even noticed among Bonnie's brood."

"That's very true." Emma looked across the field, where all the children were gathered by the creek, hunting for frogs.

"He fits right in among the other children. He seems to thrive with some playmates around."

The thought that Aaron should have a younger sibling flitted into Paul's mind, immediately followed by confusion.

Where on earth had that thought come from? Where would Aaron get a younger sibling?

Paul's eyes strayed to Emma beside him, her plain brown dress covered in black soot and ash. She had stood by his side these last few weeks as they sorted through what they could and destroyed the rest. She had worked hard to keep the animals taken care of while the men made plans and gathered materials to rebuild. And she had done it all with no complaint or question, just quiet strength.

The first time he'd seen her, he had thought her to be pretty. But in this moment, it was like he was seeing her for the first time all over again.

The sun was setting behind her, illuminating the pile of hair pinned on top of her head and making it shimmer like gold. Her cheeks were flushed pink from hard work and sunshine and her hands were stained black with soot from the house.

She wasn't just pretty. She was stunning. Inside and out, Emma was a beautiful person.

Paul had the sudden urge to grab Emma by the shoulders and kiss her. He would have done it if he had thought that it wouldn't shock the life out of her. He was unsure if she had ever been kissed before or if she had any interest in kissing him at all.

"I should go back to Bonnie's. I need to clean up and help with dinner." Emma looked down at her filthy hands and dress, hold her skirt out to the sides to examine the damage she had done to it by climbing through the ashes.

Turning to escort Emma back across the fields, Paul took her hand and tucked it into the crook of his elbow as they walked. Her eyes shot up to his in surprise at such a courtly, familiar gesture, but when he only smiled down at her and kept walking, she seemed to accept it. As they neared the creek, Paul thought he might have even felt Emma lean into him a bit.

"Emma, would you like to join me for a walk outside after dinner?" he asked before they were in earshot of the children, who were now playing a game of chase.

Her brows shot together, forming a line in the center of her forehead much like his, but before she could question why he was asking, he continued. "I think it's time we get to know one another a little better. I feel as if you know quite a lot about my life, but I know very little about yours. I'd like to know more about your father."

"Oh," she replied, her face softening at the mention of her father. "I would love that, Paul, thank you."

As they passed by the children, Emma patiently gathered them up and sent them home to complete their evening chores and to wash up for their dinner. Paul admired her laughing patience with the children, regardless of the age.

Twelve-year-old Rachel was clearly enamored of the pretty blonde who was only ten years older than herself, and Emma handled it with grace. She handled rambunctious six-year-old William with the same smile and calm, even when he failed to listen completely to instructions. She was a natural caretaker, a natural mother.

Paul shook his head to clear that thought from his mind. It seemed to be straying in the direction of marriage and children suddenly.

***

The walk that Paul and Emma took that evening was the first of many that fall. As the days shortened and the land grew dark earlier and earlier in the evening, they would wait for the children to all fall asleep then bundle up and walk under the light of the moon and the stars.

They nearly wore a path between the house and the creek during that autumn once they had fallen into a natural rhythm and found a favorite spot. In the middle of a small grove of cottonwood trees, the pair would stop and turn to one another, Emma resting her back against the rough bark with Paul's hand beside her head, leaning close enough to her to kiss.

The first time he kissed her, she had frozen for just a second, and he was momentarily afraid that he had done something wrong, offended her in some way or misread the direction of their relationship. But then she melted into him, her hands resting on his chest as she lifted herself up on tiptoe to meet his mouth more easily. He made sure to keep any kisses relatively chaste, knowing how easily a simple kiss in the intimacy of the moonlight could become overly amorous.

When the night grew too cold, or one of them began yawning, they would make their way back to the house hand in hand. Emma told him of growing up with only her father, of her best friends Hallie and Georgina, and of her love for God and Christ. And though Paul had strayed from his relationship with God for the year after Laura had died, Emma helped him to find his way back.

As the days and nights both turned colder and the snow blanketed the ground, they would choose to stay inside by the warmth of the fire, reading the Bible and praying together.

Which is why Paul was surprised that Emma was not suspicious one cold, snow covered January evening when he insisted they go for a walk in the snow the very minute Aaron was down to sleep for the night. He did all he could not to show his nervousness and excitement, and he must have done a fairly good job of it, because she simply said, "That sounds lovely. I'll get my cloak."

Paul took Emma's hand, tucking it into the crook of his elbow as they walked across the meadow between the house and the creek in companionable, comfortable silence. The icy snow crunched under their feet and sparkled like diamonds in the moonlight.

She leaned into him as much as was possible as they walked, enjoying his physical heat as well as the warmth of their affection for one another.

She was so lucky to have found a decent man who was also such a good father and provider for his family. The fact that he always sought to also include his father-in-law truly revealed his strong sense of honor and virtue. After growing up with her father as her only family, Emma had a great appreciation for the family she had fallen into here in Colorado Springs.

They reached a stand of cottonwood trees near the creek and Paul pulled them to a stop. Emma leaned her back against the cold, rough bark of the tree, still holding Paul's hand. Typically, Paul would place a hand beside her head and lean against the tree that way.

This time, however, he surprised her by stepping back and taking both of her hands in his. He took a deep breath and grinned at her, looking like the cat that had caught the canary.

It was at this moment that Emma became suspicious. "Paul, whatever has gotten into you? You are as excited as Aaron gets when there are sweets nearby."

"I am much like a child with sweets nearby because you are here, my sweet," he replied. As Paul was not usually one for such fanciful language, Emma giggled at his silliness. "And I would like it very much if you would be my sweet, my Emma for the rest of my life. You have made every aspect of my life better, and I know that you will only continue to make me a better, happier, more faith-filled man."

The words "my Emma" struck in her heart. Emma felt the spirit of her father lingering nearby, as if he were placing a hand on Paul's shoulder, giving the younger man his blessing.

"Emma Clement, will you do me the honor of becoming my wife?"

She felt a tightness in her chest from the emotions spilling out of her heart. The intense heat of love for this man filled her. She sent up a quick prayer of gratitude to the God who had sent her to Paul, and for the words that she was sure were a sign of approval from her father.

"Of course, I will, Paul! I would love nothing better!" She threw her arms around his neck, and he held her close. His lips brushed her cheek, the warmth of his breath in the cold evening air sending a shiver down her spine.

He leaned his forehead against hers and they looked into one another's eyes, both exuding such happiness that it overflowed into laughter. Still laughing, he grasped Emma by the waist and lifted her up off the ground, spinning them both around in celebration.

As they had walked back toward the Higgins cabin, they had discussed the particulars of the wedding.

"I think a spring wedding would be lovely," Emma told him, thinking of how the land came alive with color in the springtime. She imagined the bright green of springtime grass, the leaves on all the trees, the vibrant colors of the wildflowers that bloomed in the fields and meadows across the Colorado countryside. Her mind painted a picture of herself, in a lacy white dress, walking through a field of red and pink wildflowers with Paul by her side.

"Then a spring wedding you shall have, my love," Paul replied, still euphoric from his proposal and Emma's response. "We should have the house finished by then, as well. Perhaps we can move right in as a newly married couple."

"What a splendid symbol that will be of our brand new start," she said. "A new home and a new family to begin the new season of spring."

Epilogue

One year later

October 1874

The smooth dough rolled beneath Emma's hands as she worked it back and forth across the flour covered kitchen counter. She hummed tunelessly as she looked out the window in front of her, watching Aaron carefully collecting eggs from the chickens out back. He was now very proudly six years old and had demanded to have chores to complete all by himself.

Emma smiled at the memory of the small birthday celebration they had held at Bonnie's house last fall for Aaron. Bonnie had created another delicious and ornate pie, this time featuring a Noah's Ark and the multitudes of animals, which the Gilberts and Higginses had shared amid laughter as John and Earle competed to see who could tell the most outlandish story.

"Did I ever tell you all about the time our house was overrun by Indians?" Earle asked, nonchalantly, knowing that he immediately had captivated everyone's attention.

"Indians?" Aaron exclaimed, the pie he was eating practically falling out of his gaping mouth. He was enthralled by any story his grandfather told.

"It was in the early days here, back in about '45, I'd guess." Earle leaned back in his chair, settling himself in for the storytelling. "We'd just finished building the house, and so we

were living out here on this wide-open land without a soul around for miles, or so we thought. I was in the barn tending to a horse when I heard my Amelia outside calling for me. She sounded a little more worried than normal, so I ran outside as quickly as I could. And what did I find when I ran through the barn door, but a passel of Utes on horseback!"

"Were you scared?" little William Higgins asked, leaning forward in his seat.

"I was a little at first, but they weren't running at us like they were going to attack. They were just riding calmly across the field," Earle assured the children. "No, they were just coming to see who had built this lovely house on what had once been their land. A couple of them could speak some English, and so we had a little talk."

"You talked to the Indians?" Aaron's eyes were open wide, an expression of absolute hero worship on his face.

"Sure did. They were right nice, too. I told them that I simply intended to farm the land and raise some horses and cattle, that I was no threat to them or their way of life. We agreed that if neither of us raised arms against the other, we would have no quarrels. And so, we've lived here in peace ever since."

"I thought you said overrun, Earle!" John accused. "You made it sound like you fought off a whole tribe of Indians single handed."

They had all laughed at John's complaint but agreed that Earle won the contest and awarded him the last piece of pie.

Aaron and Emma had spent the fall and winter living with Bonnie and her family, who were so kind and gracious in their time of need. The men, however, had stayed in the bunkhouse with Holt and the farmhands so that they could spend their days cleaning up the burned house and rebuilding a new one.

The new house was a little smaller than the last—only one story instead of two and made of stone rather than wood. Paul had wanted to ensure that this house would not be as easily destroyed as the others. There was one large kitchen and sitting room, so that the evenings could be spent all together in front of the fireplace, and four bedrooms—one for Earle, one for Aaron, and one for Paul and Emma to share with one to spare.

Paul and Emma had been married in the spring, after a few months of courtship spent growing together in God's love, praying, and reading the Bible together on Bonnie's porch in the evenings or sitting before the fireplace sharing stories with all the children. They had taken long walks through the snow, bundled up and sharing their hopes and dreams for the future and tales of their childhood exploits.

Paul began to smile more freely and became animated as he told her stories of his childhood adventures in the countryside. She, too, was feeling happier than she ever had in her life now that she had a man who loved her. He had said as much on Christmas Day as they shared simple gifts with Aaron and Earle.

She loved their little house. She liked being close and cozy with her family, which a flutter in her stomach reminded her was now growing.

She placed a floured hand on her stomach, reveling in the feel of the swelling mound she found there and the knowledge of a new life growing within her. A new son or daughter would greet them in the spring, and it was just now becoming visibly evident. She knew many women went to great lengths to disguise a pregnancy, but to Emma, it was such a blessing and a source of happiness that she had no desire to hide it.

Leaving the dough to rise under a kitchen towel on the counter, Emma went out the porch to sit with Earle until Aaron returned with his basket of eggs.

Unlike the year before, Earle no longer sat rocking in his chair on the porch all day, staring out toward the road. Much of the time, he could be found helping around the farm in some way. But on many days, Earle sat on the back porch watching over the fields and the animals as he worked on some small project or another. It turned out that he was quite good at repairing bridles and saddles as well as woodworking. Emma had been shocked to discover that much of the fine furniture she had admired upon her arrival to the ranch had indeed been crafted by Earle himself.

Earle's current project was to expand upon Aaron's collection of small animals. He had already replaced the horses and cows that had been destroyed in the second house fire, and now Aaron had a herd of goats and sheep along with a chicken and rooster in his menagerie.

The current animal had Earle cursing under his breath and squinting at the book in front of him for reference. When Emma had found a book full of animal drawings and stories at the general store recently, she had been so excited to bring it home for Aaron. She had not, however, anticipated that he would then want to add elephants and lions to his animal collection.

"What in tarnation is this creature, anyhow?" Earle asked Emma, holding up the long-necked giraffe. "This thing can't be real. It's absurd."

"And God made the beast of the earth after his kind, and cattle after their kind, and every thing that creepeth upon the earth after his kind: and God saw that it was good." Emma smiled at Earle as she sat in the chair beside his, looking over his shoulder to the drawing of the animal so tall that it could eat leaves straight off the trees.

"This is an animal that only God and its mother could love." Earle shook the wooden animal in Emma's direction, then went back to shaping its long legs with his small whittling knife.

She chuckled at Earle, for whom she had no title—he wasn't her father or her father-in-law, but he was equal to either in affection and importance in her life now. He had truly opened up in the last year, revealing a man full of vigor and spunk. She had even had the extreme pleasure of witnessing his expert fiddle playing at this year's town picnic.

"Perhaps if you make two of everything, we can have a model for my lesson on the story of Noah's Ark at Sunday school this week," Emma joked, a smirk raising one corner of her mouth.

"Oh, no, you don't." Earle shook his head, smiling at Emma's teasing. "I will not be talked into crafting another of these nonsensical creatures. And do not even contemplate any more of those elephant things. Those large ears and the long nose. It's even more impractical than this long-necked beast."

Emma laughed out loud at Earle's silliness as Aaron came trotting back to the house.

"Emma! I got seven eggs! And none of them pecked me today!" He had grown so much taller in the last year that Emma had needed to let out the hem of his trousers twice, and she noticed that they were starting to look too short once more. Unfortunately, there was no more fabric to let out now, so it seemed that she would have to make him a new pair.

"Very well done, Aaron." She reached one arm around the boy, squeezing him to her side. "You're getting so big. And so responsible. I think you're going to be an excellent big brother."

"I will!" He set the egg basket down at Emma's feet. "I'm gonna teach my little brother how to climb trees and catch frogs and run fast."

"And what if it's a girl?" Emma asked, ruffling his brown hair.

He paused for a moment, as if he had not considered the fact that the baby may not turn out to be a boy. "Then I'll teach her how to climb trees, too! But she may not like catching frogs as much. I'll make sure she's always safe and protect her from all the scary monsters."

"That sounds just perfect."

"Scary monsters like this one?" Earle asked, holding out a roughly completed giraffe. "I still need to smooth out some rough edges, but what do you think?"

"What is *that?*" Aaron exclaimed, rushing to his grandfather's side to look at the picture in the book.

Emma took the eggs into the kitchen, leaving the two men to discuss the exotic animals of the jungle.

As she organized some items in the small pantry off the kitchen, Emma contemplated her Sunday school lesson for this week. She and Paul had returned to the church soon after the house fire. When the young woman who had been running the Sunday school got married and moved away after Christmas, Emma had leapt at the opportunity to offer her services to the children of the church.

Last week, they had learned about the story of Jonah being swallowed by the whale and discussed why it was important to be obedient when your parents asked you to do something. She had even allowed Aaron to bring his wildlife book and show all the children what a whale looked like.

The children were all amazed that such a large fish, one big enough to swallow a man whole, truly existed. Until that moment, they had all thought it was something made up just for the story, like a dragon or a unicorn in a fairy tale. They had all been so fascinated by the animals in the book that she decided a lesson with Noah's Ark would hold their attention as well. She had to be sure that it did not become a lesson about strange new animals, however.

The Bible story told of Noah, a faithful follower of God, who was instructed by God to build a great ship and to fill it with two of each of the animals of the earth. Though he was not near the water, he followed God's orders and tried to warn others of the coming flood, but no one would listen. After seven days, the rain began to fall and the land became flooded. Noah, his family, and all the animals were saved from the rising waters, but those who did not follow God were drowned in the flood.

To Emma, the story of Noah's Ark was a story about how important it was to remain faithful in the face of hardship and to always trust in the Lord's plan. Even amid the raging flood waters, Noah and his family remained faithful to God, trusting that he has a plan for them and that he would save them in the end. This reminded her of how she had lived her life in the last year. She had faced the death of her father, often feeling as if she would be pulled under by the waves of grief, and trusted that God would lead her to where he needed her next.

When he led her to Paul, she faced challenge after challenge from Paul's resistance to God's love and from Aaron's difficult behavior, but she had trusted in the Lord. And in the end, He had sent Emma her very own dove and olive branch, a sign of hope among the suffering, when she and Paul had prayed together over Aaron's sick little body.

Now they prayed together every day, at every meal, and read the Bible together each night. They attended church together every Sunday, especially now that she taught Sunday school, and were active members in all church activities.

A few weeks earlier, Emma had glanced across the aisle during the service and noticed Shaw McCormick and his new wife Mary Lou in the next pew. After the house fire, Shaw had chosen not to move back home immediately so that he could help to build a new farmhouse but began writing letters to Mary Lou and visiting her in town as often as she could.

Shaw had discovered very quickly that there had never been another suitor, but that his mother had tricked him into coming to his senses and marrying the girl she felt he was meant to be with.

Once the house was completed, Shaw had proposed to Mary Lou and found a job and a house in town to settle down.

Emma had noticed over the previous weeks that Mary Lou's waist seemed to be expanding, and so she smiled over at Shaw, who had caught her eye with his, and mouthed her congratulations to him. He smiled proudly back at her and then, clearly smitten, turned his adoring eyes to his wife.

***

That Sunday at church, the Gilberts all sat together in their pew listening to Pastor Newton's sermon about the wedding feast at Cana, when Jesus turned water into wine. Paul smiled at Emma, knowing that she, too, was remembering that this passage had been read at their wedding. To Paul, it seemed that not only had Christ performed a miracle at Cana by transforming something ordinary into something wonderful, but He had performed another miracle by leading Emma to him and Aaron and

Earle. He had transformed their shared grief and suffering over the deaths of their loved ones into something wonderful.

He had made a family whole once more.

As Pastor Newton went on, Paul attempted to stay focused on the words of the wise man but could not help but reminisce about the details of their wedding day. The ceremony had been held in this very church, with the spring air wafting through the open windows, carrying in the aroma of the blooming daffodils and daisies.

He stood up at the front of the church in a brand new gray suit that he had ordered from the tailor in town. The stark white of his new shirt glowed against the deep blue of the woolen waistcoat. He had never considered himself a vain man, but he was quite pleased with his appearance in this suit. It fit him well and the blue of the waistcoat highlighted his eyes in a way that even he had taken note.

Aaron stood beside him in a matching suit, fidgeting among the unusual number of layers he was required to wear for this event. He also claimed that his new shoes were pinching his toes, but Paul assured him that he simply needed some time to break them in. His son looked quite handsome, and Aaron was very proud to be allowed to stand up at the front of the church as Paul and Emma said their vows.

The creaky old upright piano in the corner of the church suddenly changed its tune, from a subtle background melody that reminded Paul of watching a butterfly float on a breeze to a commanding chord that announced to one and all that the bride was ready. He looked up from his son and down the aisle to the church door to find Emma standing at the back of the church with her hand on Earle's arm.

They slowly came toward him, and he ceased breathing or thinking at all. His heart was full to bursting at the sight of his beautiful bride. She, too, had a new dress for the occasion. It was a frothy, lacy confection in lavender and white, with a bodice that nipped in at the waist to highlight her tiny waist and a neckline that draped across her chest in such a way that he could see the delicate bones around her feminine shoulders. Her warm blonde hair had been intricately curled and styled so that some was pinned up on top of her head and some hung loosely about her shoulders.

His only thought was that she looked like an angel, an absolute miracle as she grinned at him all the way up the aisle.

It was a short aisle, and yet time seemed to move in slow motion as Earle escorted Emma to the front of the church and declared that he was there to give this bride away. Paul didn't feel as if he took a full breath until Emma's hand was tucked into his elbow and they faced the pastor together.

And now Paul looked at his wife again, noticing how she held Aaron's hand in the pew as she bowed her head, and the congregation began to pray together. The sun was coming through the windows in such a way that it seemed to bathe her in a honey glow. Her hair sparkled beneath its rays, and Paul knew that she would always be this beautiful to him. It was not her physical appearance that made her so lovely. It was the way she shined from the inside out. Her strength. Her patience. Her faith in God and in others.

He thought of the vows she had recited at their wedding, holding both of his hands firmly in hers as she looked confidently into his eyes.

"In the name of God, I, Emma take you, Paul to be my husband, to have and to hold from this day forward, for better, for worse, for richer, for poorer, in sickness and in health, to love and to cherish, until we are parted by death. This is my solemn vow."

She had lived up to every promise thus far. He was so proud to have Emma as a wife. To have someone who would place her trust in him, but also to challenge him when he needed it.

Their only true disagreement in the last year had been over Caleb O'Kelley.

The night of the fire and Paul's gunshot wound, which had healed so well he forgot about it most days, Annie had dragged Caleb with her out into the darkness and run for the mountains. Emma had at first been understanding and proud that Paul was willing to forgive as God instructed us to. But she had later become worried that Caleb could show up again and attempt to hurt Paul again or do something to Aaron.

"I couldn't stand it if something were to happen to you or Aaron, Paul! I feel as if I am always expecting some tragedy to befall you at the hands of Caleb O'Kelley!" she had exclaimed one evening in frustration.

Paul put his hands on her shoulders and quoted the Book of Matthew. "Take therefore no thought for the morrow: for the morrow shall take thought for the things of itself."

She looked taken aback, her eyes widening and swinging up to meet his.

"What? Are you still so surprised that I can quote scripture?" he asked.

"No, that's not it at all." She placed her hands flat on his chest. "I had a dream last night about that passage! Really, it was the whole Sermon on the Mount, with Jesus speaking to the crowds of people, but—" She paused for a moment, gathering her racing thoughts. "Oh, Paul, you're right. Worrying over it will do no good. I should endeavor to enjoy each day and face each challenge as it comes, rather than fussing over the possibilities of things that may never come."

He hugged his wife tight to his chest and reminded her that Boone Holliday had his men on high alert for Caleb. "Don't forget as well, if the man shows up in town again, he will be arrested on sight."

She nodded against his chest and hugged him back, and he swore he would never grow tired of the feeling of this delicate, yet strong woman held against his heart.

As it turned out, there was no need for Emma's worry, because there had been no trace of Caleb or Annie. As the year went on, Emma became more confident that the O'Kelleys were truly gone and would likely never return.

The pianist struck out the opening chords for the closing hymn, and Paul was brought back to the present. He stood proudly beside his family to sing out the words and proclaim his faith in God.

***

That same afternoon, after a boisterous midday meal among John and Bonnie's family, a new Sunday tradition since Aaron and Emma had moved out of their house, Paul and Emma walked across the fields toward home hand in hand. The fields had turned golden with the onset of autumn, and the leaves on the trees were resplendent in their yellows and reds.

Earle and Aaron walked a few yards ahead, hypothesizing about the lives of the strange creatures in Aaron's new book. Aaron had become especially interested in the multitudes of different types of birds illustrated in the book, and Earle knew enough about animals to help Aaron hypothesize about the purpose of the animals' large beaks and colorful feathers.

"I saw that you were a little distracted during the service today," Emma said to Paul, without accusation, merely curiosity. "Where was your mind wandering this morning?"

"I was remembering our wedding day and how beautiful you looked." He smiled and quickly kissed her temple. "How beautiful you always look and always will look to me."

"Those are some quite romantic words, Mr. Gilbert," Emma teased, lightly elbowing his side through his brown woolen jacket. "You might make a girl vain with talk like that. But I do hope there is more that you like about me than just my stunning beauty."

"I did not say stunning." Paul yanked on a strand of Emma's hair and laughed as Emma feigned offense, knowing that he was teasing her.

He gathered her closer against his side and squeezed her shoulders. "Every day, I am so grateful to God for bringing you here. You saved me. You saved us all. And your beauty goes deeper than your pretty face and your shimmering blonde hair. It is a beauty that comes from within, from your faith and your love for others. And I know that will never fade, even when your face is full of wrinkles and your hair has gone gray."

Emma stopped and looked up at him, with tears in her eyes. Her pregnancy had made her more prone to extreme emotions, and she had recently begun crying in any instance of extreme happiness.

"Paul Gilbert, that is the most wonderful thing you've ever said to me." She leaned up and kissed him. "I love you so much. And I am also grateful to God for bringing me here because you and your family also saved me."

Paul turned their bodies so that they looked together at the green fields of the ranch and their cozy new stone house. He wrapped his arms around Emma from behind and placed his hand on her swollen belly. He felt a strong kick from within and smiled, knowing this baby would be hearty and healthy. "What do you think of the name Frank for a boy?" he asked.

She gasped with happiness and grinned up at him over her shoulder. "Oh, I love it! It would make me so happy to pass on my father's name. And he would be so proud to have his namesake also carry your last name. He would have liked you so very much." She paused and picked at her fingernails, looking a bit guilty. "Do you have any girls' names in mind?"

He chuckled, knowing the look on her face. "No, but I get the impression that you might."

Rather than directly answer him, she asked an unexpected question. "Do you remember the Bible story that sent me here to you? The one I read before I saw your advertisement in the newspaper?"

"The story of God speaking to Aaron and Miriam?"

Emma nodded. "And do you remember the vision I had when Aaron was so sick last fall, the one with the little girl?"

"And Jesus healing all the sick children?" He finished the story for her, knowing exactly which vision she was referring to and now also knowing what name she was thinking of for their potential future daughter.

Emma turned around and looped her hands around the back of Paul's neck. "What do you think of the name Miriam for a little girl?"

Paul squeezed his wife affectionately and kissed her cheek, holding her close to him as he looked out over his land and his family, all the blessings God had provided.

"I think Miriam sounds perfect."

THE END

Also, by Olivia Haywood

Thank you for reading "**A Godsent Governess for his Tormented Family**"!

I hope you enjoyed it! If you did, here you can also check out **my** **full** **Amazon** **Book** **Catalogue** **at:** https://go.oliviahaywood.com/bc-authorpage

Thank you for allowing me to keep doing what I love! ❤

Manufactured by Amazon.ca
Bolton, ON

40698658R00181